PENGUIN BOOKS
CAN I TELL YOU A SECRET?

Evelyn Cosgrave lives in Limerick with her husband and two daughters. When she's not writing, she works as a teacher. Her first novel was *Desperately Seeking . . . Can I Tell You a Secret?* is her second novel.

GW00692295

Can I Tell You a Secret?

EVELYN COSGRAVE

PENGUIN BOOKS

PENGUIN BOOKS

Published by the Penguin Group
Penguin Books Ltd, 80 Strand, London WC2R ORL, England
Penguin Group (USA) Inc., 375 Hudson Street, New York, New York 10014, USA
Penguin Group (Canada), 90 Eglinton Avenue East, Suite 700, Toronto, Ontario, Canada M4P 2Y3
(a division of Pearson Penguin Canada Inc.)
Penguin Ireland, 25 St Stephen's Green, Dublin 2, Ireland (a division of Penguin Books Ltd)
Penguin Group (Australia), 250 Camberwell Road,
Camberwell, Victoria 3124, Australia (a division of Pearson Australia Group Pty Ltd)
Penguin Books India Pvt Ltd, 11 Community Centre, Panchsheel Park,
New Delhi – 110 017, India
Penguin Group (NZ), 67 Apollo Drive, Rosedale, North Shore 0632, New Zealand
(a division of Pearson New Zealand Ltd)
Penguin Books (South Africa) (Pty) Ltd, 24 Sturdee Avenue, Rosebank, Johannesburg 2196,
South Africa

Penguin Books Ltd, Registered Offices: 80 Strand, London WC2R ORL, England

www.penguin.com

First published by Penguin Ireland 2009
Published in Penguin Books 2009
1

Printed in England by Clays Ltd, St Ives plc

ISBN: 978–1–844–88148–2

www.greenpenguin.co.uk

Penguin Books is committed to a sustainable future
for our business, our readers and our planet.
The book in your hands is made from paper
certified by the Forest Stewardship Council.

To James

Spring

Angela O'Regan looked round the room and smiled to herself. Who would have thought she'd ever have an eighty-fifth birthday party? She'd nearly given up on living half her lifetime ago, and now look at her, blowing out the candles on a cake shaped like a bicycle (some daft person had remembered that at one time in her life she was never off her bicycle). It was too much really; a woman of her age should be sitting quietly in a chair by the fire dozing, hardly aware what day or year it was. But that was the thing, she didn't feel like a woman her age, she felt much more like a girl.

'Go on, Granny, blow! You're going to have to do better than that!' Susan, her middle granddaughter, screamed from the far end of the table.

'Then give me a bit of help, child,' Angela retorted. 'I haven't got the puff I once had.'

'All right, then,' said Felicity, the eldest granddaughter, 'let's all go together. One, two, three . . . HAPPY BIRTHDAY, GRANNY!!!'

Angela sat back and let her daughter-in-law take over the cutting of the cake. Maureen liked to take charge and it wouldn't have dawned on her that Angela might enjoy presiding over her own cake. 'Pass your plates up,' she called out brusquely as if she was doling out broccoli at a children's tea. 'Someone get the pastry forks. We might as well use the good stuff.'

Susan left her position by her boyfriend's side and went

to the bottom drawer of the mahogany sideboard. Angela thought she was looking pale, not that she wasn't always as white as a sheet, but this was more than mere lack of pigmentation. There was a lack of warmth in her cheeks. And wasn't she the one they were all watching and waiting for an announcement from? She was about to move back to Limerick with Paul, and they were on the lookout for a house. The big day couldn't be far off. It made Angela smile the way the young people did everything backwards now. The sex came first, the house came second and only then did any of them think of getting married. But Paul had an air about him of a man who was about to settle down. You could tell he'd done his running around and was ready to take on the responsibility of being a married man. The kids took so long to grow up these days; you sometimes wondered if they'd ever make it.

'Are these the ones?' Susan asked, holding up a battered blue velvet box.

'They were my mother's,' Angela told her. 'They were a silver wedding present.'

'You should throw out all that junk, Granny,' said Marianne, the youngest granddaughter. 'Or sell it. You'd get a great price at one of those antique fairs. I'll bring 'em if you like.'

'Those are heirlooms, Marianne,' said her mother dryly. 'Some of them will be yours one day, but for now they're still very precious to your granny.'

'I was only mentioning it. I don't want any of that old stuff, anyway. It's mouldy and smelly.'

'Marianne, mind your manners. And pass me your plate.'

Marianne really was a caution, thought Angela. She was twenty-six years old and still behaved as if she was fifteen.

Still dressed that way too, although Angela knew that the combat trousers and the couple of T-shirts she was wearing on top of each other were what she considered dressing up. She'd let a couple of her piercings close – the one in her lip and the one in her eyebrow. Angela had always admired the little nose stud. That thing on her tongue she tried not to think about. And she'd completely given up asking her what she was doing with herself now. Every time she saw Marianne she asked her how the job in the clothes shop was going, or the job in the café, or how she was getting on with her course in reflexology or in lighting design or marine biology or papier mâché . . . she'd had to give up. It wasn't her place to say anything, of course – she just hoped Tom and Maureen would say something before it was too late and that girl was lost altogether.

'Lovely cake, Mum,' said Tom, who was already halfway through his slice.

Angela turned to her son, who was seated at his wife's elbow.

'You like your cake, Tom.'

'That I do.'

'I'll bet the bicycle idea was yours.'

'You have me there! I thought you'd like it.'

'Ahh, you're just a big eejit, Tom.'

Everyone had dressed up for the occasion, but Tom was the only one who looked overdressed. It wasn't at all that Angela thought men shouldn't wear pink, it was that they shouldn't wear *baby* pink. And, yes, she knew that the little man waving his stick meant that this was a very good jumper – hadn't Maureen pointed it out to her often enough – but there had to be something more suitable for a man approaching sixty. She mightn't have minded quite as much if she had been convinced that this pansy pullover was his

3

own choice; but, of course, Maureen had dressed him. She'd been dressing him since she turned up at Angela's door thirty-five years ago.

Maureen herself looked very nice. She always did. She'd always spent a fortune on her back. She had lovely trousers on her today, casual but cut very nicely, and a colourdy top that was very good at hiding the bit of a tummy she had. Her hair was done in a new way – cut in short waves that travelled up her cheek – and it helped to soften the hard edges of her face. She never wore too much make-up, just the right amount to brighten her up. Oh yes, Maureen kept herself very well, she had to give her that.

'I think it's time for the champagne now, Granny.' Felicity smiled at her across the table. Felicity was a fabulous girl. She'd always been the sensible one – even Susan could be flighty at times – but you could always rely on Felicity. Not that Angela saw much of her now that her job in London kept her so busy, but Felicity was always the one to call to remind her that the clocks were going forward or that there was a cold spell forecast or that the Brown Thomas sale had started. She was great at giving out information, not so great at revealing anything else though. You wouldn't have a clue what was going on in her personal life – not a boyfriend or even a date was ever mentioned. And she was the oldest of them – thirty-three now – probably the most attractive of three good-looking girls. Her naturally blonde hair and sparkly blue-green eyes and the lovely clothes she wore made her stand out in a crowd. Yet there wasn't a sign of her getting married. Not that marriage was the be-all and end-all of everything, especially not nowadays. Women had so many more options than they'd had in Angela's day and Felicity was particularly career-driven. Tom had explained to Angela that when a big multi-national bought out the company

4

Felicity worked for, she'd be a very wealthy woman. You had to admire that kind of drive and ambition in a person. Still . . . when the nights were cold . . . Angela could only look back on her own marriage, brief as it had been, and think of it as the happiest time in her life.

'Oh, don't be wasting it on me, love,' she said, realizing that Felicity was still looking at her expectantly.

'Don't be silly, Granny, this is what I got it for.'

'I know, but it's so expensive. You should keep it for yourself. Any old rubbish would do me. Sure, I don't know the difference.'

'Nonsense! An occasion doesn't get any bigger than this.'

'OooooohhhhhhHHHH!!!! HAPPY BIRTHDAY, ANGELA!!!!' The cork popped and the champagne began to flow.

'Not too much now – I've already had all that wine,' said Angela.

'Don't give Daddy any. He has to drive us home,' said Maureen.

'Cheers!' said the three girls in unison.

'Happy birthday . . . Mrs O'Regan,' said Paul.

'Oh, this is nice!' said Marianne. 'Did you bring another bottle?'

'I did,' said Felicity. 'But you're not getting your hands on it.'

'Oh, Fliss! Don't be so stingy. I never even got a birthday present off you this year.'

'You most certainly did! I sent you sterling. What you asked for!'

'Oh yeah, right, thanks. Did I thank you?'

'No, you didn't actually.'

'Well . . . thanks.'

'You're welcome.'

'Marianne, come here and have the rest of mine, love, I can't be doing with all this alcohol – but it is absolutely lovely, Felicity. Thank you so much for bringing it.'

'You're welcome, Granny.'

'And thank you all for all my beautiful presents. I don't deserve any of them.'

'Oh, Granny!'

'And Paul. There was absolutely no need for you to give me anything. It's a lovely scarf, I'm sure I'll wear it all the time.'

'You're more than welcome, Mrs O.'

'He picked it out by himself, too,' added Susan.

'Isn't he marvellous! Did I tell you Gavin will be home soon?' Angela said to Maureen as she took away her half-eaten cake.

'You did, Angela.'

'It'll be lovely to see him again. It's been so long.'

'Oh, that boy . . . he always makes life hard for himself.'

Angela couldn't hide the excitement she felt at the thought of Gavin's return. She'd always had a soft spot for him, ever since her first glimpse of him as a baby with those bright blue eyes, that pudgy little mouth and that expression on his face, so like his mother's, of absolute trust in everyone round him. It was so easy to see how Frank had fallen for Grace.

'And it was a shame Luke couldn't make it. He works very hard, you know.'

'Luke always pleases himself. I don't know if those boys will ever turn out right.'

'Who's that?' asked Susan, catching the end of the conversation.

'Your O'Regan cousins.'

'God, I haven't seen them in a hundred years. What are they up to now?'

'Well, Gavin's on his way back from Sweden and –'

'He'd have been here only that he's coming home for good so soon – he couldn't get the time off,' offered Angela.

'And Luke's still in the States. I doubt he'll ever come home.'

'You wouldn't expect them home just for an old woman's birthday party. Sure, even Kay couldn't manage it.'

Angela's daughter had made every effort to get home for her mother's eighty-fifth, but seeing as her sister-in-law was organizing the event and had moved the date around to suit herself, it had become impossible in the end for Kay to make the party. She was planning a more extensive visit to her mother later in the year.

'Tom will come over and give the grass one more cut tomorrow,' said Maureen, changing the subject quickly.

'Oh, that's great. There's fierce growth at the moment.'

'That'll have to be it for a little while then because we're bringing the mower down to Ballyconnell. There's a huge amount of work to be done in the garden there and we'll need the good mower. We'll eventually buy another one, but there's just so much expense at the moment.'

'Of course, love. Sure, it's so exciting for ye with the new house.'

'Oh, it'll be marvellous, Angela. A new lease of life.'

'Aren't ye great to be doing it?'

'A life-long dream. You have to grab your dreams.'

'You do, love, you do.' Angela was silent for a moment as she contemplated her son and daughter-in-law grabbing their dreams at the seaside. 'And have *ye* seen any nice houses, Paul?'

'Well, you know, things are a bit up and down at the moment, Mrs O'Regan. With prices falling we'd do better to hold on for a little while.'

'Things are so hard these days for young people trying to buy a house. It was never so hard in our day.'

'Ah, well, you know, nothing's cheap. But if you're crafty about it you should be able to do well.'

'Have you seen anything you liked, Susan?'

'What, Gran?'

'Any nice houses? Anywhere you think you'd like to settle?'

'Mmmm, nothing much really . . . We haven't looked at that many yet. It'll be easier after we move down.'

It struck Angela that Susan wasn't all that excited about the prospect of buying her first home with her boyfriend.

'And ye're going to rent for a while?'

'Yeah, I think we'll get one of those new apartments in the city centre. There's some beautiful ones just gone up on O'Connell Avenue. You know, that lovely building that used to be the county council? They're supposed to be fabulous.'

'They're very expensive,' added Paul.

Susan flashed him a look.

'We wouldn't be renting for long . . . I just think it would be nice to be living in the middle of everything, like you do, Gran.'

'Much good it does me now to be in the middle of everything.'

'You know what I mean. I'm not ready for the suburbs yet.'

'Nothing wrong with the suburbs, Susie,' said her mother. 'That's where all life happens. We can't be sharing houses like students all our lives.'

'I know but . . .'

'Sure, it'll be for the pair of them to decide what they want,' said Angela, giving her granddaughter a warm smile.

Susan smiled at her granny, ignoring her mother's frown.

'I don't know,' said Tom expansively, spreading his arms along the table, 'in my day things were done differently.' His eyes were wide with an expression of bemusement, his lips curling at the corners.

'Oh, Dad, please,' said Susan. 'We know all about your day; your day was a hundred years ago.'

'I'm only saying things were done . . . in a certain order . . . in my day. Isn't that right, Mam?'

'Leave me out of it,' said Angela. 'Let the young people do things their way.'

'Isn't that right, Paul?' continued Tom, with a wink in his direction.

'Oh, erm . . . erm . . .'

'In my day a man took charge. There's certain things in life that only a man can do . . . if you get my meaning.'

'Dad,' said Susan with a sustained whine, 'would you shut up!'

'Oh, now . . .'

Somehow, Tom had passed the point of harmless joking. Paul's gaze hadn't left the crumbs of cake on his plate since Tom had started talking. Susan was caught between trying to give her father dagger eyes and scanning the rest of the room for help. No one else knew where to look or what to say.

Suddenly Paul cleared his throat.

Susan went white.

'Well . . .' he began, 'it has been on my mind . . . and Susan is . . .'

'Oh fuck!' gasped Marianne.

Paul went to stand up, but the legs of his chair caught on the edge of the rug and caused him to fall backwards a little. His face was purple and he couldn't tear his gaze away from the crumbs on his plate.

'I . . . ah . . .' he began again. 'I . . . ah . . .' Eventually he shifted his focus to his girlfriend of three years, cleared his throat again, and, as if someone had finally given him the answer in a television quiz show, the words began to flow.

'I would like to ask Susan to marry me,' he said. 'It would make me very happy.'

I

A year or so later . . .

Susan was frantically ringing the doorbell. She wasn't even sure how she had got here, but now that she was here she couldn't go back. She began walloping the knocker. Nothing. She tried peering in the windows but that was useless – bloomin' net curtains. She was beginning to root in her bag for her mobile when the door opened.

'Susan, sweetheart, what a lovely surprise!'

'Oh, Granny,' she said, and burst into tears.

It didn't take long for Angela to gather up her grand-daughter and set her down in the living room with a large glass of brandy. She had been listening to her granddaughters' woes and crises ever since the days when the three girls used to call in after school. As soon as they were legal she replaced the warm milk with brandy, but otherwise her handling of their crises had remained the same: she listened, she proffered the drink, she made a few soothing noises and soon everything was all right again.

But this time the old formula didn't seem to be working.

'Oh, Granny,' Susan said again, polishing off the brandy with a sniff, 'it's all a huge mess. I don't know what I'm going to do.'

'Take a deep breath now, and tell me all about it.'

'But it's a mess,' she wailed. 'I've made a mess of everything.'

'Just tell me about it, sweetheart. Is it to do with Paul?'

'I've left him! I just walked out today and said I wasn't coming back. I didn't even know where I was going when I left. I just ended up here. Is it OK if I stay for a while? Just a little while, until I get myself sorted?'

'Of course, dear, you stay as long as you like. Now, would you like another drop of brandy?'

'Oh, thanks, Gran, that would be lovely.'

Angela poured another double for her granddaughter and a little one for herself. 'Now, do you want to tell me why you have walked out on Paul, or is it private?'

Susan put her glass on the table and lowered her eyes. She seemed to be deliberating furiously; her forehead was knotted and her lips were fixed in a bloodless pout.

'I . . . it was all . . . we had this big row,' she said at last.

'Oh?'

Susan scratched her head as though it was crawling with nits. 'I sort of – I . . .'

'Take your time, lovey. You don't have to tell me if you don't want to.'

'No, no, I do want to. It's just, it's . . .' She looked hopefully up at the ceiling and then began scratching her head again, 'not very easy.'

'Did something happen?'

'Well, a while ago . . . I . . . did something, and . . . a couple of hours ago I . . . told him about it.'

'What did you do, love?'

'Oh, Granny, don't hate me, please don't hate me.'

'I could never hate you. Don't be silly.'

'I know, but . . .'

'Take a deep breath.'

'There was this wedding. You remember? That couple we used to live with, Niall and Stephanie?'

'I remember.'

'At their wedding I – did something.'

'Yes?'

'I sort of . . . I sort of slept with somebody.'

'Oh.'

'Please don't hate me, Granny.'

'I don't hate you. I'm a little surprised, that's all.'

'Please don't be surprised! And don't be disappointed. Oh God, don't say you're disappointed in me!'

'I only mean I'm surprised because I thought you were happy with Paul.'

'I was – I mean – I thought I was, but . . . Actually, I think, maybe I wasn't.'

'So did Paul throw you out?'

'What?'

'When you told him.'

'No! You see, that's the thing. He didn't throw me out. He forgave me!'

'Isn't that a good thing?'

'You'd think, wouldn't you? What's wrong with me, Gran?'

'There's nothing wrong with you, love. You're in shock, for a start. Here, I'll get you another little brandy.'

'Thanks, Gran. You're so good to me.'

As Angela took Susan's glass she noticed that her hands were shaking. Poor girl. She really was in a state. And in a right mess too, like she said. It was only a little over a year since she'd got engaged. In this very house. That had been an odd thing – Tom kind of forcing the issue and Paul clearly not having a clue. She remembered it well. Paul had made his declaration – though you'd never have thought, by the way his eyes had gone buggy and his skin had come up in lumps, that he'd just asked the love of his life to marry him – and then Susan had looked up meekly from her plate and said, 'Sure, why not?'

After that it was all screams and hoots and congratulations and more of Felicity's lovely champagne. Paul actually apologized later for stealing her thunder. As if, at her age, she had an ounce of thunder left to steal! But she'd thought Susan was happy. She'd thought this was what she wanted. Now here she was, having been unfaithful to him and walking out on him!

'So you didn't want him to forgive you?' she ventured, setting down the brandy beside Susan.

'I should have, shouldn't I? I mean, if you really love someone and you make a mistake, then of course you want them to forgive you. And I thought that's what I wanted when I sat down to tell him. I didn't want there to be any secrets between us, you see. But then – it was so quick – he didn't even have to think about it! It was as though I'd told him I'd finished the last packet of crisps or something.'

'He said nothing to you at all?'

'Well, no. He sort of said he couldn't believe it and what was I thinking and he said fuck a lot, but under his breath, not really *at* me. And he kept walking in and out of the kitchen. But – I'd expected a lot more shouting . . . and crying. It all seemed too calm.'

'And then what?'

'Then he said that he understood there'd been a lot of change lately and he presumed everything would settle down once we had our house. That's what he said, Granny – can you believe it!'

'Oh, lovey, we all say things that come out funny sometimes. What you need now is a good night's sleep. The back room's all made up and I'll bring you up a cup of hot milk and a couple of digestives. Here, take this week's *Hello!* — .. help you relax.'

'But really,' continued Susan as she was bundled out of the room, 'wasn't that just the weirdest thing to say?'

Angela reflected, as she watched Susan climb the stairs two at a time, that any man who had just been told that he'd been cuckolded had every right to behave a little oddly. But there wasn't anything to be gained by pointing this out to her slightly hysterical granddaughter.

2

Susan was sitting up in bed wearing one of her granny's nightdresses (she had neglected to pack a bag) flicking through the pages of the magazine, but not even a shot of a half-naked Daniel Craig could hold her attention. It had all happened so fast. Her only instinct had been to run. If she hadn't got out of that flat she would have exploded. As she stood in the middle of the kitchen floor she'd felt a tingling in her hands so strong that she'd had to clench them into fists to prevent herself from grabbing the plates from the press and firing them at the wall, one by one, each crash scoring her a gold medal. And they weren't even her plates. She'd wanted to scream like a harridan until someone called the guards, convinced a heinous crime was being committed. She'd wanted to take the knives out of the drawer and stab them between his eyes. It was frustration she felt, just like any delinquent acting out their issues in the town centre on a Saturday night. Only she was too well brought up to actually do any of it.

How could he do that? How could he just forgive her? Had he no respect for himself at all? Clearly he had absolutely none for her. What was it she had said to him as she was walking round the kitchen in circles trying not to go to the knife drawer? That she wished she had never met him, that she had wasted years of her life with him and she needed to move on now before it was too late? Had she really said all that? And had she really meant it? Paul had stood there with a packet of biscuits in one hand and a jar of coffee in the other, motionless, voiceless. She couldn't get that image out of her head; the impotence of it galled her. Why wasn't he smashing things? He was a man – he wasn't supposed to be able to control his urges like she was. Oh Paul, she thought bleakly, and his urges . . .

She spread her legs wide in the small double bed so that one foot touched either edge and then brought them close together again. She sighed. It was good to be in this room again; she couldn't remember the last time she'd slept here. So much had changed recently. She had moved house, moved city, changed jobs, got engaged, lost daily or weekly contact with all her friends. And why exactly? Well, of course, it was all part of growing up, being sensible, starting a real life – her mother was right, you couldn't pretend you were a student all your life – it was just that it had happened so quickly. As if, overnight, she'd gone from eating spag bol while watching *Big Brother* on a rented telly in a room with cigarette burns on the carpet, to having Sunday roast in a house that smelled of paint with a man who said he was her husband and with whom she was having a conversation about who would give up work after the baby arrived.

She sighed and picked up the magazine again. She loved a good nose into a glossy – she liked to imagine what it would be like to wear those clothes, have those lips, meet those friends, live in that house, have sex with those men. Although the truth was that it was rare enough for Susan to find herself truly lusting over any of these things. If asked, she'd say the nicest house she'd ever been in was her granny's; her favourite clothes were the jeans and shirts she wore when she was relaxing on a Saturday and her ideal man was . . . now that she thought about it she wasn't sure. George Clooney maybe, or Johnny Depp, or what about the new Mr Darcy, what was his name again? McFadden or something? It was quite a while since she'd been heavily in lust with a fantasy man. Was that, she wondered, because her every need had been satisfied or because she was so far from having her needs satisfied, she had forgotten what they were?

Susan had never considered herself to be fascinating, but there had been a time when she had been capable of spontaneous behaviour – like the time she and three of her classmates ran naked round the Aula for a dare. Sure, it was night time and there was only the four of them there, but they did it. Now, if somebody suggested a midnight run in the buff, the first thing that would occur to her was that she might step on something, or catch a chill. She sighed. How had she let herself get this way?

It had all started in a shared house in Ranelagh. After her year of travelling, she came back to Dublin to take up the job she'd been offered in the tax office. At the time she'd happily batted away the fairly constant stream of jokes about her job with the confident assertion that she was living in one of the most happening cities in the world and her work was merely a means of experiencing all it had to offer. Yet, somehow, after a year or so of exploring a handful of Dublin pubs and nightclubs, her job, uninvolving though it was, took over her life and in the evenings she did little other than explore the TV listings.

She had found the Ranelagh house through a friend of a friend. For Paul it had been a similar experience: a friend of his was moving out, so he moved in. The location was perfect for access to work and town, and the area itself was extremely pleasant to live in. It was one of those rare house shares where everyone had the room they wanted, everyone had similar ideas about domestic hygiene and everybody liked the same TV programmes. There was another girl,

Stephanie, and another guy, Niall. Stephanie and Susan worked together as did Niall and Paul. The girls got the bus to work and the boys drove in Paul's car. They would all arrive home at roughly the same time; someone would put the kettle on and make tea for everyone; someone else would have picked up some food and started a little gentle cooking; someone else would open a bottle of wine and someone else would tell a story that had them all in stitches. They were good times. At weekends the four of them were inclined to go out together on Saturday nights. Often the girls went shopping during the day while the boys went to a match, and on Sundays they stayed home together to nurse their hangovers with the Sunday papers and a big fry-up. When Susan thought back on her life with Paul it was those times, pre-relationship, that seemed the best.

Then, all of a sudden, everything changed: Stephanie and Niall got together. One minute all four of them were just having a laugh, the next Stephanie and Niall were all over one another. It couldn't but make a difference, even though they all tried not to let it. They still did a lot of things as a foursome, but there was no avoiding the fact that the other pair would sometimes go out by themselves, or that they often went to bed early, and so Paul and Susan were inevitably thrown together more. And that was how it always seemed to Susan when she thought about it: they had been flung together like ingredients in a bowl, but nobody had paid any attention to the recipe. If they hadn't been so much in the habit of spending all their free time together they might never have looked at each other and thought, Hey, why not? And they certainly wouldn't have ended up, one Friday night, during the ads of *The Late Late Show*, turning to each other and letting their lips collide. Susan wondered if they were ever truly attracted to each other or whether it was just comfort and convenience and a desire to make up the foursome again that drew them together.

That's when they had sex for the first time – during *The Late Late*. Pat Kenny was interviewing Brian Kennedy, but despite that, their libidos remained high. There had been something in the atmosphere all evening: Stephanie and Niall had gone out straight after work; Susan had done some late-night shopping, so Paul had come home to an empty house. As soon as Susan walked in the door he was hopping on one leg trying to do things for her. He made her a cup of coffee with biscuits he had bought specially. While she was drinking that he ran out for a Chinese take-away and a bottle of wine. He had stopped off at the video shop but hadn't been able to make a satisfactory choice. A thriller seemed wrong and he didn't know enough about romantic comedies to take the risk. Hence, they ended up watching *The Late Late*. Susan had gone along with Paul's new-found attentiveness without taking too much notice, but when he started to edge closer to her on the couch and when his breathing became noticeably heavier and when he kept altering his position as if he couldn't get comfortable, she started to wonder if something was about to happen.

She had truly never thought about Paul that way before. He had always seemed somewhat asexual to her, even though he was obviously a very masculine sort of man. He was tallish and had an athletic build. His strong jaw was softened by a warm smile and his eyes, though often frustratingly inexpressive, were genial. There was nothing wrong with him, he just wasn't the sort of man to appeal to Susan instantly. She was convinced at the time, however, that all the best relationships came about between people who weren't instantly attracted to each other (having just had a fairly disastrous fling with a co-worker she had been lusting after for months), and you only had to look at Stephanie and Niall to feel the love between them. And so, with all these thoughts in her head, and Paul getting closer on the couch, Susan concluded that if he was keen, then she might as well be keen as well.

Somewhere, deep within her, Susan was painfully committed to a non-specific notion of 'romance', yet when it came to choosing men, or even knowing what she wanted in a man, she was never able to realize her fantasies. Paul wasn't the man she dreamed of, but he was the man she knew she'd end up with . . .

Their first kiss really was just a collision of their lips. Susan couldn't ignore Paul any longer, so she turned to him and he immediately moved forward so that his face was perfectly parallel with hers. They looked at each other somewhat dubiously, then closed their eyes and moved into the kiss.

Susan didn't feel anything. She had thought she might get a little tingle as soon as she felt his breath, but there was nothing other than a slightly out of body feeling that was a little uncomfortable. Paul, however, seemed to be feeling plenty. He lunged forward and promoted the kiss from mere lip contact to fully blown French-style tongue gymnastics. Susan was quite surprised, but now that she had started, she figured she might as well keep going. So she gathered her knees under her, wrapped her arms round his neck and kissed Paul as if he were someone she had been lusting after for months.

They were like a ball rolling down a hill, gathering more and more momentum until they had to stop or they would end up smashing into pieces. Wild-eyed and breathless, Susan managed to pull away for a moment to ask Paul if he was sure that they should do this. Paul was not in the mood for conversation, but he did know where Susan was coming from. She had to know whether this was a Friday-night fling because they were home alone, healthy and horny, or if this was the beginning of something lasting.

'I think you're great,' he said, 'you're really hot.'

'Thanks,' said Susan, but that wasn't exactly what she was looking for.

'No, really,' he said, 'I've been thinking about you for ages. I really think we'd be good together.'

'You do?'

'Fuck, yeah! We know each other really well. We know we get on great. You're really hot.'

Susan was trying desperately to hear what she wanted in Paul's words, and while there was nothing wrong with what he was saying as such, it just didn't have the magic she would have liked. Maybe she shouldn't have started talking at all and just let it happen. Because she did want it to happen; in the time they had been kissing she had worked out that this was a good thing. All of a sudden the idea of Paul slotted into place. She hadn't met anybody she liked in ages – apart from the guy at work and pure lust didn't count – and she was feeling the need to be in a relationship. It wasn't because she was desperate for a man, or that she was incapable of functioning on her own, it was simply because it was nice. Going out with someone was nicer than not going out with someone, and Paul was the nicest someone she had met in a long time. She disagreed, however, about knowing each other really well. They might have been living in the same house for over a year, but she felt she had never had a real insight into who he was. But that was one of the best things about being in a relationship: it allowed you access to the next layer of a person, and allowed them to peel a layer off you. Yes, all of a sudden Susan got very excited about the prospect of being Paul's girlfriend, and she was willing to waive his lack of romantic diction in favour of getting right down to some hot and heavy love-making.

The first time wasn't particularly good but that was to be expected. They certainly didn't know each other's bodies well and it emerged that they had very different styles. Susan loved to be wooed slowly; she liked long lingering kisses that travelled all over the body and she liked foreplay to continue until sex seemed like the most natural thing in the world.

Paul, on the other hand, was impatient. He liked to get in there and get on with it, but he was more than happy to engage in a bit of cuddling afterwards. He considered himself quite a good lover because his penis was ever so slightly above average in length and girth, and because, on occasion, his lovers had faked it a little too enthusiastically. Once Paul got up a head of steam, he was rather single-minded in his approach and there was little chance of his partner getting there for real. So far he had never been with anybody long enough, or with anybody who cared enough, to tell him that his technique left a lot to be desired.

And so it was the first time with Susan; as soon as they resumed after their little chat, Paul launched himself into the act. Only the necessary clothing was removed, and after very little further effort he had his orgasm before Susan had even positioned herself comfortably beneath him.

It was not good for Susan, but she wasn't giving up. She hadn't had a whole lot of experience, just enough to know that if she wanted this to work, she would have to make some changes. She wasn't signing up for night after night of bad sex, no matter how convenient it was.

They were lying on the couch half dressed, sweaty and a little unsure of what to do next. Pat Kenny, still mute, had moved onto the big car prize of the night and was just about to call Brian Kennedy back to make the draw when Susan found the remote under her left buttock and switched the TV off.

'Why don't we go upstairs?' she suggested, in a tone she hoped would signal that if he had thought that was good, then he hadn't seen anything yet.

'Sure,' he said, in a tone that seemed to suggest he would like to go to sleep. Susan was tired too, but if she let the night pass with only the previous ten minutes to recommend Paul to her, they might never get any further.

Firstly, she suggested they share a shower. There was nothing sexier than a shower-clean naked body (actually, there was nothing sexier than a raw earthy sweaty one, but Susan knew they weren't there yet). Thankfully her own bed was nicely made and the sheets were only a few days old. After drying each other off, she threw him down on the bed and began to kiss him all over, very slowly and very sexily. He went nuts. But she wouldn't let him in until he had done the same for her. It drove him even crazier. Then she insisted that she went on top and worked at her own orgasm before she let him throw her on the floor and find his own. It was very successful. As they lay panting by the foot of the bed, they wrapped their arms about each other and Paul kissed the top of Susan's head.

'I love you,' he said.

'I love you too,' she said.

Susan wasn't sure if he meant it, or if she meant it when she said it back to him, but she was confident that sooner or later they would both mean it. Once they had climbed back into bed, she nestled against him, not sorry that he was there.

The first year or so of their relationship was quite good,

and most of the time they got along perfectly well. Yet Susan needed to feel some tension somewhere, something that would suggest that her world would fall apart if she ever lost this man. But they didn't seem able to generate that kind of intensity. Apart from having reasonably regular sex, they could still have been housemates.

And as time wore on, the sex became tedious. Susan tried not to focus on what wasn't working because she still wanted to be with Paul, but she was disappointed in the sex. She had expected that the thrill might wane with familiarity, but she felt she could reasonably hope for a little more. Paul easily reverted back to his streamlined approach and Susan found her mind wandering on the occasions when he sidled up to her and began his routine. At first she was able to maintain her interest by fantasizing about other men. She didn't think there was any harm in imagining that it was Johnny Depp's arms around her, or that it was Captain Jean-Luc Picard of the *Enterprise*, breaking his rule to make love to a junior officer (after all, a healthy fantasy life was highly recommended by experts and quacks alike), but after a while even that became too much of an effort. When she started making shopping lists or thinking about something funny somebody had said during the day she knew there wasn't much va-va-voom left in their sex life.

Yet neither of them seemed to have any ideas. Their habit had always been to look to Niall and Stephanie – Susan couldn't escape the idea that herself and Paul were merely their sidekicks – and so when Niall and Stephanie got engaged and started looking at houses, Paul began to think that getting on the property ladder was something they should be doing too. He'd never mentioned marriage though . . .

*

Susan woke the next morning to the sound of birds singing and the smell of coffee brewing. Suddenly, as the events of the previous day flooded in, she was consumed by a sense of panic. Yet, as her eyes adjusted to the muted April light coming through the muslin curtains, she began to relax a little. As a child she had spent hours lying on this bed staring at the rows of pink flowers interlocked with pink ribbons until her vision became blurred and all sorts of weird shapes emerged from the walls.

She got out of bed and looked at herself in the dressing-table mirror. Apart from the ridiculous nightie (it seemed to contain more material than all her clothes put together), she didn't look too bad. Susan wasn't vain and she never peered at herself too closely, but she had half expected to see some horrific change reflected in her face. Yet there were no new lines, no disfiguring scars, not even much of a shadow under her eyes. Breaking up seemed to be good for her complexion.

She turned round and boldly pulled back the curtains. She was symbolically letting in the light not only on a new day, but on a whole new life. She was going to embrace that light and let it illuminate a brand new world for her.

She was busy being poetic and portentous in her head when she noticed a figure entering the gate at the foot of the garden. It was a man, wearing wellington boots and a waxed jacket that was too big for him. He was carrying something that looked like an inside-out kettle and he was dragging another odd-looking contraption behind him. It was unlikely that he was a burglar – he didn't look the type and a quarter past seven in the morning was hardly peak burgling hour. Susan figured he was probably the gardener – Angela had a gardener now that Tom had moved to

Ballyconnell. Just as she was beginning to turn away from the window, he looked up. He saw Susan and remained looking at her for barely a second, yet it seemed longer than was to be expected from a mere gardener. She was suddenly aware of her billowing and translucent night attire, yet she continued to stand at the side of the window with her hand on the sill, until she heard the noise of the bolt on the back door being opened.

She decided not to go downstairs if there was company, so she climbed back into bed and took up her magazine once again. However, the glossy pages were beginning to bore her; there were only so many celebrity interviews one could read without feeling that it was all a bit pointless. She began to fantasize about what it would be like if she and Paul were a celebrity couple: their break-up would have to be kept from the press, they would have to remain tight-lipped about the details and she would have to make fleeting appearances in public wearing designer jeans and dark glasses. She smiled at the thought. She picked up a biro from the bedside locker and began to make a list. Whenever Susan felt things were getting a little out of control in her life, she resorted to her list. A list of things to do steadied her and made her feel that her life had some structure. Crossing things off the list made her feel that she was (if only benignly) the master of her own destiny. To do:

1. Return to flat and rescue remains of former life.
2. Buy Granny a really nice present.
3. Ring parents and tell them the news (maybe).
4. Find out who gardener is and make plans to bed him in the green-house.

Before she could start on 5, she heard the back door open

again and, rushing to the window, was in time to see the gardener walk back down the path. His hands were in his pockets this time and he seemed to be in a hurry. Susan wished he would turn round and look up again (as if she was actually going to say anything . . .) but he didn't. Oh well, she thought, it can wait till tomorrow . . .

Susan had been in two minds about coming out on Friday evening but eventually she'd let the girls persuade her. Tiffany's bar had opened only recently and was attempting to be very sophisticated with its chandeliers and wine lists, fancy mirrors and raised balcony over the river, but in fact it was just a comfy pub which served a good pint and decent wine. Getting out again during the week was one of the things she was enjoying about being back in Limerick. Her home city was on a scale that suited her; in Dublin she used to feel like the gombeen girl up from the country but now, as she placed one foot pointedly in front of the other, she felt almost cosmopolitan. Bringing her back to Limerick was perhaps the one good thing Paul had done for her . . .

She'd also let the girls persuade her into a little late-night shopping. 'You know me,' her friend Bernie had said, 'I'm no shopaholic, but I'm a firm believer in a little retail therapy for the lovelorn.'

It wasn't too hard, in the end, to let them drag her into Brown Thomas where they did a hit and run on all the cosmetics counters.

'They go with your hair,' said the girl at Chanel of a luminous palette of colours she had just applied to Susan's sea-green eyes.

'It's such a healthy look,' said the YSL girl of the blusher she had applied to the apples of Susan's cheeks.

'All you need to do is match your lipstick to your skin

tone,' chimed the pair at Clinique, presenting Susan with three of the most beautiful lipsticks she had ever seen. After spending most of her life avoiding the girls at the cosmetics counters, Susan was charmed to see what they could do for her. How long was it, she wondered, since she'd looked in the mirror and been truly happy with what she'd seen?

Next they dragged her to Cruises Street where she was shunted into Carmel's favourite boutique and told not to come out until she had at least one complete outfit. Susan usually bought half an outfit because she felt guilty about spending too much money. So she would buy the top and leave the skirt, or buy the pants and leave the top, and then find, when she went home, that she had nothing to go with the top or the skirt and end up buying more disparate bits the following week because, when she opened up her wardrobe, she had nothing to wear.

But this time was different. Carmel found her the top – a gorgeous blend of heathery greens and warm russets – in a soft silk that rested suggestively on her breasts. Bernie handed her the cropped trousers that picked up the colours of the top so perfectly but it was the sales assistant who presented her with the pièce de résistance – the absolutely fabulous shoes. Susan gasped when she added up the price tags. What would Paul think of her spending so much when they were saving for a house? But then she remembered . . .

It only truly dawned on her later, as she was strolling down Charlotte Avenue to meet the girls, that she was single again, that Paul wasn't part of her life any more, that her life as she had known it for the past four years was over. It should have scared her; it should have terrified her; yet she couldn't ignore the slow bubbling of excitement that was beginning to manifest itself all over her body. It wasn't just the new clothes or the make-up; she was experiencing a very real lightness in her step that she hadn't felt in a very long time. Maybe part of it was having unloaded her problems to Angela – maybe part of it was having unloaded her guilty secret to Paul – but most of it seemed to have something to do with having left Paul. It was losing him, leaving him behind, that was giving her this sense of her world having opened up again.

Bernie hailed her from a table by the window; it was still just bright enough to be able to appreciate the view. This was something Susan was grateful for: the girls. She had been so lucky to find a pair like these. From her very first day in the revenue office they'd been warm and welcoming. There was no nonsense about them; they were simply glad to have some new blood about the place. Bernie was in her mid-twenties, perennially in and out of love, but having no serious interest in settling down. Carmel, who was technically Susan's boss, was thirty-two, and beginning to think she would never find a man. She was also getting broody (all her sisters had recently had babies) and at times she was comically single-minded. Susan found each of them, in their different ways, refreshing and easy to be with. Now that she'd moved and saw so little of Stephanie she was glad to find female company she could relax with. Seeing them now, though, decked out in their best stuff, waving to the window seat they'd saved for her, she felt a little guilty. She hadn't been entirely straight with them about her break-up with Paul.

'Suffice to say,' she'd said when she caught up with them at work that morning, 'that it's completely over, and it's all my fault.'

They'd pressed her for details, of course, but she couldn't quite get her tongue round the words: Oh yes, I'm a big slut and I'm also a horrible bitch and a small bit of a nutter – I throw away a perfectly decent man, and all I can say is *phew*! She knew she'd tell them the full story eventually, but she needed to live with the truth herself for a while before she gave it out to the world at large. It was different telling Angela – no matter what she did, her grandmother would never think badly of her.

'Sit here,' said Carmel. 'I'm just off to the bar for another one of these.' She was holding an empty bottle of wine precariously as she struggled to get off her high stool while still holding onto her bag, her phone, and the slit in her dress.

'Australian Shiraz, fourteen and a half per cent, twenty euro a bottle. You in?' asked Bernie.

'Why not!' said Susan. 'Wine puts me on the floor, but why the hell not!

'So . . . how're you feeling?' asked Bernie as Carmel limped off to the bar.

'Oh . . . OK, you know. It's a bit weird, but I'm fine. It was the right thing to do.'

'You're allowed to have second thoughts, you know.'

'I know, but that's the weirdest thing. This feels like a thought I should have had a long time ago. It makes me feel a bit stupid, actually.'

'That's nonsense!'

'No, it isn't. It's like, well, if this was so obviously the right thing to do, why did it take me so long to do it?'

'Oh, come on, we're always slow when it comes to these things. It's never easy to see the obvious when it's right in front of you.'

'But I think I must have been sleepwalking. For four years! That's a long time not to be fully awake.'

Bernie smiled. 'We all do a bit of it. I mean, if you presume that this is the man for you, you don't go questioning it every day. You just presume. And if nothing goes wrong, then you keep on presuming.'

'Yes . . . it still makes me feel stupid, though.'

'Here we go!' Carmel was waving a large white napkin along with her other paraphernalia. 'You'll never guess what I got!'

'I thought you'd stopped doing that,' said Bernie.

'How else am I going to meet men? You scare them away if they come over to the table.'

'Real men don't give out their phone numbers to nutty women they meet in the pub.'

'He looks pretty real to me.'

All three pivoted on their stools to catch a glimpse of an excessively tanned man standing by the bar who was now deep in conversation with an excessively tanned woman.

'Maybe he's *not* the one,' said Bernie with a little more feeling than was necessary.

'What are *you* smiling at? You've no business to be smiling at my pain.'

'What?' said Susan. 'Was I smiling?'

'Yes, you were,' said Bernie. 'Quite a wicked little smile.'

'I was just thinking . . .' The barest half smile leaked out again.

'What were you thinking?'

'Oh, it's nothing . . . just . . . well . . .'

'Well what?'

'Well . . . there was just this guy . . .'

'What! You've not broken up with Paul five minutes and there's already "this guy" . . .'

'Oh, it's just someone I saw from my window – my granny's gardener, for God's sake – and it just struck me

32

that . . . well . . I haven't done that in a long time.'

'Done what?'

'Look at a guy and think . . . you know.'

'Go on!' said both girls, taking deep swigs from their glasses.

'That's it. I've only seen him a couple of times – for a split second – but I saw him again this evening when I was getting ready. I mean, I couldn't even really see him – he had his back to me and his hair was falling over his face . . . but he had nice arms, you know, not too muscular, but nicely toned.'

'And . . .'

'There is no "and", it just made me wonder what it might be like to . . .'

'What it might be like to *get it on* with the gardener!' added Carmel helpfully.

The three girls roared with laughter, nearly knocking their glasses over.

'Oh yes, *gettin' it on*,' mimicked Bernie, as she started rocking back and forth in her seat. Carmel suddenly choked on her mouthful of wine, spraying the other girls and the occupants of the next table before nearly falling off her stool. And Susan sat there calmly, imagining what it might be like to get it on with the gardener.

It was just then, as the three girls were beginning to recover themselves, that Susan looked up and saw Paul standing at the bar.

3

The following morning, while Susan was still in the middle of a slightly erotic dream (something to do with potting sheds and garden hoses), Angela was deep in conversation with her daughter-in-law.

'You should have done something, Angela,' Maureen chided.

'I think all the doing was long over before she landed here, Maureen.'

'That girl is never done making a mess of things. Do you remember her leaving cert?'

'Her leaving cert was a long time ago.'

'Have you spoken to Paul?'

'Of course I haven't.'

'Well, somebody should.'

'It's for them to sort out.'

'You can't rely on Susan to sort anything out. She needs to be told what to do.'

Angela thought that Maureen was far too quick to tell her daughters what they should do. Was it any wonder they were always keeping things from her?

'She seems pretty adamant about this. I don't think we should interfere.'

'Oh Angela! If only I wasn't so far away.'

'Will you be coming back?'

'I can't at the moment. We have too much on. But you should do something. Talk to her. Make her see sense. She won't do better than Paul, you know.'

'I don't think Susan sees it that way.'

'I don't know what other way to see it. She's just going to rot in that tax office.'

'Susan will sort herself out.'

'I wish I had your faith, Angela, I really wish I did.'

Susan appeared in the kitchen looking attractively dishevelled.

'I'd better go now, Maureen, love, there's someone at the door. I'll give you a call later in the week.'

'Do, Angela. I worry so much . . . and get Susan to ring me.'

'That was your mother,' Angela said, putting the phone on the table, 'and before we go any further – I'm afraid I told her. I didn't mean to – it just slipped out.'

'Oh God! Did you tell her what I did?'

'Lord, no, love, I just said that you were here. That you and Paul had a row. Everything else is your business.'

'Thanks, Gran. Actually you've saved me a job. I'm not up to my mother at the moment.'

'Whatever I can do, lovey. But she is worried about you, you know.'

'I know. Mum always means well, even if it doesn't always come across that way.'

'And I'm worried about you too.'

'There's no need to be, honestly, Granny, I'm fine.'

'Still . . . I mean,' she said, handing Susan a cup of steaming coffee from the pot, 'do you think . . . you'll go back at all?'

'No.'

'Won't you at least talk to him?'

'I met him last night. In the bar.'

'Oh?'

'And you know what? I had nothing to say to him.'

'Nothing at all?'

'Nothing.'

'But surely he had something to say to you?'

'He wanted to talk all right. He wanted me to come over today and have a big, long-drawn-out, utterly pointless . . .'

'You can understand that he wants to talk.'

'But it's all been said. I mean, he should hate me. He shouldn't be able to stand the sight of me. I did something absolutely horrible to him and he just wants to continue as if . . . well, as if I never did what I did.'

'And why did you do it, love?'

Susan lowered her head.

'I don't know. I was very drunk.'

'That doesn't make it better.'

'I don't think I'm trying to make it better.' She sighed heavily. 'I don't know, Gran. But it wasn't a good sign, was it? Things mustn't have been right if I could . . .'

'And what now?'

'I don't know that either. I suppose I have an awful lot to think about. I really appreciate you letting me stay here while I get my head together. This house always makes me feel . . . safe.'

'You're welcome to stay as long as you like, love.'

'Thanks, Gran.'

'But you know, do think about it properly. Make sure you're doing the right thing. If Paul can forgive you for – your little infidelity – then he probably really loves you.'

'I don't know.'

'Real relationships aren't easy. And it's when they're at their most real that they're the hardest.'

'What do you mean?'

'Maybe you're having a little difficulty adjusting to the idea of getting married.'

'I'm fine with that – or at least I *was* fine with it.'

'Sometimes you don't even realize these things. I had pre-wedding jitters.'

'Really?'

'I remember sitting in the kitchen with my mother, just like we are now, and I started blubbering like a starved infant. My poor mother didn't know what to do. But she sat down beside me and waited until I stopped. Then she just asked me if I was all right. And do you know what I think it was? I didn't want to leave my mammy. I was totally in love with your grandfather, but all of a sudden I realized that I wouldn't be sitting there with my mother in the mornings any more, that it wouldn't be her I'd come home to in the evenings, and even though I couldn't wait to be married and be living with your grandfather, all of a sudden I was afraid of the change. My life was about to become so different.'

Susan laid her hand across her granny's and gave it a little squeeze.

'I know it's different nowadays. You've all been living together and doing everything there is to do, but it's still a big step. Just think about it, lovey. You might have the jitters and not even realize it.'

'I will think about it.'

'And now, what about a bit of breakfast? I put a few things in the fridge – a couple of fresh croissants, a packet of rashers, some sausages, eggs and that orange juice with the bits in it.'

'Oh, Gran . . .'

'I'll leave you to do the cooking yourself. I want to get on with my dusting.'

'That's great. You're brilliant. But leave the dusting, I'll do it for you later.'

'No, love, I enjoy the dusting. I like to do the jobs I'm able for. I'll find something else for you to do, don't worry.'

Susan continued to sit at the table sipping her coffee. Her head was already beginning to feel better. She hadn't had a night out like that in ages and she couldn't remember the last time she'd had so much fun in a nightclub. She'd danced late into the night to music she didn't recognize surrounded by people she didn't know. It had been exhilarating.

But was that what she wanted her life to be now? Going out to pubs like Tiffany's and staying out in the clubs till the small hours in the hope of meeting someone? Getting all excited when some overdressed ponce asked for her number? Nights like last night were only fun if you didn't have an agenda.

She looked round the kitchen; there was no evidence of Angela's breakfast of cereal and toast apart from the coffee pot which was still brewing silently on the hob. That was the biggest thing she was aware of now – the silence. It was as if, since breaking up with Paul, all the background noise in her life had stopped and it was only now that she was able to hear her own thoughts. That wasn't a good sign either, was it? If you equated life with your boyfriend to having the TV on and the dryer going? Surely the love of your life should constitute a symphony at the very least?

That's when she noticed that the gardener was back.

She sat there for another while just looking at him. He was wearing jeans and a casual shirt over a T-shirt and gloves to protect his hands from the rough branches he was taking off Angela's privet hedge. He seemed lost in the work, cutting at a slow pace, allowing the branches to fall at his feet and periodically gathering them into small heaps. She had a better view of his face from this angle, although his hair did tend to fall across his eyes. He was definitely a bit older than her, but not much. She wondered what it must be like to do that kind of work – out in the open air, your own boss (more or less), communing with nature – Susan checked herself before she went any further. She knew she'd no more give up the centrally heated comfort of her office than she would be able to mow a straight line in the grass. She was more the kind of person who appreciated nature from the other side of a pane of glass. Yet there was something about the way he seemed so at ease with the work that made her feel there was more to it than simply cutting and shearing. He knew what he was doing, he was confident, and the result clearly gave him satisfaction.

She decided to go and talk to him. What did she have to lose? And where was the harm in a little friendly conversation? She grabbed another mug from the press and, pausing for a moment to check that her fake silk dressing gown didn't reveal anything it shouldn't, filled the mug with coffee and walked casually out the back door.

'Hi,' she said cheerily, 'I'm Susan, Angela's granddaughter. I'm staying with her for a while. I thought you might like a cup of coffee.'

He looked at her, a little quizzically, before responding.

'Hi,' he said.

'It's black,' said Susan, hardly pausing to allow him to speak, 'the coffee. Do you take milk and sugar? I can run inside and get them for you.'

'No,' he said, still looking puzzled, but laying down the shears and putting his hand out for the coffee, 'black is fine.'

'So,' Susan said, as he took a sip from the mug, 'you're my granny's gardener?'

'Ahm, yes,' he said slowly, 'I do a bit of gardening for your granny.'

He was smiling now. Susan couldn't imagine at what, and began to wonder if her dressing gown was gaping or if her hair was in a worse state than she had thought. She gave the gown a tug across her chest but decided to keep talking.

'So, have you known Angela long?'

'Yes, Susan,' he said, 'I've known her all my life.'

'What?'

Susan wasn't sure which was more surprising – that he used her name so easily or that he had known Angela for so long.

'Yes,' he continued, a little hesitantly, 'ahm . . . she's my granny too. I'm your cousin Gavin.'

'What?'

'You know, Gavin O'Regan? Frank and Grace's son?'

'Oh my God, Gavin!' Susan's eyes kept getting bigger and bigger as she realized what a fool she must look.

'Well,' he said, 'it's been a while.'

'Oh my God, Gavin!' she said again. 'Of course, I see it now. I'd heard you were back all right.'

'Just a few months. I got delayed.'

'But, yeah, it has been ages. The last time I saw you must have been . . .'

'It was at Mum's funeral.'

'Oh God. I'm so sorry. I mean, I'm sorry I didn't recognize you. I mean, I'm sorry about your mum too.'

'That's OK.'

'And ahm . . .'

'You were in Australia when Dad died.'

'Yes, I remember. I couldn't get back. I wasn't even in Australia, I was on the way. I think I was in Vietnam.'

'You sent a card, and a lovely letter.'

'Oh, good. I mean, that I sent a card.'

'I know.'

'I can't believe we haven't been in touch.'

'Oh, you know, time passes. You were away and then I was away for a few years.'

'Of course, how was . . . ?'

'Sweden.'

'Yes, yes, I knew it was Sweden. Was it good?'

'It was good for work. A bit boring otherwise.'

'Ahm, Gavin, I really feel like an eejit. I'm really sorry. I recognize you now but you do look different.'

'Don't worry about it, Susan,' he said smiling, 'it's been, what, twelve years?'

'I can't believe Granny never told me it was you!'

'Oh, she was probably having a bit of fun.'

'Bit of fun indeed! I'll kill her!'

Gavin laughed out loud.

'Anyway, it's good to see you. And thanks for the coffee.'

'Oh, you're welcome.'

'So . . . are you around for long?'

'I don't know . . .'

'I might see you again before you go.'

'Oh yes, I'm not going soon. I just . . . I'm . . .' Susan realized that she was in a mess in a number of ways, and that retreating into the house was the best she could do at the moment.

'It was really nice meeting you again. We must have a proper cup of coffee and catch up.'

'Definitely.'

'I'd better go.'

'See you.'

He handed her back the mug.

'Thanks.'

Gavin picked up the shears and went back to work.

Susan charged back into the house hollering for Angela.

'Gran? Gran? Where are you? Gran?'

Angela emerged from the living room, Pledge and duster in hand.

'What is it? What's wrong?'

'Why didn't you tell me it was my cousin Gavin who was your gardener?'

'But I did. I was talking to him the very night you arrived.'

'What?'

'Yes. I told you I was talking to him on the phone that night. He does all my gardening.'

'No, Gran, you just said you needed to get some gardening done. You never mentioned it was Gavin.'

'Didn't I? I thought I did.'

'No, you . . . I . . .'

Susan realized she was beginning to sound hysterical over a gardener and that she was in danger of making her granny nervous. Angela occasionally forgot things, but no more than she had ever done.

'Oh, you probably did mention it, but I didn't hear you. I was so wrapped up in myself I wasn't listening straight. So he does a lot of work for you?'

'Gavin's a life saver. Since your dad has been in Ballyconnell so much, Gavin has looked after everything. I'd be lost without him.'

Now that Susan thought about it, she did recall her parents mentioning that one of the cousins was going to look in on

Angela while they were away, but she hadn't associated the geeky boy – who had presumably grown into an even geekier man – with the figure she had seen from her bedroom window the previous morning.

'Gavin's brother, Luke, he's in the States then?'

'That's right, he's doing very well for himself over there. We don't see much of him, of course.'

Susan was piecing together the various bits she had been told over the years but had hardly paid attention to. Now she remembered hearing that one of the brothers was in Europe somewhere, and that the other had gone to the States, but she hadn't kept track of who went where. And there had been something else her mother had hinted at, something she was supposed to keep quiet, but she hadn't been interested enough at the time to pay any heed. Now she was bursting with questions.

'So, what is it Gavin does again?'

'He's an engineer.'

'And he's what, thirty-three?'

'Thirty-five.'

'Is he married?'

'No, he's not married.'

'And does he have a girlfriend?'

'Aren't you very nosey all of a sudden?'

'I'm just curious. I'd kind of forgotten about Gavin. I'm just . . . catching up.'

'Oh, you're fickle all right, forgetting about the cousins you spent so much time with when you were children.'

'Oh, Granny, that was a million years ago. We've all changed so much since then. But I kind of like the idea of having a grown-up cousin.'

'I'm sure Gavin's delighted to have you too. I'd be lost without him. Now, are we having a cup of tea, or what?'

Susan filled the kettle and rooted in the press for chocolate biscuits. Yes, she thought to herself, much better to have lost a gardener and gained a cousin.

4

On Tuesday evening Susan was strolling slowly up Charlotte Avenue, enjoying the evening air and peering into people's gardens as she passed. She had always liked this side of town; as children and in their teens she and her sisters had spent a huge amount of time here. The three of them had gone to school nearby even though there was a perfectly good school not ten minutes' walk from their own house on the other side of town. But Maureen didn't think that a co-ed community school was the right educational milieu for her daughters, so she insisted on sending them across the river to the nuns. They'd railed against it at the time – why did they have to get up so much earlier? What was wrong with the school all their friends went to? Why did they have to be different? But Maureen's mind wasn't for changing. In the end they'd been perfectly happy – even Marianne, whose official line had always been that she hated all author-itative institutions, grudgingly admitted that it was all right. And of course, one of the best parts was calling in to Angela every evening on their way home.

She slowed her pace even further and had to do a double take on her surroundings. She was having a déjà vu moment, almost as if she had slipped back in time and was walking home to Angela's after school. She had to look down and make sure she wasn't wearing the uniform that never quite fitted because it was a hand-me-down from Felicity, and that the bag she was carrying was indeed the semi-ugly brown leather thing that Paul had given her for Christmas, and not the green canvas wreck she'd held fast to for five years. She shuddered. Perhaps it was her brain's way of telling her it was time to move on and stop sheltering at her granny's. Time to get out the paper and look at flats and work out how she was going to handle the next phase of her life. She sighed. She was often a bit slow on the uptake.

She mentally returned to the list she'd made the night of her arrival at Charlotte Avenue to see how she was faring:

1. Return to flat and rescue remains of former life.

Well, that had been weird. She'd gone back to the flat in Dooradoyle before going to work that Friday morning. Turning the key in the door her mind was flooded with all sorts of insanities: what if Paul was still there? What if he were so upset at her leaving that he wasn't able to face work? What if he were lying in the bath right now with his wrists cut, gasping his last breath? She rushed through the door, her own breath held, but she found everything as she had left it, if not a little tidier. There was no sign of Paul. The living area had been neatly arranged after what looked like a night spent watching the telly: the remote was lying in position on the arm of the couch; yesterday's newspaper was folded at the television listings and was positioned on top of the coffee table. In the kitchen one plate, one knife, one fork, one spoon, two mugs and a cereal bowl were resting on the draining board. In the bedroom the duvet had been pulled up and smoothed out; Paul's pyjamas were folded under his pillow as were hers, still undisturbed. In the bathroom the bath contained a few hairs but was otherwise free of human evidence. It was almost as if she had never lived here. She was sure she had left some clothes lying on the floor and her make-up had definitely been in a mess on the shelf over the sink; now it was gathered neatly into a little toilet bag and hung on the back of the door. Was Paul trying to get rid of her?

It didn't take long for Susan to fill the trolley bag she'd last used for holidays. She wasn't inclined to accumulate large amounts of clutter; when she grew tired of her clothes she threw them out; when her magazines were read she recycled them and when something lay around the house gathering dust she found a reason to break it. However, as she stood in the hallway ready to close the door on the flat for the last time she was uneasy with the thought that the whole of her life with Paul, some four years, was being carried away in a medium-sized piece of luggage from Dunnes Stores. It seemed rather pathetic if that was all her life with him had amounted to. Surely there was more to her and more in her than what she had experienced with him?

2. Buy Granny a really nice present.

She hadn't managed to do that yet. But she had been good about not making extra work. Granny really was fabulous. Susan had done exactly as Angela had suggested and tried to work out if this whole thing was just an attack of pre-marriage nerves. Was Paul's instant absolution evidence of the strength of his love for her, or was it merely a sign of his need to get on the property ladder? Small and all as her salary was, it would still make a difference in getting a big mortgage. But no, that was far too cynical. Either way, though, she didn't think it was nerves. Or if it was, then it was time her nerve endings got in

47

touch with each other and woke her up to what her life had become.

3. Ring parents and tell them the news (maybe).

Well, Granny had done the initial telling but she'd had to have the 'conversation'.

'I don't understand you at all,' her mother had said before Susan had finished her first sentence. 'If you've had a fight with Paul, why aren't you over there making it up with him?'

'It's not a fight, Mum, it's over. We're not together any more.'

'That's rubbish, dear. Get over there and sort it out. You don't break up with someone over a silly fight.'

'It's not a silly fight. It's over.'

'That's nonsense. It's not over. You've been going out for nearly five years. You'll be getting married soon.'

'MUM! It's over!!'

'Don't shout at me, Susan.'

'I'm not shouting. I'm only saying.'

'And *I'm* only saying that one argument doesn't mean a relationship is over. You have to work at things. Marriage is all about compromise.'

'We were never married, and I've never stopped compromising!'

'Susan, lovey, you know very little about life.'

'What's that supposed to mean?'

'You know what you should do now? You should get Paul to come down here for a little break. The air here is so pure it would help you to see everything more clearly. Daddy and I are very upset that you've never seen the house.'

48

'I'm working. It's hard to get away.'

'You're not working at the weekends. Why don't you come down this weekend?'

'Why don't you come up to Limerick?'

'We're done with Limerick, love. All that pollution isn't healthy.'

'Limerick's not polluted! You should try living in Dublin for a while.'

'I don't know why anyone would live in Dublin. It's just madness to live where there are so many people. Do you know that if the whole country was as crowded as Dublin the population would be forty million? Sure, wasn't that why you and Paul left Dublin – so you could start a family in a cleaner environment?'

'What are you t– Oh, never mind. Look, I'll see about coming down.'

'I hope you're not being a strain on your granny. Angela's getting very feeble these days.'

'Granny's not getting feeble and, no, I'm not being a strain on her. I'm pulling my weight, Mum.'

'I just think it's very strange altogether, piling in on top of Angela like that.'

'I don't really want to be on my own at the moment.'

'You should be buying your own house, Susan. And you should be living in it with Paul.'

'Oh honestly, Mum, I really have to go.'

'Well, don't come crying to me when you –'

'Bye, Mum.'

'Susan?'

'Granny's calling me. I have to go.'

By the time she got off the phone she was exhausted. But at least she could cross it off her list.

*4. Find out who gardener is and make plans to bed him in the green-
house.*

She hadn't done that, obviously. Bed him in the green-
house, that is – she did know who he was now. But if he
hadn't been her cousin . . . Oh well, she thought, it was
probably OK to give up a fantasy man if it meant she gained
someone she could have fun with.

She resolved to start a new list as soon as she got home,
beginning with looking for a flat and learning to drive. It
had been on her mind for ages that it was finally time she
got mobile. How had she let herself get late into her third
decade and still not be able to achieve forward momentum
behind the wheel? Sure, her mother's attempts at teaching
her as a young teen had been terrifying, and obviously it
had been so much easier, in Dublin, to use public transport
and, yes, she had just let Paul do all the driving when she
was going out with him, but now it was becoming ridiculous.
She *had* to learn to drive.

As she approached number 9 she could see the front door
was open and the sound of voices was coming from the
front room. One voice was definitely Angela's and the other,
she thought, might be Gavin's.

'Hello!' she hollered expectantly, walking into the room.

'Hello, love,' said Angela, 'come here a minute, we need
your advice.'

'Hi!' Gavin said, turning round to take in Susan.

'Oh?' she said. 'What do you need me for?'

'I'm getting this room painted, was I saying that to you?
Gavin is going to do it for me, and I don't know what to do
about the colour. This room gets very little light so it needs
brightening up, but I'm blind from looking at these cards.'

Gavin handed Susan the sheaf of colour cards, pointing

out the sections featuring whites, creams, magnolias, ivories and golds.

'They're all nice,' said Susan, not paying them much heed. 'What do you think, Gavin?'

'Whatever Angela wants, but I know that this burnished apple white here goes on very nicely.'

'Yeah,' said Susan, looking more closely, 'that does look nice. I think you should go with that, Gran.'

'Great! That's sorted then. Will you get me that one so, Gavin? I'll go and put the kettle on, I'm parched. Will you stay for tea, love?'

'Ahh . . . I will, Gran, thanks.'

As soon as Angela had left the room, Susan turned to Gavin.

'I want to apologize for being so rude the other day. If I'd thought for a second . . .'

'It's no big deal, we've all changed.'

Susan couldn't believe how different he seemed. Of course she'd never known him all that well – an age difference of seven years was as good as a generation when you were a child, and besides, Gavin had always been very aloof. His younger brother, Luke, was the one she remembered. He was only a year or two older than Susan; he was funny and boisterous and good at sports. While Luke had all the cousins in stitches doing impressions of their elderly relations, Gavin would be hiding upstairs listening to heavy-metal music and sorting through his Top Trumps. Whenever he did surface you could hardly see him under his mop of greasy hair, or behind his jam jars of glasses. Oh yes, Susan thought, you have certainly changed.

'But Granny had mentioned you were home,' she said. 'I've been so wrapped up in myself lately, I haven't been paying attention to anything.'

'We all get that way sometimes.'

'So . . . are you enjoying being back?'

'Yeah . . . it's been nice getting in touch with Granny again. I was hoping to meet your parents, but they seem to be away.'

'Oh, that's them – off in Ballyconnell all the time. You kind of don't expect your parents to go surprising you like that at this hour of their lives. You expect them to be still there when you surprise them.'

'Yes . . . I . . .'

'Oh God, sorry, I –'

'It's fine. Angela tells me you're back in Limerick for good?'

'Yeah. Yeah, I moved back with my . . .' Susan waved her hands about as if expecting to fashion the right word out of the air, 'my fiancé. But we broke up.'

'I'm sorry.'

'I'm not heartbroken or anything. I probably should be – I have nowhere to live, an uninspiring job – and absolutely no hobbies.'

'No hobbies?'

'Well, you know . . . if I'm going to fill out forms looking for new men, I'm going to need a couple of hobbies.'

Susan wasn't sure what was making her behave so flippantly. Perhaps it was the fumes from the sample pots Angela had left open all over the room.

'Tea's up, kids,' roared Angela from the kitchen.

'I love Angela's teas,' Gavin said as they were making their way to the kitchen, 'they're absolutely delicious and absolutely healthy at the same time. I can never make food like that.'

'Mmm,' agreed Susan, 'she seems to be able to get the balance right.'

Over tea – omelette, green salad and fresh home-made scones – the cousins began to catch up.

'I hear Felicity's making real waves in the dotcom sector,' said Gavin.

'Oh yeah. She's shit hot. I mean, I don't really understand it all, but they have this website – you might have heard of it? Thegoss.co.uk? It's full of celebrity gossip and stuff, but anyway they're gearing up to sell it. For a fortune. I mean, she might actually be a millionaire. I know that doesn't mean what it used to, but it'd still be kinda cool to have one in the family.'

'Wow! She was always heading places.'

'Oh yeah, Felicity is so focused. She wouldn't let anything distract her from what she wants.'

'And what about Marianne?'

'She never stops moving around – always changing jobs, always changing men. She's in Cork at the moment. She started some course, but it got cancelled.'

'Ahh, lots of sisterly love and affection I see,' said Gavin, laughing.

'Well, you're no better with Luke. I remember the two of you trying to kill each other. Literally. At least we never punched each other.'

'I never punched Luke. I wasn't allowed to. He was a sneaky bastard, though.'

Susan laughed.

'We get on OK, nowadays,' he continued. 'It helps being three thousand miles apart. So what are your plans,' he added, 'now that you're back in Limerick?'

'Oh, not much. Learning to drive, I think, is the first thing. I'm ashamed to admit I've never learned.'

'Do you know what I was thinking?' said Angela.

'What, Gran?'

'Well, I was thinking that seeing as you're here and seeing as Gavin's here, he might teach you to drive.'

'What!'

'I think it'd be a great idea. It's time you learned, love. I should know – I was forty before I learned to drive.'

'I know I need to learn, but you can't just ask –'

'It's no problem,' said Gavin.

'But you can't –'

'Oh, I know Gavin wouldn't mind. And he's a very patient teacher. He taught me how to send email.'

'But even so . . .'

'Honestly, Susan. I'd be delighted.'

'But I haven't even got a provisional licence – or any insurance!'

'We won't leave the industrial estate – you'll be fine. And you can apply for a licence tomorrow.'

'That's settled then,' said Angela. 'You can use my car. It's nice and small for beginners.'

'Mine might be better,' suggested Gavin. 'The Micra's a bit too small, Gran, it's only got a one-litre engine, and the gear change is a bit stiff. And I think my insurance covers other drivers.'

'Well, OK . . . are you sure you don't mind?'

'Really. It'd be fun.'

'That's settled then,' said Angela. 'Now, who wants one of my rock buns?'

They decided to make a start on the lessons that very evening, so, after doing the washing-up, the pair of them set out for Gavin's flat. As they were walking down the garden path to the back lane, Susan was struck by the tidiness of the garden and the rows of shrubs and flowers she wished she knew the names of.

'You really do an awful lot for Granny,' she said.

'Oh, you know, I like to give her a hand.'

'Yes, but you're very generous with your time.'

'Honestly, it's not a big deal. She's the only family I have in Limerick and I like spending time with her.'

'Of course,' said Susan, 'I'd forgotten that. Well,' she added with genuine tenderness, 'now you have me as well.'

'Yes,' he said without looking at her, 'now I have you as well.'

It was scarcely a five-minute walk to Gavin's building, a large converted Georgian house opposite the park.

'Hey,' said Susan, 'why don't you show me round while we're here? If you don't mind, I mean – there's no hurry with the lesson, is there?'

'No, but we don't want to leave it too late.'

'I'm just curious about this building. I've always wanted to get a look at these apartments.'

'No problem, just please ignore the mess.'

But Gavin's flat wasn't the least bit messy. His front door opened onto a small hallway, lit by a skylight, off which were doors leading to a very sizable living area (comprising kitchen, dining and living room), three bedrooms (one of which was large and had two windows facing the park, another of which was used as an office-cum-study), and a large airy bathroom with another skylight that offered a distant view of the river. The apartment was a mix of clean modern lines and rather quaint antique fussiness, yet it was a mix that worked. Because the rooms were spacious and bright, they could take the chunky new furniture, and because the flat was a classic Georgian design, it could take the older pieces that must have come from his parents' house.

'This is really nice,' said Susan, swinging round from the living room and entering the large bedroom.

'It's fine,' said Gavin.

'Oh!' she said, realizing she was in his room, among all his things. 'Sorry, this is your bedroom.'

'That's OK,' he said. 'Here, have a look at the view.'

Susan walked over to the large sash windows to take in the vista of the park and much of commercial Limerick behind it, but she didn't fail to take in the snow-white duvet cover or the books on the bedside locker or the shirt that was draped over a chair by the window. She felt the intense privacy of his space, but there was nothing in Gavin's demeanour to suggest that he was uncomfortable with her being there.

They went next into the room which he used as a study. It was painted, like all the others, in what Susan assumed must be burnished apple white, which gave all the rooms a sense of cool airiness. There was a computer and desk against one wall and, on the facing wall, several guitars were arranged on stands. In the middle of the room were two chairs, a recliner and an old-fashioned Queen Anne. Susan observed that much of the furniture in the flat was quite old, not at all what you would expect in a twenty-first-century bachelor pad.

'You play the guitar!' she exclaimed.

'A little.'

'You must play a lot, you have a load of them!'

'Well, they're all a bit different. This one's a Spanish guitar and this is a regular acoustic, although it's meant to be a twelve-string. And these two are electric, but I only play one of them, and that one there is a bass.'

'I thought a bass was huge, like a cello.'

'That's a double bass. This is a bass guitar, you know, part of the rhythm section.'

'I didn't know there were so many different kinds of guitar.'

'There are tons more.'

'Wow! Can I touch them?'

'Of course. Here, try the acoustic,' he said, lifting it from the stand and handing it to her.

'So,' she said, holding the guitar as if it were a missile, 'do you play in a band?'

'There's a local band I used to play with that are still knocking around. Their bassist is away a lot so they want me to fill in when they have a gig.'

'You play gigs? Where?'

'I haven't played any yet, but there's loads of music venues around town.'

'I'll have to come and see you play. Play something now.'

'Aren't we having a driving lesson?'

'Oh, there's no hurry. Play something.'

'Another time. Here, make yourself comfortable, I'll be back in a minute.' He disappeared into the bedroom leaving Susan perched on an amp in the middle of all the guitars, wondering what it would be like to be a rock chick.

Gavin was only gone five minutes, but when he came back he had changed from his painting clothes into indigo jeans and a crisp white shirt. Susan observed that his long frame was quite slight, yet an almost tangible strength seemed to emanate from his limbs. She couldn't imagine him lasting very long in a boxing ring, but she could see him holding something very heavy for a very long time.

'Come on.' He smiled. 'The light's beginning to go and dusk is the worst time of all for driving. You won't be able to see a thing.'

'Maybe we can go tomorrow; I'd love to hear you play.'

'Oh, Susan, I'm really not in the mood to play the guitar.'

'All right then, but you have to tell me the next time you have a gig.'

'Sure, I'll let you know. Now what about this lesson?'

'What about a cup of coffee?'

'Susan!'

'I'm sorry, Gavin, I'm being a baby. I'm just a little bit nervous about getting into the car. I haven't had any time to think about it.'

'You'll be fine. We'll just go out to the industrial estate and drive up and down for a while.'

'You know, I've never left second gear. In all the lessons I've had, I've never managed to get out of second gear.'

'That's OK.'

'No, it's not OK; it's moronic! I'm nearly twenty-nine and I can't even manage to – roll down a hill. I have a degree, but I can't – well, actually, it's not a very good degree. But I mean, half the people on the road are gob-shites and yet somehow or other they've all learned to drive.'

'Hey,' said Gavin, clearing a couple of newspapers from the couch, 'let's have a cup of coffee so and maybe we'll leave the driving till Saturday morning. The evening's a bad time to start anyway.'

'OK. Sorry for wasting your evening.'

'Believe me, Susan, I had nothing else planned.'

As Susan settled herself onto his two-seater couch, and looked round the airy room, she realized that his parents were a big presence; an entire bookcase was full of his father's volumes, the paintings on the wall were by his mother, and several photographs of both of them were propped on the original marble mantelpiece. Susan didn't know whether or not to mention them; she hadn't spoken to him about his parents since that first day in the garden when she had made such a fool of herself. Yet she couldn't ignore them; Frank and Grace had been a big part of her life at one time.

'Your mother was beautiful,' she said as Gavin handed her a mug of coffee.

'She was,' he said, taking one of the photographs from the mantel.

'And you look like your dad.'

'You think so?'

'Yes, round the eyes, I think.'

'Hmm, maybe,' he said, putting the photo back.

'I suppose you still miss them?'

'Obviously I wish they were still here, but it's not as bad as it was in the beginning. You do move on.'

'I suppose. I sort of miss my parents and they're only sixty miles away. But when I'm near them for longer than ten minutes they start to drive me mad.'

Gavin laughed. 'That's the way all right. So, Susan,' he added, sitting beside her on the couch, 'what's the big mystery with your sudden return to Charlotte Avenue? Angela's been very cloak and dagger about it.'

'What! You mean she hasn't told you?'

'No. She hasn't said a word.'

'Well,' Susan leant forward and took a deep breath, 'I came back to Limerick with Paul, my fiancé – I'd mentioned that. We'd got transfers, you know, with decentralization, and we were saving for a house. And it was all fine, but then . . .'

Susan knew she couldn't continue. Just like she couldn't say it to the girls, she couldn't bear the thought of Gavin – so nice, so sweet, such a good person – knowing that she had been a . . . that she wasn't as pure as the driven snow.

'But then . . .' she continued, 'well . . . I . . .'

'You don't have to tell me.'

'No, it's no big deal. He . . . cheated on me. That's all. No biggie. Common-place stuff really. But that was it, you know.'

'That's rough. I'm sorry.'

'It's OK. It's a bit weird at the moment . . . everybody feeling sorry for me. But it was the wake-up call I needed. If something's not right, then it has to go. Anyway, enough about me – are you going out with anyone?'

If Gavin was surprised by the question he didn't show any sign of it.

'No. Not for a while now.'

'Why not?'

'I don't know. Why ever not? Just not meeting the right person, I suppose.'

'And not willing to settle for the wrong one?' suggested Susan.

'What? Oh yeah, I suppose so.' Gavin looked disconcerted.

She got up and walked over to the window. She stood with her back to the light, her mug of coffee in one hand, the other expansively taking in the room.

'This apartment has a really nice feel to it. You must be very happy here.'

'Happy?' said Gavin. 'I've never really thought about it. I suppose . . . I must be.'

'Come on,' said Susan, grabbing him by the arm, 'I'm going to buy you a drink. In lieu of all the driving lessons you're going to give me.'

'All right then. But you do know they don't really approve of drinking and driving.'

'Come on, smart arse – before I put my purse away.'

*

As Susan was climbing into bed that night, she reached for her list. It was tempting to just lie back on her bed and let the effects of two pints of Guinness lull her off to sleep, but she was committed to sorting her life out – on paper at least.

She'd had such a lovely evening. Gavin was so easy to be with and everything he said made her laugh. He'd reminded her of the time she sat into the driver's seat of his father's car and somehow or another managed to let the handbrake go. The car was seconds away from colliding with the dining-room window when Gavin climbed in beside her and wrenched the brake back into place. Yes, first on her list was definitely learning to drive. There it was:

1. *Allow Gavin to teach you how to drive. You'll never have a better opportunity. If you blow it this time you'll be catching buses for the rest of your life.*
2. *Think really hard about something Granny would like. In the meantime stock up the fridge, replace all the wine you've drunk and pay the electricity bill.*
3. *Don't let Bernie coerce you into bed with any strange men.*

Bernie had revealed, over lunch a few days earlier, that she had a bit of a boyfriend.

'It's Brian,' she said with a furtive glance over her shoulder.

'Brian? Brian who?' asked Carmel.

'Brian.'

'Brian? Our Brian?'

'Yep.'

'Are you sure?'

'What kind of a question is that?' snapped Bernie. 'Of course I'm sure!'

'Who's Brian?' asked Susan.

'Brian who works with us.'

'Oh, he's quite nice.'

'Yes. Yes, he is,' responded Bernie instantly, 'he's a very nice guy and I had a really good time with him.'

'So what's the problem?' asked Susan, as Carmel was still sitting there with her mouth open.

'He's just not Bernie's type,' she said, 'he's really quiet.'

'Only in big groups.'

'I used to think he was gay.'

'He's not gay.'

'But he dresses really badly.'

'Only at work.'

'Do you fancy him?'

'Yes, I do.'

'Leave her alone,' said Susan. 'She likes him. So what?'

'Nothing. I'm just surprised.'

'I'm delighted,' said Bernie. 'Now, who else has news?'

'Well, actually . . .' Carmel was struggling to keep a broad grin from breaking out all over her face.

'Oh?'

'It's nothing. I just bumped into an old college friend, that's all.'

'That's hardly news,' said Bernie.

'He was looking really good. He's just got married.'

'Great.'

'But it's not going very well.'

'Then you should leave him be to get on with it.'

'Oh, for God's sake, Rob and I were only talking,' scoffed Carmel. 'I'm not playing the other woman or anything. You're still allowed to talk to married men, aren't you?'

'It all depends on what you're talking about,' said Bernie.

'I'm only being a shoulder to cry on.'

'But you're a new shoulder. It's not like you've been his buddy for years. You don't know what's going on in their marriage. Have you ever met the wife?'

'I've met her. She's OK. I wouldn't be gone on her.'

'Well, if I were you I'd just be careful. Isn't that right, Sue?'

'Oh, listen, I'm no one to give advice. I only know how to break up relationships.'

'Speaking of relationships,' Bernie ventured with a wry smile, 'Brian has a friend . . .'

'I'm happy for him.'

'He's really nice. Alan. He's a dentist.'

'I'm even happier for him.'

'Oh, come on. Why not? It'll help you get over Paul.'

'What? You're suggesting I have a fling with him?'

'If you wanted to . . . But actually, I think you'd be good together.'

'I don't think it's very fair on Alan, to foist a woman on him who's just broken off her engagement.'

'He's mad keen.'

'What? What have you told him?'

'Just that you're really nice, and you split up with someone recently. He went through a bad break-up himself not so long ago. Ye'd have loads in common.'

'No way.'

'Come on. We could be a foursome.'

'I hate foursomes.'

'I don't really mean a foursome. It's just that Brian and Alan have done everything together for years, and now that's all changed, because Brian has me.'

'Maybe Carmel was right and he *is* gay, if he's that attached to his little friend.'

'He's not gay. Oh, come on, Susan, why not? Alan's really nice.'

'Well, set him up with Carmel, then.'

'Yeah, why not set him up with me?'

'Ye wouldn't like each other.'

'Why not?'

'Ye just wouldn't.'

'Look,' said Susan, 'I'm not ready to go dating, especially not with men who can't get their own girlfriends.'

'He's just shy. Just one date, and see how it goes? Please?'

'No.'

'Please? I'll owe you a big one?'

'I'm giving up men.'

'Just this one time?'

'No.'

Susan had the impression Bernie wasn't going to give up, but the truth was that the thought of going out on a date with a man she didn't know made her feel as though she was coming down with the flu. Maybe life had been boring and predictable when she was with Paul, but at least she'd remained healthy.

4. Take up a hobby. Even if not for internet dating websites, would be good for general well-being.

It was so long since she'd had any kind of a hobby that she didn't know where to begin. She'd never been into sport – one session on the basketball court in first year had been enough to teach her that she'd be better sticking to the sidelines – and as elocution wasn't really something you could carry into adulthood she was at a bit of a loss. Gavin might have some ideas . . .

5. Stop having momentary flashes of Gavin taking his shirt off.

She wasn't serious about this last one. Of course she wasn't having mo—

All of a sudden Susan was aware of a commotion downstairs. She went to the landing and peered down. Angela was hugging someone in the hall — a woman, a woman she knew.

5

It had been one hell of a week for Felicity. It always made her smile when her family talked about her becoming a millionaire. She had casually mentioned once that it was the hope of thegoss.co.uk to be bought out by Sony Ericsson and when she, by the way, mentioned that the price might be in the region of fifteen million, the family hadn't been able to let it go. Of course, she always shrugged it off jokingly, yet there wasn't a word of exaggeration in anything she had said. It was just that it wasn't her share of the potential fifteen million that excited her, it was the buy-out itself.

Thegoss was Tony's brainchild. Tony Whitby, part-time journalist, part-time techie, full-time wheeler-dealer. She'd met him through a colleague at her old job as advertising executive for Sainsbury's and they had got talking at a party he had thrown for people in the business. His website was in its infancy then, but had made a name for itself by being able to get the scoops milliseconds before its more traditional rivals. That was thanks to Tony's contacts in the trade. Having worked on assorted rags on Fleet Street for several years he knew the people who knew the right people, and he knew how to get their secrets. Whether they liked it or not. By the time he met Felicity he was at the point where he had to branch out if he wanted to be noticed by the big boys. That's where Felicity came in. In one brief conversation she managed to convince him that she could get him what he needed – customers to visit his website again and again and again.

'It's called CRM,' she said to him over her first-ever glass of two-hundred-pound-a-bottle champagne, 'customer relationship management. It's all about knowing who your customer is. Just like a corner shop really, except that the corner is as big as the world.'

'Go on,' he said.

'You know as well as I do why the very early dotcoms failed. Sure, they were massively overvalued, but mainly it was because they didn't care about their customers. They treated internet users as if they didn't matter, as if there would always be another person out there who didn't know that they gave a shitty service. And that's the other thing they did wrong – they forgot that the number-one thing people do online is talk.'

'And are you going to talk to all to my users?' he asked, topping up her champagne.

'I don't have to talk to them,' she said, putting her hand over her glass. 'I merely have to remember what they looked at the last time they logged on. That's how I can build up a profile of who the users are, and as soon as I know who they are and what they like, I can start selling it to them.'

'Big advertisers.'

'The biggest.'

'Big revenues.'

'And lots of attention.'

'I like you, Felicity O'Regan. I think you should come and work for me.'

It hadn't been a difficult decision. Sainsbury's paid well but she was beginning to find the work excruciatingly boring. The possibilities of the internet had always fascinated her ever since she first heard about it in a minor module on computing during her business degree in the early nineties. She wasn't a techie; she didn't have a clue how to do any of the stuff that got you onto the net, but she had a world-wide vision when it came to exploiting it once you got there. Up to now she hadn't come across an opportunity to work at the coalface. Tony was offering her two thirds of her current salary with 15 per cent equity over five years. It was an offer she couldn't refuse.

What she should have refused, though, was his offer to get into bed.

Felicity had always had trouble getting a boyfriend. At first, in college, she had no particular interest in going out with some spotty, badly dressed, inarticulate boy from her class, and because she didn't join any societies or socialize much, she didn't meet any other boys. When she went to London she was far too intimidated and far too busy to be bothered to go looking for men, but mainly she was far too intimidated. Not having made the usual attempts and experienced the usual fumblings with young men who were as shy and inexpert as she was, it was now very difficult to imagine herself in close proximity to any of the suave suits who seemed to occupy her world. It was easier to be busy all the time; it was easier to give the impression that she was above all that and if, occasionally, she allowed rumours of a boyfriend back home to go unquashed, then it was only to give herself a little breathing space. The truth was that she was lonely and would have loved someone to explore London with. She didn't make women friends easily either, especially in a job as competitive as hers. Her only contact from home, Sandra, had been going out with Fergal from the very beginning so she wasn't always free for Felicity. It had been through Fergal that she met one of the few guys she had gone out with for any length of time.

Greg was a nice guy: English, a lawyer, good-looking and interested in going out with an attractive and intelligent girl.

Felicity thought him entertaining, easy-going and fun to be with. They had a couple of perfectly nice dates: a movie (a romantic comedy neither of them could remember), lunch (trendy spot in Notting Hill), dinner (trendy spot in the Angel) and one very crowded house party. It was during the house party, when conversation was strained because of all the noise and neither of them knew where to stand or where to balance their drinks and plates of inedible canapés, that it became clear to both of them that their relationship wasn't going very far. There was simply no electricity. Neither of them said anything explicit, but they were each intelligent enough to read the signs and were actually rather relieved to see them. As Greg was dropping her off that night he did make a half-hearted play to come in for a good-night-and-good-luck-and-no-harm-done shag, but Felicity had never been interested in sex for its own sake. That was one of the reasons why she was still a virgin at twenty-six. Unusual for London perhaps, but for a well-brought-up Catholic girl from a small to medium sized city who tended to put work before a social life, not all that surprising. Or so she told herself.

Later on there was another guy, Kevin: Irish, an accountant, moderately good-looking and very interested in Felicity. They met at a party given by Sandra's work; he had also been dragged along by a friend. They hit it off instantly; Kevin was easy to talk to, if a little shy, and Felicity didn't feel the least bit intimidated by him. After the party they had their first snog and after their fourth date, their first shag. Felicity hadn't intended sleeping with him that quickly – in fact she wasn't sure if she intended sleeping with him at all – but it seemed the natural thing to do one evening after a light meal and a bottle of Pinot Grigio at Pizza Express. They had gone back to Felicity's flat and opened up another bottle of wine. They started kissing and the kissing led them to the bedroom where more kissing led them to getting naked and, without any more fuss, they were having sex. Felicity was surprised how easy it had been. After so long imagining the act (or trying not to imagine it) she had fixated a little bit on the enormity of it. In the end, Kevin just slipped his penis rather pleasantly inside her and they were off. She didn't have an orgasm that first time, but she had enjoyed it. Enough to ensure that they did it many more times over the next couple of months and enough to ensure that Felicity learned how to control her own pleasure. When she thought back on her relationship with Kevin, she always felt good about herself, as though she had followed the rules and behaved herself. She had nothing to regret.

When he announced that his company was sending him to Boston, Felicity was disappointed but not devastated. She knew she wasn't in love with him and she was happier that it should end this way rather than let it continue until they got bored with each other. She took the opportunity to visit him in Boston a couple of times, but after another couple of months and a few thwarted flights, they let it end. She still heard from him occasionally: he had become vice-president, owned his own apartment and was living with an American girl but as yet had no plans to marry. Sometimes Felicity fantasized about meeting him again and maybe having a shag for old times' sake, but she would never have actively done anything about it. It was a sweet episode in her life and was perhaps best left that way.

So by the time her relationship with Tony graduated from the boardroom to the bedroom, at least she wasn't a virgin any more. That would have been too embarrassing. Felicity found it hard to pinpoint exactly when things escalated between them. She would never have dreamed of thinking sexually about any man she worked with – especially not her boss – but somewhere in her subconscious she had probably logged Tony as eminently fuckable. He wasn't her type – if she even had a type – and he was the type that every sane woman ought to avoid. He was a bad boy. You knew instantly that he'd slept around and that he probably didn't have a huge amount of respect for women (but it wasn't his fault; he was merely a product of his upbringing). Yet there was enough charm in his smile and sufficient twinkle in his eye for you to believe that, at the back of all the bluster and the smooth talk, he was really a vulnerable man, crying out to be loved by a good woman. And Felicity was the very best of women.

She had been aware of a few of his short-term liaisons; women who were with the company only temporarily, or visitors who had a finite slot in his life. Tony liked to have all the thrill of the chase and the capture, but none of the messy aftermath. It was so much better to feign regret at an airport than to break a heart in the corridor. So the situation with Felicity was different.

She may not have been watching *him* all that closely but *he* had always kept one eye on *her*. She was interesting from many points of view: professionally she came with an incredible pedigree; personally she was very attractive. Despite the tailored suits and the manicured hair there was something provocative in the way she interacted with people – as if the corporate persona could dissolve at any minute to reveal a debauched sex kitten. Perhaps Tony was merely projecting, but he convinced himself there was enough of it there to keep him interested. She was also unusual in the way she related to her colleagues; she got on perfectly well with them, yet she kept herself a little aloof. Tony formed the impression that here was a girl who would know how to be discreet.

Even so, it was quite a long time before Tony acted on any of this. In the meantime he had enjoyed the odd coupling from his very wide acquaintance, but there came a time when he was bored with the casualness and, perhaps, the easiness of these affairs. He was ready for something more risky. It didn't take long for him to determine that his object, while not entirely alert to the possibility of an affair with him, might not be completely opposed to it either.

Felicity couldn't help being excited by the protracted gazes that began to emanate from her boss or the, all of a sudden, pseudo-awkward collisions in tight spaces that required whispering body contact, or the now quite common smiles she got from him at the most unexpected moments. She couldn't help feeling herself singled out and didn't want to think any further than the excitement it generated.

In the end Tony's approach was singularly unoriginal; he made his move at the Christmas party.

She had never been a fan of office parties and often made up excuses not to attend them, but this year was different. This year she wanted to be in the middle of everyone, dressed to kill and not afraid to play the femme fatale. If Tony wasn't afraid to follow through with his antics at the office then she wasn't afraid to meet him halfway. She had never felt such a thrill as she stepped into her new Agent Provocateur underwear and skilfully zipped up the party dress that went just low enough and just high enough to send all the right signals. The heels were the high point of the outfit in every way: four-inch stilettos, strappy, Italian, ridiculously expensive. Her blonde hair was a little blonder than usual and tumbled about her shoulders in delicious waves. If Tony didn't make his move tonight, then someone else would and, as she got into her taxi, Felicity really didn't care who it was.

He had been waiting for her. He knew she was a typical no-show at Christmas parties, but he also knew she was about to break her pattern. He left her alone for some time before he approached, but kept her within his radar. Tony loved his little rituals; he prided himself on his ability to delay the moment of gratification for as long as possible. It deepened his pleasure. When he did approach her they were each mildly intoxicated; Felicity still had control over her actions, but she was on the threshold.

'Hello,' he said, when suddenly only the two of them remained where there had been a group, 'it's good to see you here.'

'I don't usually do Christmas parties,' she said.

'I know. But I thought you might make it this year.'

'Oh?'

'Yes. I think you knew this year's party would be a good one.'

'Well, so far it's fairly average.'

'It hasn't begun properly yet.'

'So when does it begin? I might have to go home soon.'

'You should wait until after midnight at least.'

'Is that when you bring out the good champagne? This stuff really isn't what I've come to expect from you.'

'So you have high expectations of me, do you?'

'Always.'

'Well, I'll have to see that you're not disappointed then.'

'I'd hate to be disappointed after having looked up to you for so long.'

He leaned a little closer and whispered into her ear.

'May I just tell you that *you* have not disappointed me tonight. I have never seen anyone look sexier.'

'Well, thank you. I fancied a change.'

'Can I tell you what I fancy?'

'I really don't think you should.'

He leaned in again.

'Then I'll just have to show you.'

'I don't think you should do that either.'

'I'm not any good at drawing pictures . . .'

Felicity laughed out loud, aware of how ludicrous the exchange was, but enjoying every second of it.

'OK, then, Mr Whitby, we'll have to see what we can do. But first I need to say hello to some of my friends.'

And she walked away from him, her stilettos clicking across the room, feeling giddy and empowered beyond belief.

She joined a group who were discussing the best clubs for after-hours drinking but she had no interest in the conversation. What she really wanted to do was ring Sandra and tell her what had just happened and what she thought was about to happen. Part of her delighted in knowing that nobody else in the room had any idea what was going on, but she longed to tell someone how she felt. She went to the ladies to check her make-up and to gaze at herself in the mirror – this shocking girl who was about to do something very bad indeed. But fuck it! she thought. For once in her buttoned-down life she was going to do something reckless. Of course he was only interested in her because she was there and hadn't been conquered yet. Of course he'd probably turn round tomorrow morning – if he even stayed that long – and tell her it had been great but he didn't think they should do it again. Of course the situation could become untenable afterwards – she might even have to leave the most exciting job she'd ever had. But fuck it! It was a bit like drinking at lunchtime: you knew it was a bad idea, you knew you'd end up paying for it later, but there was something so gorgeously decadent about it, you couldn't resist.

On her way back to the party Tony met her in the corridor, her coat across his arm. He was already wearing his.

'I thought you might take me back to your flat,' he said. 'This party isn't so good after all.'

He held her coat for her and she said nothing as she put it on, and still said nothing as she walked ahead of him down the stairs and out into the air. There was a line of taxis waiting and they got into the first one; she still hadn't said anything. As soon as Felicity had given her address, Tony ran his hands up her legs and beneath the lace of her new underwear. She said nothing. He began to kiss her neck and her ear and told her again that she was the sexiest woman he had ever seen. By the time they reached her flat, Felicity was in no doubt that she was entirely complicit in what was about to happen. If the spectre of tomorrow morning had been looming before her, it was long gone, replaced by the cascade of sensation she was receiving at Tony's every touch. She still said nothing.

In fact Felicity didn't speak beyond a faint whimpering and moaning until they were lying on her bed, spent and gratified, after Tony had succeeded in giving her a very profound orgasm. He had said very little except to assure her that he had condoms and that he was healthy. The notion of protection hadn't even occurred to Felicity; for someone who liked to be cautious in these matters, she had experienced uncharacteristic abandon. It was, without a doubt, the best sex she'd ever had. She'd never been so aroused and if she'd been asked during the moments immediately before, during or after her climax, she would have said that, yes, of course she was in love with this man. Lying beside him afterwards, her habitual caution had taken over again, and if asked she would probably have remained circumspect, but given that nobody was asking, she could indulge any feeling she wanted.

And so the following morning arrived and Tony turned to her (so much more exposed now that his narrow shoulders were no longer covered by an expensive shirt and that his carefully groomed hair had lost the protection of its products), and revealed that he was falling for her.

'Better keep it quiet though,' he said, rummaging on her bedside table for his phone. 'Don't want to make the other girls jealous.'

Felicity knew that anything he said outside the office was unlikely to be trustworthy. But she liked the feeling she got waking up in her tidy apartment with the kind of man who would make her mother go into a sustained conniption. It was a pleasant, edgy sort of feeling, and she decided she could handle it.

The only expectation Felicity had was that this fling with her boss would not last long. She had always been a realist and the reality has always been that philanderers do not make promises and they most likely break your heart. But she was getting what she wanted: the thrill, the intoxication, the dynamism that came from feeling that she had come into herself at last.

Her only mistake, really, was believing that what he said inside the office was any more trustworthy than what he said outside it.

6

Felicity was Susan's favourite. She was everything anyone could want in an elder sister: she was gentle, protective, indulgent and informative. She had minded Susan as a baby, and as a young child she had looked out for her and seen that she got fair treatment from her parents who were often blind to the antics of their manipulative youngest daughter, Marianne. Felicity gave Susan her old dolls, her old clothes, her old lipsticks and, on one occasion, her old boyfriend. She told her things her parents never would have (like anything to do with sex) and kept from her parents the things they were better off not knowing (like the time Susan got drunk on a bottle of Mateus Rosé she'd thought was cranberry juice).

They had remained close despite the growing physical distance between them. Felicity went to college in Dublin when Susan was starting secondary school; she went to work in the City in London when Susan was starting college in Galway. They still met at family occasions, they phoned each other, they emailed, they got on with their lives but always with reference to each other. In fact the months preceding the arrival of the two girls on Angela's doorstep was probably the only period of their lives when they hadn't been in good contact. Susan had been preoccupied with her move, her house-hunting, her infidelity and her split from her fiancé; Felicity, it turned out, also had a lot on her mind.

*

'Susan!' Felicity exclaimed. 'What are you doing here?'

'I'm staying with Granny. It's off with Paul. What are you doing here?'

'I . . . I came home for a holiday.'

'Well, it's great to see you.'

And Susan gave her sister the sort of hug that made up for months of failing to talk.

It didn't take them long to catch up. Angela opened a bottle of wine and the girls chatted while she put on a feed of rashers and sausages. Felicity explained that she'd been working so hard in the last few months she'd lost contact with everybody, and when she finally had to take a break she could think of nowhere more soothing or relaxing than Limerick.

'I would have thought you'd have headed to the sun,' said Susan.

'Sure, I'm like you with the sun – I can't take it. But I wanted to come home to switch off; I haven't the energy for an actual holiday. And I definitely couldn't face Ballyconnell and Mum and Dad.'

'I know. I have Mum breathing down my neck trying to get me to get back with Paul.'

'What happened?'

'Oh – I'll tell you later.'

'But are you OK?'

'I'm fine. There's fear of me.'

'But why didn't you tell me?'

'I'm only getting it straight in my own head. So how long do you have?'

'A while. I decided to take a proper break this time, no more of this rushing back after two days. They can survive without me.'

'Great! It's so good you're here.'

The two girls sank back into the soft texture of Angela's sofa and sighed with contentment. It was rare for Felicity to just turn up out of the blue; she often had to fight to get away even for the big holidays like Christmas and Easter. Her longer breaks were usually spent in exotic locations. She liked to ski in Switzerland, she liked to shop in New York, and even though she didn't like the sun, she liked spending time in places where she could expensively avoid it. She worked very hard and in time-honoured tradition she liked to play hard as well. As Susan watched her drink the ice-cold wine as if it were some kind of elixir, she could only think how fortunate it was that Felicity's holiday co-incided with her own little holiday from herself.

'So, what's new with you?' she asked. 'Are you still seeing that guy?'

'Which guy?'

'You know, the one you said had a yacht but no manners?'

'Him! Oh God, no! I only went out with him those two times. I had thought there might be hidden depths, but there weren't.'

'So, anybody else?'

'Oh . . . not really. No one that matters.'

Angela came back into the room carrying towels and a bundle of sheets.

'Now, my dears, if I give you the sheets, you might make up the bed. I can only do that sort of work in the morning.'

'Of course, Gran,' said Felicity. 'I'll look after myself. I'm not going to be any trouble, I promise you. Whatever about Susan here, I do know how to tidy up after myself!'

'Now, now, I'll have nothing said against Susan, she's been a treasure.'

'I'm only joking. But really, Gran, sorry for crashing like this. I couldn't face going to an empty house.'

'Sure, I'm delighted to have you here.'

The two girls made up the bed in Felicity's room and climbed onto it with their bottle of wine. Susan couldn't help noticing that Felicity looked tired, or, if not tired exactly, then maybe a little faded. Or something. She couldn't put her finger on it.

'I can't believe you're here,' she said. 'It's been years since we were alone together in this house.'

'I know! It's weird. But it's nice weird. I've always found this house very therapeutic. It must be the calm energy Granny generates.' Felicity rearranged herself on the bed. 'So, Susan,' she said, moving closer to her, 'do you want to talk about it now?'

Susan shifted around, stretching out her legs, picking up a magazine and putting it down again.

'Well, I might as well tell you. I'm a big, slutty bitch, and Paul is better off without me.'

'What are you talking about?'

'I slept with someone.'

'Oh!'

'Yeah. Not good, is it?'

'I didn't think you had it in you.'

'No, neither did I. Until I did it.'

'So who? When?'

'It was at Niall and Stephanie's wedding.'

'Ouch!'

'I don't think they knew about it. Though it was the bridesmaid's boyfriend.'

'Susan, what were you thinking?'

'I wasn't thinking, was I?'

'What happened?'

'It started with a snog. In the garden. And Paul saw us.'

'Did you and Paul have a fight?'

'No. We never fight. Not proper fighting, only bickering, that he ignores anyway.'

'Were you trying to pick a fight?'

'I don't honestly think I was. I think I just really fancied having a kiss with this guy. And I was very drunk.'

'I should hope so!'

'It's not funny. Paul was really embarrassed.'

'Well, of course he was! And then what?'

'Paul was all forgiving about it. He knew I was in bits. So we went back to our room so I could sleep it off. But later . . . well, I got up again. And bumped into the guy . . . and went back to his room . . .'

'Susan!'

'I know, I know . . . I feel awful about it. Or at least – I do feel awful, for myself, that I did that. I mean, I'm not proud of it. But . . . this is the thing . . . I don't fully regret it.'

'What do you mean?'

'It's the thing that woke me up. I didn't sleep with that guy because I was drunk. I slept with him because I wanted to. And when I told Paul about it, I think I wanted him to scream abuse at me and throw me out. But he didn't. He wrinkled his nose a bit, and forgave me.'

'Because he loves you.'

'I don't know if that was the reason.'

'What else?'

'I don't know. I don't know if Paul ever really loved me or if he just decided it was time to settle down and I was the one who happened to be around.'

'That's a bit callous.'

'I don't think he ever meant to be callous. I don't think

he was aware of it. I mean, look at our engagement. He had no notion of asking me to marry him until Daddy practically told him to. In all the times we'd talked about buying a house he never once mentioned marriage. And in the year we were engaged, we hardly did a thing about organizing a wedding. Any time I mentioned it, he just said he'd leave it up to me.'

'Most men are like that.'

'Yeah, they are, and that's fine. Because usually the women they're with are happy to go and organize it all and as long as he meets them at the altar on the day, they've no complaints. But I didn't just want to get married. I'm not sure I even care about getting married; I want to feel I'm with someone who absolutely wants to be with me. For me.'

'I guess we all want that,' said Felicity wistfully.

Susan sighed.

'But you know what?' she said, turning around to face her sister.

'What?'

'I really enjoyed that kiss. It was the best kiss I'd had in years!'

'That's because it was illicit.'

'Maybe, but I also think it was just a bloody good kiss. Paul's a useless fucking kisser!'

'Susan!'

'It's true. And he's a useless fucking lover too!'

'Oh dear!'

'You see. I told you he needed to be got rid of!'

'Oh, hon,' said Felicity, wrapping her arms around her little sister, 'I don't know whether to laugh or cry. You poor thing, having to suffer all that bad sex and all those useless kisses.'

'Oh, please laugh. I don't want to start crying over him.'

'But, Susan, didn't you ever talk to Paul about any of this? I mean, there must be more to your relationship than some under-par sex?'

'Not a lot really.'

'And have you spoken to him since?'

'Just the once. We met by accident. He was all keen for having it out. For forgiving me all over again, but I wasn't up to it.'

'You really do owe him something of an explanation.'

'I know. And I will. I'm just breathing a little free air for a while. I'll talk to him soon.'

Felicity gave her sister a hug.

'And I thought you had your life all sorted.'

'Me? My life's like my washing basket – disorganized, out of date, a little bit stale and very, very dirty!'

'You're not so bad.'

'It's so good to talk to you, Fliss. You look tired, though; I think I've worn you out with talk.'

'I'm fine. I just had one of those weeks – you know.'

'I know. How's work?'

'Work's a balls! But never mind about that for now. Listen, Susan, don't be so hard on yourself . . . everybody makes mistakes.'

'I know. I just hadn't made such a big one in a very long time. Here, I'll let you get to sleep. See you in the morning. I'll make you pancakes.'

'Night, Sue.'

As Susan made her way to her own bed her thoughts returned to that night at the wedding. The kiss, in the garden, had been an accident. She had wandered outside for some fresh air and found him (Donal . . . or was it Derek?) having

83

a cigarette. They had been introduced earlier and had spent some time on the dance floor with a big crowd. She had noticed him. He was a nice-looking guy, certainly, but nothing amazing. However, as he pulled on his cigarette and made casual remarks about the wedding, he began to appear very attractive. Susan wasn't sure what it was, his nonchalance maybe, the way he really didn't seem to give a fuck about anything. He made a very stark contrast to Paul in all his carefully thought out carefulness . . . And then he began complimenting her: small, sideways things, like how awful the bridesmaids' dresses were, but how nice hers was, and what a good dancer she was compared to the way most people just threw themselves around the floor. And then he just said it:

'I'd really like to kiss you.'

And she said, 'Then why don't you?'

It was almost as if it was someone else's voice, or at least as if someone else had made her say it. But once it was said, she became that person. He leaned in and pressed his mouth against hers. She liked the pressure of his lips and responded by gently biting his lower lip. He suddenly threw away the cigarette and launched into her mouth with his tongue. She was surprised, but not entirely displeased, by his smoky breath and soon their tentative kiss had morphed into a full-on guns a-blazing snog.

That's when they were discovered. Susan hadn't given a second's thought to the fact that they were only yards away from the function room and there were many other smokers and walkers about. She heard a throat clear and looked up to find Paul standing a couple of feet above them on the veranda.

'Oh!' was all she said. Donal or . . . Derek seemed to understand fairly quickly what was happening and sidled off into the bushes.

'I'm sorry,' she said then, but only because it was the least that was expected of her.

'It's OK,' he said immediately and put his arm round her. 'You've had an awful lot to drink.'

She began whimpering, but it wasn't out of remorse, it was more out of confusion and perhaps frustration. He guided her back inside the foyer where he got her a cup of tea and a slice of wedding cake. As far as he was concerned, that was the end of it.

But for her, it was only the beginning.

She'd been quite drunk, but not so drunk that she didn't know what she was doing, or that she couldn't remember every detail. After the tea and cake Paul suggested they go to bed. She was in no position to argue, so she let him drag her off to their room where they watched some TV before falling asleep. However, Susan never went fully to sleep and got up some time later. She got dressed and, leaving Paul snoring heavily, went out in search of the party.

She found the last stragglers in the residents' bar. She also found him there. The bride and groom had gone and he was the only person she recognized in the group. So she had another drink and added a comment or two to the generally disjointed conversation, but after a while it was just the two of them apparently having a very meaningful exchange about their childhoods.

The suggestion to leave the group was his. As they walked along the deserted corridors he explained that his girlfriend, the bridesmaid, had heard about the kiss and so had locked him out of their room. It wasn't a problem though, as his friend had given him the key to his room.

'Don't worry,' he said, 'he's pissed off his head, he won't hear a thing.'

Susan was fully aware of the seediness of what she was

doing, but neither that nor her boyfriend sleeping elsewhere in the hotel would put her off. The friend was indeed off his head; he was sprawled untidily across one of the beds. They sat on the other one. They kissed for a while, but Susan couldn't quite work up the magic of their earlier clinch. He began searching his pockets for something and then checked the lockers. Eventually he found what he was looking for in the friend's wallet: a condom. Susan wondered later, if he hadn't had the presence of mind to go searching for one, would she have? He not only produced the condom but he opened up his fly and put it on. He seemed quite proud of himself as he stood before her, his dress shirt falling open, his zip undone and his penis sheathed and standing to attention.

This was the only time Susan thought she might leave. The sexiness of the experience, such as it had been, was slipping away. But then he began kissing her again and this time she did feel the excitement. So she lay back and let it happen.

Given the amount he must have drunk it was amazing he was there at all, and despite the fact that they couldn't get each other's names right (he kept calling her Sarah) and that zero time was spent on any appreciable foreplay, it wasn't the worst experience in the world. He couldn't quite manage an orgasm of course, and after one final effort he collapsed on top of her. He slid off immediately and went to sleep. Susan pulled herself from the bed, and as she was rearranging her clothing, the thought struck her that maybe, seeing as neither of them had an orgasm, it didn't really count. She dismissed the thought immediately – her morals were surely better than those of the average American president. She opened the door and went back to her room. Paul was still snoring.

No, it certainly wasn't her proudest moment, but as she said to Felicity, it had served a purpose. So maybe there was no harm done.

7

Susan decided it was time to bite the bullet and just do it. It had been a long time coming, but now it had arrived. It certainly wasn't going to be easy, it could end up an even bigger mess, but that was a chance she had to take. It was the right thing to do. She opened the door and approached the desk.

'I need a hair cut,' she said. 'I need it so badly.'

Susan hadn't been to a proper salon in years, and hadn't had a decent haircut in even longer. She was never able to decide what to do with her hair; she knew that short styles suited her best, but she never had the guts to let anyone cut it really short. She kept hankering after a longer style but never had the patience to let it grow past the point where it was utterly wretched-looking. That was where she was now – the point where her hair was utterly wretched-looking – and she had to do something about it. This time, though, she was determined to go further than she had ever gone before.

'Have you an appointment?'

'No. I just decided this minute. I was th–'

'Wait a minute and I'll see if there's something. You should really make an appointment.'

'Oh, I know, it's just that –'

'There's a cancellation at two o'clock. If you take a seat there, Val will be over to you.'

It was only half past one but Susan didn't dare suggest that she'd come back in half an hour. When Val came over Susan knew she had better be there. So she took a seat, picked up a magazine she'd already read, and began to read, furiously. When Val eventually came over, at twenty past two, Susan was deep into the recipe pages.

'So what are we doing?' Val said.

'Ahm . . . I'm getting it cut.'

Susan had never had a consultation before.

'Yeah. How?'

'Well, I'd like something a little different.'

Susan looked round the salon at the other stylists with their heavily tinted hair, streaks of red and purple, sections of shaved head and sections of extensive extensions and realized she'd have to clarify her definition of different.

'I just want a cut,' she said tentatively, 'you know a straight-forward cut, but I'd like it to be . . . sort of . . . Well, I'd like it to suit me – if you know what I mean. And I don't want any colour – if that's OK?'

'That all your own colour?' asked the stylist.

'Yeah. I don't think I have any grey yet.'

'No, it's good. How short do you want to go?'

'Ahm . . . well . . .' Susan was working herself up to it. 'As short as you think would be good.'

'We could go quite short. You have a high crown and we could go sort of pixie style, you know, maybe a little bit Keira Knightley?'

'Whatever you think.'

Which one was Keira Knightley again? Was she the one in the pirates film or the one who was in rehab?

'OK. So we'll do that,' Val said, walking away and hollering at a younger girl to come over and wash Susan's hair.

She tried to view the experience as cathartic. For every swipe Val made at her black mane she visualized a day of her life with Paul being hacked away and a new, sleeker, more confident version of Susan would begin to appear.

If only it were that easy.

Afterwards, as she paid for her new do (seventy-five euro!), she tried to convey to Val, by the tone of her voice and by her repeated use of the words *fabulous* and *wonderful*, and by leaving a very extravagant tip, that she had done a truly wonderful thing. It was the equivalent of her new wedge heels and halter-neck sundress (bought earlier that morning to celebrate the fact that it was finally summer). Susan was a new woman walking high over the rest of the world. But Val merely sniffed and told her to condition more.

She was still on a hair-spray high as she rounded the corner of Cruises Street and bumped into Carmel.

'Oh my God, I'm so glad I met you!'

'Hi, Carmel. Nice to see you too.'

'I have so much news! Have you time for coffee? Or what about a drink? I think my news calls for a drink!'

'Actually, I'd murder a cup of coffee. It's a little early for drinking.'

'OK, whatever. Coffee's fine. Where'll we go? Somewhere quiet.'

'What about Rollo's? It's usually quiet enough.'

'Fine,' she said as they started walking. 'So how are you anyway? Love the hair.'

'Oh, thanks. I just got it d–'

'I've been meaning to get mine cut for ages but I can't decide what to do. I'd never have the guts to go as short as yours – that is *so* short. Oh, here. Here's a table. Will we sit here?'

'Here's fine.'

So,' she said, once Susan was seated opposite her, 'Rob and I slept together.'

Susan really didn't know what to say: Was it good? Did

you come? Did he wear a condom? What were you thinking? Are you insane? Have you lost your mind?

She really felt she had more to be thinking about than her friend's dodgy love life and that she was the least qualified person to have thoughts on anyone's relationship, yet she hadn't been able to help forming a theory about this old friend of Carmel's.

She hadn't ever met him, but from everything Carmel had said (she'd been talking a lot about him in between tax returns), and taking into account that Carmel was probably overlooking a lot of the bad stuff, he emerged as a weak individual who hadn't a clue in the wide world what he wanted, and was more than happy to let Carmel wreck her head trying to sort things out for him. Susan knew the type. They were usually of just about decent enough quality to attract nice girls like Carmel. Often they were good-looking, though not in a way that would stop traffic, more in a way that would please your mother (and in the way that would fade with age). They always had regular jobs. Possibly they were quite well paid and might even have some real estate to add to the package. They were well brought up, they treated you well (until a crisis occurred), they knew how to be generous and generally made you feel as though you had done well for yourself. Their only fault (until the crisis occurred) was that they were boring. Boring in the pub, boring at the dinner table, boring in the bedroom, boring at the breakfast table.

Of course, for a lot of women, boring isn't a problem, not even in the bedroom, as long as the other things are there. (Susan realized that, until recently, she was probably one of these women.) Yet it wasn't until the crisis occurred that these boys' biggest flaw became apparent: they took themselves dreadfully seriously. As soon as someone like

Rob had even the slightest doubt that he might not be blissfully happy in his new marriage, he began to see it as a wide-reaching catastrophe that had to be examined with earth-stopping gravity – rather than as merely a mild adjustment to a change in circumstances. (The real problem with Rob and his wife was that they were having a little trouble getting used to sharing a house. They hadn't lived together before the marriage, despite sharing a bed four nights out of seven, and neither could quite get used to having the other and the other's stuff around all the time. They had foolishly thought that by saving the thrill of cohabitation for marriage, they would also save themselves the newlywed fatigue that some of their friends had suffered from. Rob and his young bride had got it wrong, however. They knew they loved each other, but at the moment it was hard to stand the sight of each other all the time.) Being inclined to believe the problem was only his, Rob took his troubles to the first person who showed any sign of interest in them – Carmel.

'Oh!' was what Susan finally said.

'So,' Carmel asked, obviously needing more, 'what do you think?'

'I don't know what to think. I mean, I really don't think it's a good idea. He's married, Carmel. He's still very married. Where does it leave you?'

'Oh, his marriage is over. He as good as said it.'

'But did he say it?'

'He didn't have to.'

'I'm worried about you, that's all. It's never a good idea getting involved with married people. It's not right anyway, apart from how it's going to affect you.'

'It's different if the marriage is over.'

'Carmel, his marriage has hardly begun.'

'I thought you'd be pleased.'

'Why on earth would I be pleased?'

'I love him.'

Susan sighed.

'I hope you don't love him. For your sake, I really hope you don't.'

'Don't be so pessimistic. It's going to work out. Plenty of people leave their wives and are blissfully happy with other people.'

'Maybe, but not without a whole lot of heartache in between.'

'Well, I'm happy anyway. I'm sorry you can't be happy for me.'

'Ask yourself this: why are you telling me this in a whisper so low I can barely hear you? Why are you going to beg me not to tell Bernie when we see her on Monday? And why haven't you told your mother that you've met someone nice?'

'How did you know I haven't told my mother?'

'I didn't. But of course you're not going to because Rob is married, and what you've just done is add to the mess.'

'I really thought you'd be more understanding.'

'I'm sorry if I'm not being what you want, but I honestly think that the best thing for you to do now is break up with him. Feed him any sob story you like, but break up with him. Forget about him. He's not the guy you think he is, because he's going home to somebody else each night. I'm not saying it's your fault – he's clearly being a total bollocks – but you need to get out now.'

'I can't. I love him. And he loves me.'

Susan sighed.

'I don't know what else to say to you.'

'Then say nothing. I'll do this on my own.'

'Oh, Carmel, look, I don't want you to feel like you're on your own, but I can't pretend this is a good thing. There are other guys out there, you know.'

'Yeah, well, I haven't met them.'

'You will. Look, I'm single again. We can have a bit of fun going on the man hunt.'

'You've got Alan chasing you.'

'I've no interest in Alan.'

'But he's still chasing you. He's not chasing me.'

'I'm sure there's an Alan out there to chase you too!' Susan smiled beseechingly at Carmel. 'Come on, let's order some chocolate cake. I won't say a word to anybody and you just think about what I said. OK?'

'OK. But I really do love him, you know.'

'I know.'

Somehow, Susan's high had evaporated and all she could think about was her own dodgy love life. Who was she to criticize anyone!

Of course, the hair cut and the new clothes and even the ninety-seven euro fifty she'd spent on new make-up weren't going to be enough to dispel the real cause of Susan's gloom.

Paul had texted her again. He still wanted to meet, but she couldn't bring herself to call round to that flat and put it to Paul that she had never really loved him. It scared her to think that four years of her life had disappeared with him. It was as if that time had entered some kind of wormhole and been swallowed up. The Susan of those years was part of another dimension now. Why couldn't Paul understand that and just move on?

8

Susan and Gavin were walking gingerly along the grassy track that wound steeply down towards the sea. Ballyconnell beach was an offshoot of a much larger bay, and while the bay was sheltered and ideal for swimming, this stretch of cove was entirely exposed to the Atlantic winds. It was these winds and the break from the overhanging cliffs that made Ballyconnell such a good surfing beach. Gavin was explaining this to Susan as they picked their way along the path.

'But it must be so dangerous,' Susan said.

'Well . . . it can be. But not if you know what you're doing. I mean, you'd need to be a fairly decent swimmer and you wouldn't want to take chances.'

'It must be exhilarating.'

'It is. When it's good it's the most amazing feeling in the world. You feel like . . . like . . . you're in control of everything. The bigger the wave, the scarier the swell, the better the thrill. It's sort of as though you're the master of the universe!'

'I'm just sorry you didn't bring your board with you. I'd love to see you go out there and get all wet and masterful!'

'I'll bring it the next time. And I'll bring one for you too!'

'No thanks! I prefer to get my thrills on dry land.'

They had ended up in Ballyconnell purely by accident. They had started out by driving at a crawl round the local industrial estate in second gear. Halfway through the lesson

Gavin suggested they try third gear again and when the moves to and from third gear went so well, he suggested they try for fourth.

'Oh God, no! I'd never get back down from fourth. Let's leave fourth for the next lesson.'

This was Susan's third driving lesson. The first lesson had begun very well. Gavin drove them to the industrial estate and parked in a quiet area behind one of the larger factories. 'You won't see a car here for hours,' he said. 'So feel free to let rip.'

'Don't say that,' said Susan. 'I'm really afraid that's just what I'll do.'

'Just relax into it. You can't do any damage. You have to be able to drive before you can do any damage.'

'There's always a first time,' said Susan, fastening her seatbelt in the driver's seat. 'My mother brought me out here when I was sixteen and I'm convinced I crashed the car without ever switching the engine on.'

'I'm sure you didn't!'

'Even if I didn't, my mother keeps telling me that I did!'

'I promise that even if you do crash, with or without the ignition on, I'll pretend it never happened.'

'Good! That's the kind of driving instructor I need.'

'OK, then. Will we give it a go? Put your left foot on the clutch and turn the key.'

Susan managed to get into second gear on that first day and cleared a good hundred metres without a shudder or a stall. On their second lesson she repeated the success of the first within ten minutes, but then she was very timid about chancing third gear.

'I remember third gear,' she said. 'I could never get third gear. I'd try to slide up and over, just like you said, in one smooth movement, but as I'd go up I'd get lost and I wouldn't be able to find the over. Then the car would stall and my mother would start shouting and that would be it for the day. It was awful.'

'Sounds awful. No wonder you're so bad.'

'Hey!'

'Only joking . . . Why didn't your father teach you how to drive? He strikes me as much more suited to that sort of thing.'

'He would've been. But Mum thought she was a better driver than him. He never passed a test, you see. He got his licence during some amnesty or other, whereas she learned the hard way and had to take her test three times. She said that made her a better driver.'

'And was she?'

'She was a slower driver. She used to sit hunched up to the wheel peering through the windscreen as if she was half blind or something. And I swear she never looked in her mirror. But of course, Dad would never criticize. If Mum believed she was the better driver then it must be true.'

'Yes . . . your dad always had a real goddess complex about your mother.'

'Don't talk to me! Whatever she said, *ever*, he always agreed with, even when she was talking garbage. I'd love to find a man who'd always agree with me no matter what.'

'No way! I'd say you'd be bored silly with a man who wouldn't challenge you.'

'I dunno. I wouldn't mind trying it for a while.'

Yet, as Susan tried again and again to get into third gear she wondered if that wasn't exactly what the problem had been with Paul. He hadn't ever challenged her. About anything. It wasn't that he always agreed with her and he certainly didn't have a goddess complex about her, but he never said or did anything that made her re-evaluate herself. He never called her on her moods or gave out that she was being unreasonable (even when she was – like the time she insisted they buy expensive ski jackets even though neither of them had any intention of going skiing). And when she did the ultimate unreasonable thing and slept with someone else, he just went along with it. Was that why she did it in the first place? Just to try and provoke a reaction from him?

'There you have it! That's it! Just up and over – just like your mother said.'

'Hey, that's great! I did it! I got into third gear! Oh – aren't we going very fast? How do you get back down again? Is it down and over? Is it over the other way? Oh God, I don't know what to do!'

Gavin was eventually able to coax her down from third gear but it had been such a frightening experience that, by the time of their third lesson, she was very disinclined to attempt it again.

'You know what you need?' Gavin said, in an attempt to promote fourth gear. 'You need to get out on the open road.'

'I'm not ready for the open road! The open road isn't ready for me!'

'You'll be fine, honestly. It's hard to get a proper feel for driving when you're in a place like this. We'll get you out on a nice strip of quiet road and you'll see how easy it is.'

'Oh God, are you sure? I'm so afraid I'll wreck your car.'

'I'm not that attached to this car. Come on, I'll drive us out of the city and you can take over then.'

That was how they ended up in Ballyconnell. The dual carriageway that began on the very edge of the city heading for Clare seemed the obvious choice. Susan was delighted to allow Gavin to climb as far as fifth gear and even to hover very close to the speed limit, but every time he suggested she might take over the wheel, she suggested he drive just a little bit further. Soon they had left behind the dual carriageway, the new bypass and the very nice strip of quiet road that he had had in mind originally, and found themselves only a couple of miles away from the beach.

'What!' exclaimed Susan, reading a signpost. 'Ballyconnell – five kilometres! How can we be five kilometres from Ballyconnell?'

'One of the fundamental laws of physics, Susan. If you drive you will get there!'

'Oh, shut up! I don't want to be in Ballyconnell. What if I bump into Mum and Dad?'

'You won't. Their house is much closer to the other bay.'

'Have you been to their house?'

'No. But I know where it is.'

'Oh.'

'I do talk to your parents occasionally, you know.'

'I know. I just didn't realize you listened to them too.'

'You really have a very bad attitude.'

'Me! I do not!'

'You're very unfair to your parents, especially your mother.'

'I am not! You just don't know them. You only know the public side. When they're all "Nice to meet you and, my, haven't you grown!"'

'You're so easy to get a rise out of.'

'That's unfair! You're supposed to be my friend.'

'I'm sorry, I *am* your friend. Haven't I brought you to the seaside? Come on, let's get out and walk down to the beach. The surf should be good today.'

They had just reached the end of the track and on climbing a low sand dune, the sea opened up in front of them.

'Oh wow!' said Susan. 'This is nice, this is *very* nice. I'd forgotten how nice this beach is. Maybe I do see why Mum and Dad have disowned Limerick.'

She immediately took off her shoes and ran headlong into the breaking foam.

'Jesus Christ, it's cold!'

'Get out of there, you idiot,' said Gavin, following with her shoes, 'the water down here doesn't warm up till August.'

'But it looks so good.'

'Then climb back up here and look at it.'

They settled themselves in a crook of one of the rocks which gave shelter while still allowing them to appreciate the full wildness of the sea's swell.

'I still can't help feeling they're going to appear any minute,' said Susan, peering across the length of the beach as she brushed the sand from between her toes.

'Who? Your parents? Honestly, at this time of the year they're much more likely to go to Ballyhoddin Bay. It's not half as wild as here.'

'You sure you haven't been making secret visits to them?'

'And what if I had? I'm entitled to keep up with my aunt and uncle.'

'No, you're not! That would just give them more reason to give out about us. You know, I tried to visit them but Mum was so busy with all her stuff that she couldn't fit me in.'

'Did you try very hard?'

'Well . . . maybe not very hard. But you wouldn't either if you knew she was going to try and persuade you to marry your old boyfriend you've just dumped. I just don't want to hear it.'

'Is that because you secretly *do* want to marry your boyfriend but you just don't want it to be your mother's idea?'

'What? Oh God, no! Things are so over between me and Paul. So over. Sure the main reason we broke up –'

'Yeah?'

'Well . . . there were a million reasons really – apart from – but mainly that . . . well, we're just so different really.'

'Oh?'

'Just take us on holidays: firstly we decide to go to Marbella, because our friends Niall and Stephanie went there, but neither of us actually has the wit to say that we don't really like sun holidays. Then once we're there, I like to get up early, go for a nice walk in the shade, maybe do a little gentle shopping, maybe visit a place of historical or cultural interest . . . You know, nice, simple holiday stuff. Then maybe have dinner over candlelight and just watch the world go by.'

'Sounds lovely to me.'

'Yes, but what Paul likes to do is the complete opposite. He likes to sleep late, but once he's up, he won't sit still again. He has to be golfing or playing tennis or beach soccer or he has to be swimming or surfing or scuba diving or playing tag rugby or canoeing or potholing or whatever. And then in the evening he just wants to have a quick shower and an even quicker meal and then drink pints in whatever nightclub is the loudest.'

'That sounds awful!'

'I know there's nothing wrong with it. It's just that it's

different from what I like. And I know loads of couples manage to make the differences between them a good thing – you know, he learns embroidery and she learns how to wrestle – but we could never do that.'

'Sometimes, I suppose, there just isn't enough there.'

'If we had got married, I'm sure it wouldn't have lasted. And nobody wants that – a failed marriage. I know my mother thinks we don't take marriage seriously, but the truth is we take it much more seriously than they ever did. They jumped into marriage with the first person who held their hand at the dance hall. They were all probably as horny as hell, but the only way they could sleep with someone was to marry them.'

Gavin laughed.

'I've never heard it put quite like that before, but you probably have a point.'

'Of course I do. When I get married . . . I want . . . Well, actually, I've no idea what I want. But it certainly isn't Paul.'

'Then you definitely did the right thing.'

'So what about you? Felicity told me you were nearly married once.'

'Did she now?'

'Yeah. She said it was years ago, when you were only a boy and you didn't know your own mind.'

'Did she really say all that? Maybe it's just as well Felicity isn't here today.'

'You're not cross, are you?'

'No, of course not. That's just the thing, it *was* years ago. So many years ago.'

'What was her name? Pamela, was it?'

'Yeah.'

'So tell me more.'

'There's not that much to tell.'

'Oh, come on, you know about my disastrous relationship, you have to tell me about yours.'

Gavin laughed again.

'What? You've shown me yours, now I have to show you mine?'

'Something like that.'

'Well,' he said, stretching his legs out on the sand, 'I met Pamela at a party. I didn't know who she was, but she, apparently, had been hearing about me from her best friend's boyfriend who worked with me at the time.'

'So she had been spotting you?'

'She seemed to like something about what she was hearing. I have no idea why Colin was talking about me in the first place . . . but, anyway, she asked me out on a date.'

'What! She asked you out?'

'Yeah. Is that so rare?'

'Yes! It bloody is! How many women have asked you out?'

'Ahh . . . just the one actually.'

'There you go. And she turned out to be a fruitcake.'

Gavin smiled.

'Nothing so sweet as a fruitcake.'

'Oh.'

'Look, it was a long time ago.'

'You don't have to talk about it if it's painful for you.'

'Oh, it's not painful, it's just so irrelevant.'

'Felicity said she wasn't very nice.'

'Felicity says a lot, doesn't she?'

'She didn't mean it in a bad way. Just that she wasn't a nice person, like you. You know, that ye weren't really suited.'

*

In fact, Felicity had been blunter than that when they'd talked on that first night. She'd been surprised to know that Gavin was back. 'I haven't seen him in years,' she said. 'Is he still mad about Led Zeppelin?'

'You know he plays in a band?' Susan had said.

'Oh, does he still? He was always messing around with some band or other.'

'Yeah, we must go the next time he has a gig.'

'Mm, I wouldn't mind seeing Gavin play. I saw him once years ago. He was going out with someone at the time.'

'Oh yeah?'

'Yeah, I'd forgotten about her. She wasn't the kind of girl I would have expected him to be with. Or maybe it was more that I hadn't ever seen Gavin with any girl before. She was very glamorous, very sociable, very un-Gavin like. He wasn't exactly a babe magnet in those days.'

'No?' Susan had been mildly surprised.

'Well, like you say, he was this hairy dude who was good at maths and liked music from the seventies when everybody else was into the Cure and Depeche Mode. I suppose he was one of those late bloomers, you know, the ones nobody takes any notice of until suddenly, one day, they go out and get a decent hair cut and buy themselves a pair of jeans that actually fit, and by then the music they like has become cool again, and suddenly everybody's taking notice.'

'And that's how it was with Gavin?'

'Well, I think so. I didn't see that much of him, but I remember coming back from college one weekend and . . . he was different.'

'And that's when he met Pamela?'

'Yeah. She was just so . . . loud and abrasive, and bossy, *so* not his type. But, I suppose, from his point of view, if an attractive woman makes a play for you, you're hardly going to say, "Uhh, no thanks, I'd really rather remain a virgin until I'm forty."'

Susan giggled.

'I dunno what it was, Sue, attraction is a strange thing.'

'I just can't see it. I can't see him with someone like that. So what happened?'

'That was the worst part. I don't know how long exactly they had been going out, but it wasn't that long. Maybe six months. Maybe a year. Anyway, all of a sudden they announced they were getting married.'

'How come I never heard about this?'

'I think you were in Australia.'

'But why didn't anybody tell me?'

'The engagement didn't last very long. There was all this fuss within the family. Nobody liked her and they all thought Gavin was far too young to be getting married. Frank and Grace had passed away by this time and I remember Dad going all head of the household on it and taking him aside to give him a fatherly chat. Mum was acting as if this was the worst catastrophe that could ever befall him. I mean, worse than his mother and father dying within two years of each other. That's probably why she never said anything to you: she was hoping it wouldn't happen. And then it didn't. Pamela dumped him. She went off with some guy he worked with. Some hot shot who owned the company.'

'No way!'

'Yep, that's what happened. He was pretty devastated. I don't know exactly what went on, but it was shortly after that that he went to Sweden.'

Susan looked at Gavin expectantly now, wondering how much he would tell her. He brushed some sand from his jeans and began to talk.

'Well, yeah – I mean, no, we weren't suited but . . . that didn't seem to matter at the time. I don't think I was aware of it then.'

'And ye got engaged?'

'Yeah. It was one of those whirlwind things, you know. I couldn't quite believe that she was really with me. I felt she was way out of my league. And as it turned out, I was right, on both counts.'

'No way! She was not out of your league.'

'Thank you, but my self-esteem has recovered in the meantime.'

'So was she great in bed?'

'Susan!'

'Oh, come on, you can tell me. We're cousins. Paul was useless in bed.'

'Susan, stop!'

'So . . . was she any good?'

'I'm not telling you!'

'Tell me!'

'No! It's not appropriate.'

'Oh, appropriate! Garbage! Just tell me, or I won't stop bugging you about it.'

'I can't remember.'

'Yes, you can. What kind of things did she do?'

'Susan!'

'Tell me!'

'All right! Let's just say I was grateful – OK? For everything.'

'Were you a virgin?'

'You really are a nut job, you know that?'

'Yes, and I'm enjoying being a nut job for a while. I've been far too sensible for far too long.'

'Nothing about you is sensible.'

'Good! So what happened next?'

'Next? I have no idea where we are.'

'After you proposed. How far down the line were you before it was all off?'

'Now that, I really don't remember. It was all a bit of a blur. She was the one doing all the moving and shaking, I was just along for the ride.'

'So she left you for some guy you worked with?'

'The boss, actually.'

'Wow! What a gold digger.'

'Maybe. I honestly have no idea what she was after.'

'Were you devastated?'

Gavin sighed volubly and began shaking his head.

'I suppose I was, but mainly I think I was just relieved. I knew all along it wasn't right. I just got carried away, I suppose.'

'Wow.'

He turned to her and held her in his mocking gaze.

'Now,' he said, 'are you satisfied?'

She sank further back into the shelter of the rock and ignored his attempt to embarrass her.

'It's good to talk about these things.'

'Whatever you say, Susan,' he said, grinning. 'Whatever you say.'

In fact it was good to talk about these things. Gavin hadn't talked about Pamela in several years, and even though it was a long time ago, and no matter how he protested the irrelevance of the whole thing, he still didn't know until he actually heard himself say her name again that she really didn't mean anything to him any more. He had never been quite sure what she meant to him, other than that she was the woman who gave him everything and then took it away again, along with almost everything else that had made him whole. He used to wish that he could hate her, but he simply couldn't. The truth was that he didn't blame her entirely, or even partially, for the wreck he became. He held himself responsible for being such an easy dupe. He hadn't even liked her particularly, for God's sake, and yet he had asked her to marry him, to spend the rest of her life with him. What was wrong with him, he used to ask himself, that he was so willing to jump overboard with the first woman who showed any interest in what he had inside his trousers?

And the sex hadn't been that great. He had no idea how to articulate it to Susan (how could she be so blunt, so downright inappropriate, and yet so endearing?), but while he had been grateful, he had also been a little disappointed. Having spent fifteen years or so imagining what it would be like to have sex with a live woman, he had worked up a rather exaggerated picture of how good it was going to be. He had hoped, if not his first, then at least his subsequent sexual experiences would have been more . . . holistic was the term that came to his mind. In other words, while he couldn't argue with an orgasm, he had thought there might have been a little more dialogue with the rest of him. He had thought he might *feel* more, during and afterwards. Pamela, he felt sure, didn't enjoy sex with him – in fact he wondered if she enjoyed sex with anyone; for her it seemed more a means to an end. And she had been so right in Gavin's case. As soon as she woke up his long-dormant penis, he felt he owed her. It was as simple as that. The fact that she wasn't remotely like the woman his imagination had selected for him didn't matter any more. What mattered was that *she* had selected *him*.

Susan had been staring at Gavin wondering if maybe she had gone too far. So she decided to change the subject.

'Do you like my hair?' she asked.

'Of course! That was the first thing I said to you this morning.'

'Yes, but do you *really* like it?'

'I already said I did. It suits you. It brings out your cheekbones.'

'My cheekbones? I didn't know I had cheekbones.'

'Well, you do. You have very nice cheekbones.'

'Thank you. What else do you like about me?'

'What?'

'Go on – tell me what else you like about me.'

'Susan!'

'You mean you don't like me, then?'

'Susan – I –'

'I'm only looking for some impartial criticism. Come on, you're my cousin. I've never had a brother so I've never had an impartial male viewpoint and you're the next best thing. I'm single again, so I need to know what a man thinks.'

'I'm sure *all* men think very highly of you.'

'Why, thank you!'

'You're welcome.'

Susan smiled.

'You know, you are a very good cousin. If I had known how good, I would have sought you out years ago.'

'Well, thank *you*, Susan, that's very nice to know. You also seem to be a good cousin.'

'Oh, I'm useless. I wasn't fishing. I just never knew cousins could be this much fun.'

She turned her head to one side and looked him up and down.

'I think I'll find you a woman,' she said.

'Will you now?'

'Yeah. That can be my cousinly gift to you.'

'Come on,' he said, getting up and brushing sand from his jeans, 'let's head back. If you're going to drive all the way home we'd better make a start before it gets dark.'

'What!!'

'Honestly, Susan . . .'

They stopped in the village for fish and chips (Susan lay low in the car while Gavin braved the deserted chipper) and what with a bellyful of starch and all the sea air, Susan was asleep before they hit the main road.

Gavin smiled as he looked across at her. It was so typical of her to bring up something he truly hadn't thought about in years. Now, he couldn't get that whole episode out of his head. He tried to recall Pamela's appearance but all he could see was a general brightness and shininess: her hair was bright and shiny, her skin was bright and shiny, her smile was bright and shiny. It seemed as though his brain was still dazzled by her image. She had been very attractive, he remembered that much, but she hadn't been beautiful. Her looks were showy rather than pretty and while she certainly was striking, it was more that she commanded you to look at her than that any of her features were truly arresting. It suddenly struck him as he changed down the gears on passing through the next village that Susan, for example, had completely the opposite kind of beauty. You might not notice her straightaway, and there certainly was nothing shiny about her, but you couldn't help being drawn to those green eyes and that provocative little mouth. He wondered what had gone on with Paul; was a guy really stupid enough to cheat on a girl as sweet and engaging as Susan? Of course you never knew the way a relationship could go, but he would have thought any guy lucky enough to have Susan would have done anything to hold on to her.

He sighed out loud. He thought it was rather pathetic of him to be still preoccupied by a relationship he'd had in his early twenties. But unfortunately the truth was that there hadn't been a more consuming relationship since then. When he had been in Sweden there was a girl he went out with briefly, Niamh. She was from Dublin and, like him, working on contract, so they were thrown together a lot. She was easier to talk to than most of the other women he met at the time, mainly because she was Irish (he didn't have the energy to try and impress a Swedish girl). They had a few dates – meals, boat trips, country walks – and they slept together a few times, but it hadn't been memorable. What he did recall was a slight discomfort at his efforts. With Pamela he had simply let it happen; she was clearly in the driving seat. If not exactly passionate, she was certainly erotically aggressive, but Niamh had wanted him to take charge (once she had done all the groundwork).

When they did finally end up in the bedroom of his tiny flat one night, he was rather at a loss as to what to do. They had been out with a large group from the office and all evening she had been placing her hand nonchalantly on his, or casually allowing her foot to rest against his leg. At one point when she leaned in close to tell him something funny about one of their colleagues, he could have sworn that her tongue touched his ear. They both had a lot to drink and it was rather by accident that they ended up at his flat. But once she was there the outcome was inevitable.

Niamh threw herself across his bed; without saying anything, her expectations were clear. Gavin felt the sweat run down his back and the beat of his heart accelerate, but it wasn't from sexual excitement. It was pure dread. He liked Niamh well enough, but he really didn't want to sleep with her. He just didn't think an opportunistic shag was worth the fallout it might incur. He didn't want Niamh to be his girlfriend mainly because he felt she didn't want him to be her boyfriend. He had the feeling that she already had a boyfriend back in Dublin and that he was merely a diversion for her. Another man might have found the situation ideal, but having bad memories of his first lover, Gavin didn't want to repeat the pattern. However, she was here, in his bedroom, lying across his bed. She had allowed the hem of her dress to ride halfway up her thigh and she was sticking out her chest at him. Either he had to dive right in, or run away. Never to be seen again.

So he took the plunge. He began to undo the buttons of his shirt (he was sweating so much, he was about to pass out) and he ran his tongue over his lips to test their dryness. Luckily, Niamh seemed to interpret his nervousness as anticipation and she leapt up to undo his belt buckle. He was grateful for the help, but worried that she would investigate further and find that his penis still hadn't woken up to the party. Frantically he ran the women he fancied through his head: Madonna (she had that slutty/dominatrix thing going on that he was half afraid of but couldn't quite resist). No, she was no good to him now. Now was not the time to be even half afraid. Julia Roberts (he used to like that big mouth but again, it was beginning to scare him). There was that girl in *Friends* he liked, Rachel, yes he'd think about her, she was gentle and kooky and sexy, oh yes, yes . . . very, very sexy.

By the time she had worked his jeans down over his hips, he was confident that his armoury was full. She let out a little meow and threw herself back on the bed. Now there was nothing for it. He wriggled out of the remainder of his jeans and lay down beside her. She had already worked her dress loose – a few more tugs and it was gone – and she was revealed in her matching bra and panties. She was very attractive. Gavin realized he was very lucky to be here at all. He kissed her mouth and she returned his kisses like a wild animal. He placed his hand on her thigh and let his fingers creep further and further until she began to arch her back and scream for him to get inside her. So he did, relieved that the event was progressing quickly. Removing the rest of her underwear, he worked as he thought she wanted, slowly at first, then quickening, all the time kissing her and groaning slightly. He hoped to God she would have an orgasm quickly, because he had no idea how to go about it if she didn't. Fortunately, just as he was realizing that he couldn't hold out much longer, she tossed him onto his back, writhed up and down for a little longer, and then came in a glory of screaming and moaning. He had his orgasm immediately and instantly fell asleep.

When he awoke she was wrapped around him telling him how cute he was when he was sleeping and what a wonderful time she'd had. Gavin was so pleased. He hoped that they would never have to do this again. As it turned out they did it twice more, each time a little better than the last. And then she went home to her boyfriend in Dublin.

Susan woke just as they were pulling into the outskirts of Limerick.

'Oh God,' she said immediately, 'don't tell me I fell asleep. How could I fall asleep!'

'It's OK, I really don't mind. I understand that I'm so boring it's impossible to stay awake in my company.'

'Oh, shut up. I try to apologize and you just mock me. You should have woken me up. Wasn't I supposed to drive part of the way home?'

'Yes, you were, but you seemed to need the sleep. Next time . . .'

'OK, next time I'll make it to fourth gear. And that's a promise!'

'I'll hold you to it!'

'Seriously though, Gavin, thanks a million. You mightn't think it, but I have learned so much. You make it seem so easy.'

'Hey, it's a pleasure. You're the best student I've ever had.'

'You must come over some evening for dinner. Felicity and I will cook you a slap-up meal.'

'Great, I'd love to!'

'Excellent! Well then, we'll just pick a night.'

'Any time's fine with me.'

'OK then. Maybe not this week because I still have to buy a recipe book. And maybe not the week after, because I'll have to practise. So maybe the week after that?'

'Sounds perfect.'

'Great!'

The light was fading as they approached Charlotte Avenue, and it had begun to rain. Gavin pulled into a parking space right in front of the house and as Susan was climbing out of the car she noticed that the gate was wide open and there was a pile of bags stashed sloppily against it. Susan was making a beeline for the bags when a voice from behind made her jump.

'It's about fucking time! Where've you been? I'm getting soaked here.'

Susan turned round to see the bedraggled figure of her younger sister rising out of the bushes.

9

It started the minute she appeared at the front gate. Somehow or other Marianne had formed the notion that Gavin was a taxi driver and intimated by a nod and something that sounded a bit like a whistle that he was to carry her bags up to the house.

'That's Gavin, you eejit!' said Susan. 'Carry your own damn bags!'

'Gavin who?' she said with a shrug. 'And why can't he carry my bags anyway?'

'Gavin, our cousin.'

'Oh God, Gavin! Gavin, hi!' she said, peering into the car. 'I'd forgotten about our Limerick cousins. I thought you were all away.'

'Hi, Marianne,' said Gavin, emerging from the car. 'I was away but I came back a while ago. So how are you? Nice to see you again.'

'Mmm. Hi! Nice to see you too. Which one are you again?'

'I'm Gavin.'

'No, I mean are you the rugby player or the music geek?'

'Marianne!'

'I'm the music geek.'

'So, are you going to carry my bags or what?'

'Sure. These are all yours?'

'Yeah. I don't know how long I'll be staying, so I sort of took everything.'

'Marianne, you –'

'Oh, chill out, would you, Susan? You're always so uptight.'

Susan opened her mouth as if to let out a torrent, but not even a dribble appeared, so she turned on her heel and stormed into the house.

Apparently, the reason Marianne couldn't get an answer when she rang the bell was that Angela had fallen asleep watching Ryan Tubridy and Felicity was reading in the bath with her iPod and a glass of wine.

'You could've been burgled,' Marianne announced as her granny and sister congregated in the hall to greet her.

'Well, hardly,' Felicity said, 'seeing as you couldn't get in. So what are you doing here anyway?'

'Same thing as you. I'm here to see Granny. How are you, Gran?'

'Me, love? I'm great. Come on in and we'll get you settled. What about a cup of tea? Or you girls would probably prefer some wine. Is there any wine left, Felicity?'

'There might be a drop.'

'Excellent,' Marianne said, throwing off her shoes and settling onto the couch, 'I'm parched.'

Angela fussed round them for a while, producing two more bottles of wine from her secret cupboard (Marianne politely declined the Mateus Rosé and said she'd stick with the Chilean Sauvignon Blanc that was already open), before she announced she was going to bed.

'I like to get to the nine o'clock when I can,' she said. 'Father O'Connor says a lovely quick Mass and he's very good-looking. Night, loves.'

'Night, Gran.'

'God, is Granny still going to Mass?' said Marianne, topping up her sauvignon.

'Of course she is,' said Felicity. 'What do you expect?'

'She's an intelligent woman. I thought she might have worked out how bogus the whole thing is by now.'

'She claims she only goes to get wear out of her good clothes,' said Susan, 'and she's decided to have nothing to do with the new Pope. She doesn't trust him. She thinks he has too much hair. So she's sticking with John Paul the Second.'

'That's just daft,' said Marianne.

'It's no more daft than believing in the Pope in the first place.'

'I thought she'd have got sense by now.'

'Listen to who's talking!' guffawed Felicity. 'I remember a time when you took your religion very seriously.'

'Me? When? Never!'

'Oh yes. It was quite a few years ago now, but surely you remember that bible belter you were so attached to?'

'Oh, him. Oh, well . . . it wasn't the religion I was serious about. All that zealousness made him a really good lay.'

'It's just as well ye broke up, I couldn't see you as a minister's wife.'

'Excuse me! How do you know we're not still together?'

'Oh, come on, Marianne! You broke up with him that Christmas, remember? You came home screaming to Mum and Dad, claiming you had been brainwashed. You wanted them to pay for you to go off to some rest spa in the Cotswolds. Remember?'

'Oh yeah,' said Marianne with a half smile as it all came back to her.

'Yeah, and it wasn't until they found out the cost of the place and flatly refused to pay, that you began to recover and realized you hadn't been brainwashed after all.'

'I didn't know how badly I was going to be affected. I might have been scarred for life. You never know how deep these things go.'

'Oh, come off it!' snorted Susan. 'You have the thickest skin I have ever seen on anyone. Nothing affects you.'

'That's a cruel thing to say.'

'No, it's not. It's just the truth. You're like a rhinoceros.'

'If I'm a rhinoceros, you're some sort of an evil poison-spitting serpent that has f–'

'OK, kids, that's enough of the crazy jungle,' said Felicity. 'We should probably all go to bed.'

'Oh, don't be so boring. Go and open that Mateus Rosé, for God's sake. Stick it in the freezer for a while.'

'You want more wine? Go stick it in the freezer your-self.'

'Fine, I will!'

'Take a few deep breaths,' said Felicity as soon as Marianne was out of earshot, 'she just takes a bit of getting used to.'

'She's always the same. Did you see the way she was leering at Gavin? And the way she was ordering him about!'

'She wasn't leering. That's just her way. She's an appalling flirt.'

'Well, it was . . . disrespectful.'

'Look, I really don't think Gavin minded. I'm sure he's well used to her sort.'

'I'm sure he isn't!'

'The novelty of the forgotten cousin will wear off very quickly. If there's one thing you can rely on with Marianne, it's that she gets bored easily.'

'I just hope she gets bored tomorrow and buggers off out of here. She should go down to Ballyconnell for herself, and let Mum and Dad look after her.'

'She'll probably do that anyway. Just be nice to her for now. For Granny's sake.'

'Whatever.'

'So what'd I miss?' asked Marianne, returning with the wine and a salad sandwich. 'Oh, sorry, did either of you want a sandwich?'

'We're fine, thanks,' said Susan.

'So where am I sleeping?'

'We've decided to share, and you can have my room for tonight. Then we'll make up the other back bedroom tomorrow.'

'I don't mind sharing.'

'Oh . . . I thought it might aggravate your asthma?'

'I don't have asthma.'

'Exactly!' retorted Susan.

'What *is* your problem?'

'Don't you remember when Mum decided to turn my room into a "mini-gym", and I had to share with Felicity? You said that sharing would aggravate your asthma. I always knew you never had asthma.'

'I don't have it now! But I had it very bad back then.'

'No, you didn't!'

'OK, OK,' said Felicity. 'We all got over it. And you did get your room back, Susan.'

'Only because I demanded it. I mean, Mum hardly ever went in there, and when she did, she just huffed and puffed for about fifteen minutes. She's never forgiven me. I know that every time she gains a pound she subliminally blames me.'

'Anyway, Marianne,' cut in Felicity, 'you have my room at the front beside Granny tonight, and tomorrow you can take over the room on the first landing. OK?'

'It's all fine with me.'

'Right then, Suze, let's head to bed.'

'Goodnight, Marianne, sleep well,' said Susan, and then added, under her breath, as she walked out the door, 'Just don't go having an attack of wheezing or anything.'

'What's that you said?'

But the two girls were gone and Marianne was left to finish her pink wine and think about her day. She looked over at the bags which lay in a neat pile where Gavin had left them. He was a find; she hadn't expected to see a decent male knocking about the place. She'd been quite disappointed when she went to offer him a glass of wine and found that he'd slipped away quietly. The little she could remember of him from childhood was all duffle coat and dorkiness. He'd always been a sweetie, but now it looked as if he was a bit of a hottie too. That was a bonus; he'd do nicely when her sisters began to piss her off.

Oh, they weren't so bad; they were just boring. Goody two shoes, the pair of them. Having to put up with so much of it from her teachers when they were in school was one of the reasons she avoided them now. 'Why can't you be more like your sisters? Felicity would never have done that! I can't believe you're an O'Regan!' It was impossible for her to be herself when she was constantly compared to them. And being compared to Felicity was one thing; at least she actually did something – best leaving cert results in her year, scholarship to UCD, some shit with the president. But Susan! All Susan ever did was come second in a debating competition. Everyone expected her to do shit-hot in the leaving as well – maybe not as good as Felicity, but good – and then she goes and has panic attacks and ends up getting only average results – only marginally better than Marianne's, and she'd hardly done a stroke of work in five years. She'd had to put up with being thought less good than that, for half her life. The only person who'd ever understood what it was like was Eoin.

Maybe it had been a little foolish to just bolt like that. But she hadn't been able to stop herself. What was that expression? The floodgates had been opened and she was swept along. She didn't even know what was inside the bags she'd brought. She'd run through the flat picking up anything she thought was hers. Anything she thought was his that she deserved, as well. She didn't know what she might have left behind. But it was too late now.

10

Felicity wasn't able to get to sleep. Seeing her sister turn up out of the blue like that brought it home to her how odd her own arrival had been. One minute she was heading into the biggest AGM of her life, the next she was frantically trying to get through security at the departure lounge without a boarding pass.

'I'm sorry, madam,' the security guard said, with the utmost calm, 'you can't board without a boarding pass and you can't get a boarding pass without your booking details.'

'But I have to get home! I have to get to Shannon! I can't stay here a minute longer!'

'I'm sorry. If you want to purchase a ticket you'll have to go back to the desk in the check-in area.'

'But I have to go home! I can buy a ticket on the plane!'

'No, that is not possible. I'm afraid if you don't go back to check-in, I will have to call for assistance.'

'But I'm no threat! I just need to get home.'

Unfortunately Felicity was seen as a threat and three further security personnel appeared within seconds. She had sufficient clarity of mind to be able to see the scene as it really was and when the female guard put her hand over hers using enough pressure to break her hold on the cordon that separated her from the gate, Felicity gave up. She allowed herself to be taken to a room where someone got her a cup of tea and the same female guard asked her if there was someone she could ring.

'I just want to go home,' she whimpered. 'I've had a very bad day.'

'I know, love, we all have 'em. But you might feel better if there was someone familiar who could come here. Someone you can trust.'

Felicity snorted.

'Trust!'

'Is there anyone, love? It might make things a lot easier for you.'

Eventually she had given them Sandra's number. Sandra was still the only real friend Felicity had in London despite having lived there for nearly a decade. She just didn't make friends that easily.

By the time Sandra arrived, Felicity had calmed sufficiently so they didn't think she was a threat any more. If she was willing to go home with Sandra, they were willing to forget all about it.

'But I still need to get back to Limerick!' Felicity wailed.

'It's OK,' Sandra told the security personnel, 'she's just had a very bad day. She's not usually like this.'

'All right. Come back tomorrow after a good night's sleep. Buy yourself a ticket first, and we'll see how you get on.'

'Have you heard?' Felicity asked as Sandra led her out to her car.

'I'm afraid my spies told me everything.'

'Am I insane?'

'No, honey,' Sandra said, giving her friend a warm squeeze. 'I don't think you're the insane one at all. Come on, we'll open a bottle of wine and drink the bastard's health.'

So Felicity had spent that night tossing and turning in Sandra's spare room, while Sandra booked her a one-way flight to Shannon at the premium rate of £369.

And now? Sure, she was a lot calmer. But was she any more reconciled to what had happened than when she was causing havoc at departures?

11

Angela smiled to herself as she put on her pot of coffee. What was she doing at this hour of her life with three young ones in the house? Three young ones who were bound to make trouble, especially now that Marianne had arrived on top of them? She had been enjoying the company of the other two – they had always been easier to manage – but Marianne was a different story altogether. She was fond of her – of course she was. She loved her – of course she did. But it was hard to have her around for very long without wishing she would go away. She was like her mother in that. Though she was more fun than her mother. Oh well, Angela thought, she would stay out of it as much as possible. They were all grown-ups and could look after themselves.

She poured her first cup of coffee and put the radio on: *Sunday Miscellany.* Oh, it was peaceful and all for a Sunday morning, but it made her feel old. It was fine when you were young, you could appreciate the peace and the quiet, the time for reflection, but at her age she needed to feel there was life going on somewhere. She was always wary of having too much time to think. She switched channels: Lyric was playing something that reminded her of Lenten Mass in the days when you had to rise in the dark for eight o'clock, sit through an hour and a half of fire and brimstone before walking home to a breakfast of porridge and black tea. She shuddered and changed stations again. Today FM was playing repeats of the *Gift Grub*. She settled on that. More often than not she didn't know what they were talking about or who they were doing impressions of, but it was the tone she was looking for. She put a couple of slices of wholegrain bread in the toaster and sat by the window to enjoy her coffee.

The hot liquid trickled down her throat as she settled back into her seat. It was a while now since coffee had become an addiction. After Frank died she had been left with two options – how did they put it in that film? – either get busy living, or get busy dying. It would have been so easy, then, just to give up. Who would have blamed her? No parent was supposed to have to live beyond their children. And it wouldn't have been difficult. There were enough tablets in the house for a royal overdose – Valium, Seconol, Prozac and God knows what else. What were they trying to do to her? Turn her into a junkie in her old age? Maureen was the worst. She'd let herself in in the mornings and tiptoe up the stairs calling her name ever so gingerly as if she fully expected to find the prostrate body of her mother-in-law laid out in full state in one of the bedrooms. Angela often wondered if that wasn't exactly what Maureen was hoping for, the way she kept shoving boxes of tablets in front of her.

'I got these from my own doctor,' she'd say, setting the plastic jar down on the bedside locker. 'He swears by them himself. You should take a few. They'd do you good. You're not looking well at all this morning. You need your sleep, you know.'

Between each sentence Maureen would pause as if expecting Angela to collapse into her arms and thank her for bringing her back from the brink. But Angela never budged an inch.

It was after a few mornings like this that Angela decided she'd had enough. Enough of her daughter-in-law. Enough of being treated like a child. And enough of sleep. It was time to stay awake. That's when her coffee ritual began. She realized that it was her dreams that terrified her, or at least the thought of what her subconscious might dredge up in her dreams. Reality, she could cope with. Something awful had happened, but as long as she had the wit to face it, at least it could get no worse. So she'd brew up a pot of Bewley's strong blend (always in the house for visitors but she never used to touch it) and carry her cup round the house, from room to room, dropping back to the kitchen every so often for a refill. And thus she began to face her demons. Of course, eventually she would fall asleep, but by the time she'd nodded off in a chair or in one of the back bedrooms, she was so exhausted that she didn't have any dreams, or if she did, she was too tired to remember them.

It had become a habit with her to say, usually with a shrug and a laugh, that when her husband died, she was too busy bringing up three children to notice very much. Of course it wasn't true. But she'd been saying it for so long, that when Frank died, it was time for her to acknowledge how untrue it was.

Her world had completely fallen apart. It was as if the fabric of her life had been ripped from top to bottom, and the tear went right through her heart. But being a woman of her time, and being particularly disinclined to make an issue of her own pain, she whipped out her needle and thread and patched up the rip as best she could. It was simply what you did. And it was what she continued to do until she sent out three reasonably well-adjusted children into the world.

Frank, she considered her success, Kay her break-even child, and Tom her borderline failure. It wasn't that there was anything wrong with him, or that he wasn't a perfectly successful individual as far as any onlooker was concerned. She just felt he would have fared better if his dad had been around. He would have made a man of him; she was afraid she'd made something of a woman of him. But, sure, where was the harm really? What did it matter that he'd found himself a wife who didn't let him have an independent thought in his head? Wasn't he happy? Didn't he have three lovely girls of his own? What did it matter if he never got to make a single decision about anything that any of them ever did? Didn't their mother see that everything always worked out? And no one who saw him now, at sixty, with his ridiculous barnet of silver hair and his irritating perma grin that showed off the teeth his wife insisted he whiten ('I know dental hygiene simply wasn't as important in your day,' she'd said in defence of Tom's brand new George Hamilton beam. 'I'm not blaming you, but there's no need for him to be stuck with those yellow teeth.'), could possibly deny that he was happy. No, he *was* happy, and even happier since he'd retired and moved to Ballyconnell, but Angela just wished sometimes that he could be happy on his own terms or that he might know whether or not he was happy without his wife having to tell him so.

She smiled to herself again and drained her cup. Ever since she'd come through the bad times she'd limited herself to one cup at a time. She'd never give up the stuff (she was too grateful to it and too fond of the hit) but there was a certain amount of sleep a woman of her age needed. Frank was a great man for the coffee too. Frank was a great man for everything. Somehow all the things that bothered her about his brother had come right in Frank. Nobody would ever tell him what to do. And it wasn't because he was bullish about things (he was a very gentle man), it was simply because he knew his own mind. Undoubtedly he could be stubborn, pig-headed even, but if he made a decision, even if everyone else thought it was the wrong decision, at least Angela was always confident that he knew what he was doing. Grace was proof of that. Oh, Grace . . . lovely, daft, sweet Grace. She made him so happy . . . yet she might just have ruined his life.

She was just about to wash the coffee pot when Felicity came into the kitchen.

'Morning, Gran. Mind if I join you?'

'Sit down, love. I'll make a fresh pot.'

Angela hadn't been able to work out what was up with Felicity. But something was. It wasn't just that since moving to London she'd never managed to spend more than three days in Limerick, and now she was already a couple of weeks at home. It wasn't that her beautiful face was drawn or that there wasn't any sparkle in her pretty eyes. All those things might have been the result of tiredness or stress. It went deeper than that. Something was bothering her and it went right to her core.

'Sleep all right, love? There's a lot of noise at the front. I'm used to it but it might bother you.'

'Oh no, I like the sound of traffic. It's soothing.' She sighed as she pulled her chair closer to the table and laid her arms out in front of her. 'But, no, I didn't sleep well.'

'What's the matter, love? Something's not right.'

'Oh, it's nothing really. I've just been a bit foolish.'

'Foolish isn't the worst thing you can be.'

'It is when you should know better.'

'Often we only think we know better.'

'But I did. Right from the start.'

'A man, love?'

'I don't think I could call him a man. But, yes, a male of the species.'

'Do you want to tell me about it?'

'I think I feel embarrassed.'

'Like I said, lovey, acting foolish isn't the worst thing.'

'No?'

'Go on, love. Tell me the story.'

'Oh . . . he was your typical cad, Gran, your classic bad boy, a real charmer, someone you should run a million miles away from, screaming. Don't tell me I shouldn't have known better.'

'Go on.'

'And he was my boss.'

'Foolish, I'll give you that.'

'But he was so attractive. There was something about him . . . I don't know what exactly. I mean, he wasn't good-looking – he was old and craggy, to be honest – but you just couldn't take your eyes off him. Wherever he was in the room you had to be there too, or you might miss something. I suppose he was one of those "men want to be him; women want to do him" sort of men.'

'But he picked you.'

'He didn't pick me. I allowed myself to get in line. I'd seen enough of them go before me. What did I expect?'

'We always expect it will be different with us.'

'It was good for a while, it really was. He knows how to treat a girl – I mean – he knows how to show her a good time. I suppose I was a little star-struck. Instead of just working for his gossipy rag I was socializing for it too. And it's not as if I could care less about wags and footballers, or even musicians and actors, I just don't see what the fuss is about. But it was nice, for a while, to be in the middle of it all.'

'We always knew you'd go far.'

'Oh, Granny, it's all so false. So meaningless. None of it matters. The part of it I love is making the big deals, getting the really big advertisers on board, seeing the hit rate go up and up. I actually feel a little bit embarrassed about the content of the site, but hey, it sells. Anyway . . .'

'Were you hoping for a future with this man?'

'No. No, I really wasn't. You couldn't be married to a man like that and stay sane. But, Granny, it wasn't just that – it wasn't realizing that I wasn't the love of his life. I took my eyes off the prize. I wasn't just foolish; I was monumentally stupid. And there is no excuse for that!'

'Hey, can I get in on that coffee?' asked Marianne, crashing into the room. 'I've a fierce head on me.'

'Work away, love, I'm done with it.'

'And I'm going to have a shower,' said Felicity, getting up immediately. 'Talk to you later, Gran. Thanks.'

'Take care, lovey.'

'Don't use all the hot water!' roared Marianne after her. 'I want to wash my hair.'

Angela watched as Felicity's seat was taken by Marianne and wondered how the pair could be sisters at all. Felicity held so much in and only leaked out little bits when she was able. Marianne, on the other hand, was like a tap you couldn't turn off. Only most of what came out was a very dodgy colour.

She thought of the days when her own three were tumbling down to breakfast like this on a weekend morning. Sunday, they were all up early for Mass, of course, but Saturday was always more relaxed. Frank would usually be up first; he'd wallop down four Weetabix and head out to training: rugby, hurling, Gaelic, whatever team needed him, he'd be gone. They were mad after him. He was talented, but he also had a way with the boys he was playing with. Got the best out of them. And then there was the washing. Every night of the week, nearly, there was mud-covered kit to be washed. Some of them never got clean. Those big heavy jerseys and the shorts that hadn't been white since their first wear. It didn't matter what the weather was like; they trained and they played and they brought home their cups. He loved his sports . . .

Tom played a bit too, but not to the same extent. He'd got himself a Saturday job at a very young age. In the same builders suppliers he worked in later. He seemed to like to be working, the independence of it, no doubt, and the money of course. Although he always handed up a fair portion of it. He seemed to be in more of a hurry than the others to grow up. And to have girlfriends. He always had a girlfriend whereas Frank never mentioned anyone till Grace.

And Kay. Oh, it would be nice if Kay were here. Now that the three girls were home it was more obvious what it would be like to have a sympathetic woman round all the time. But she went years ago. Her life was in Washington; her husband was there. She was more American than Irish now. And she had to go when she did. She needed to do things for herself, not feel that she had to mind her mammy. Angela had encouraged her to go. Some people have to go or they won't be happy. Sure, she'd be home again later in the year. And she never stopped emailing.

'So would that be OK?' said Marianne. 'Gran! Gran! Would that be OK?'

'What's that, love?'

'I was wondering if it would be OK if I borrowed your car?'

'Oh sure, lovey. Where do you want to go?'

'Nowhere in particular. I just don't feel like walking.'

'That's fine, love. The keys are in the hall stand. Just put them back there when you're done.'

'Thanks, Granny. See ya later.'

Angela got up from the table and began putting the breakfast things away. Susan would sort herself out when she came down. She sighed. It didn't do any good, thinking about the past. Better to leave it alone and stick with the present. She turned the radio on again but turned it off quickly. The *Gift Grub* was over and they were talking recession now. Some people were never done trying to make you miserable.

Marianne was waiting in line at the labour exchange on Monday afternoon. She had filled in her forms and had a little interview and now she was queuing up to sign on. It had taken half the morning but then she had nothing else to do. For a while there she thought they weren't going to let her sign on, there were some irregularities with her paperwork from Cork. There was even a suggestion that at one stage she had been claiming in two places at the same time. Marianne assured them that if that's what their records showed, then it must be a mistake on their part because she had certainly never received two sets of payments. Then there were endless questions about the various jobs she'd had since signing off. There was some more fudging over her name which Marianne was able to sort out and finally they said that she had the right to claim but she had to show that she was actively looking for work. 'No problem,' said Marianne who had absolutely no intention of foisting some piece of garbage job on herself, 'I'll start looking this afternoon.'

In fact Marianne was very pleased with herself at the moment. She really had made the right decision in coming to Charlotte Avenue; to think that she had originally intended going to Ballyconnell. That would have been OK for a day or two while her mother caught her up on all the news and showed her off to her Ballyconnell friends, but even Marianne wasn't able to handle her mother's persistent interference. No, she was much better off at Granny's. And it was only by accident that her mother let slip that Susan and Felicity were there. She would never have gone if Angela had been on her own. It wouldn't have seemed right and, besides, she wouldn't have known what to say to her after the first hour or so. You never really knew where you were with old people.

Sixty-five was probably the cut-off for regular living. Up to that point you were fine – working, going out, wearing make-up, getting your hair done, shopping, you could even be in a relationship up to about sixty-five. But after that point, you were just old. And even if you were still working or going out or dyeing your hair, it was just a bit sad. You'd really be better off not bothering. Not that Angela was a sad case exactly, but she was eighty-six for crying out loud. That was the other problem with old people – you never knew when they were going to up and die on you.

She was delighted with her room. Felicity had said she would go out and buy her a duvet and a new cover in the Brown Thomas sale so she would be able to move into the spare bedroom and make it her own. Marianne couldn't remember the last time she'd had a room and a bed to herself and certainly not one as nice as this. It looked onto the back garden and got the best light in the morning and evening. Sure, the room was small, the furniture was old and the wallpaper practically alive, but it had a good feel. It felt like home. It felt like the home she only vaguely remembered.

She shuffled forward in the queue. She'd hoped she was done with the indignity of queuing up for a couple of euro, but there was simply no choice at the moment. She had absolutely no money and it was a bit early to go scrounging off her family. Nor was she willing to settle for some menial job that paid no more than the government was willing to give her for sitting on her arse. If someone could get her a decent job that paid decent money she would happily give it a go, but no one was offering. She hadn't had much luck with jobs recently, or ever. Marianne was the type of girl for whom it was often difficult to find the right situation.

She had begun her professional life hopefully enough by enrolling at art college. All her teachers agreed that she had a lot of talent and that a creative career would suit her. As far as Marianne was concerned it was the only subject she had ever done the homework for so she figured it was as good a way as any to experience college life. But it wasn't long before she realized there was quite a lot of hard work involved in getting a degree, so she gave it up. Maureen and Tom went berserk, naturally. They were a little mollified when she decided to take up a secretarial course (Marianne had a notion, at the time, of being a PA) but barely weeks into the course she was dying of boredom. It was at that point she felt that maybe she wasn't fully ready for college so she took a job at a car-hire company at the airport – just for the summer. However, summer work turned into autumn work and it might have turned into winter work if she hadn't been fired just before Christmas for giving concessions to a friend.

It was shortly after that that she tried London for the first time but found it impossible to eke out a lifestyle on what she could earn waitressing. Next she headed to Europe for six months or so until poverty sent her back to Tom and Maureen for a short stint in a local garage shop. At this point she realized that while Ireland was definitely the coolest place to live, Limerick certainly wasn't, so she tried Dublin (way too expensive), then Galway (bliss for a while, but again she ran into money problems). A boyfriend brought her to Scotland for a year and another one brought her back.

And so it went. Marianne continued to go forwards and until now, it seemed, her problems never managed to follow her. By the time she ended up in Cork she had already spent much of her twenties moving around – it wasn't her fault if people and places kept letting her down. And by the time she left Cork to come back to Limerick, she had been there longer than she had been anywhere else since leaving home. And it was there that she had been happy for the first time in her life.

So no, she didn't have any qualifications, but in modern Ireland things like mere bits of paper weren't supposed to matter, it was all about drive and charisma, both of which Marianne believed she had in bucket loads.

When she got to the head of the line she was confronted by a boy who was at least five years her junior. Marianne flashed him a smile and trusted she wouldn't have any problems.

'I hope everything's all right,' she said, almost breathily.

He said nothing, just continued to study her forms.

'They said there wouldn't be any problem,' she added.

'Sign here,' he said without looking at her.

'I hope there won't be any delay?'

'Three weeks.'

'Three weeks! But I can't wait three weeks!'

'Three weeks. That's standard.'

'But I can't wait.'

'NEXT!'

Marianne walked off in a sulk. She wasn't sure which annoyed her most, that she'd have to wait three weeks to get any money, or that the boy at the window was completely immune to her. She wasn't used to that; normally she could rely on a certain level of response from male operatives. Even the gay ones – especially the gay ones – they always found her cute. And this one wasn't gay; maybe he was just depressed.

She didn't know what to do with herself; that was the problem with not having a job and not having any money. Still, she decided to take a walk down the town. It was quite a while since she had spent any time in Limerick and the city seemed to have improved a lot. When she first left it she had thought it was the lamest place in the universe and that opinion hadn't changed much over the years. But of course it was never the city itself that was lame, it was the version of herself that had been living there for seventeen years that was lame and uncool and everything she wanted not to be. More than anything, when Marianne left the city, she wanted to rewrite her character completely, change the scenery, alter the script in every way she could. And now, ten years on, she was back and glad to see that the old place had managed to change with her.

She wandered down Dominic Street and onto Catherine Street, then down Thomas Street where she was arrested by the sale signs in the Brown Thomas window. She decided to go in and have a browse, not that she was fond of ostentatious department stores like BT. She remembered it in the days when it was Todds, family owned and still a little ostentatious. It was where they went for coffee on a Saturday, and where they saw Santa at Christmas and where, if the occasion was very special, they were bought an outfit by an actual designer (rather than making do with Dunnes as they usually did). It had a great toy department, and their mother was particularly fond of the fashion floor. Their father made a big thing every year of bringing Maureen in to Todds to buy her birthday present. They were dumped on Granny, and Tom would accompany his wife to the first floor, take a seat by one of the changing rooms (one of the first places to provide seating for weary spouses), open the newspaper and wait for his wife to appear in one stunning outfit after another. Marianne clearly remembered the glow on both their faces when they turned up, late, to collect them. They were such old fools, the pair of them, she thought.

Still, she took the escalator to the first floor and began flicking through the sale racks. None of this stuff was her style. Marianne wasn't into labels or fashion, she thought the whole thing was so conservative as to be almost right wing. She knew she didn't need a Karen Millen dress to make her look good. She was the kind of girl who looked her best in jeans and a man's shirt, or at least she thought she did. There was no denying that her figure was good – she was slim without being thin and her curves exuded a health-fulness that was very attractive – and her hair, while nothing had been done to it in years, fell about her face in bolts of brown and blonde that gave her a very contemporary look without any effort at all. As for her skin, it was immaculate. She couldn't recall ever having a spot in her life (something she loved to point out to Susan when her pale skin was covered in lumpy blotches), and she never put a thing on her face other than a generic brand moisturizer. She was just lucky that way. So Brown Thomas really wasn't the mecca it had always been for Felicity and was recently becoming for Susan. But she just felt like a nose; she just felt like trying on something very expensive that wasn't in the sale and maybe telling the assistant a story about how her boyfriend wanted to see her in it before she bought it (he has such good taste, you know) so she would pop back later in the afternoon. Yes, that was what she felt like, and maybe then she would go and have a cup of coffee with her last fiver.

In the end there was nothing worthy of the hassle of trying on and nothing that tempted her into telling stories to sales assistants. It was the fag end of the sale and even a shop as exclusive as Brown Thomas was looking tatty. There were a few weary-looking men sitting around leafing through the women's magazines; she felt sorry for them. Eoin would never hang around after her like that and she would never subject him to it.

She sighed.

Eoin.

Well, there was no point sighing or being regretful; what was done was done.

But she did miss him.

She didn't think she had ever actually missed a man before, once it was over. But then . . . but no . . . it *was* over. What else could it be now, but over?

Yet she did miss the look of him and the smell of him and the taste of him. Perhaps he was the first man she had been truly intimate with. Now there was nothing left except an impression, like the tingle on your skin after a day spent too long in the sun.

She decided not to spend her last five euro on coffee either, she needed to get out of the stuffy air of the shop (air-conditioning notwithstanding) and back onto the concreteness of the street. She automatically turned up and kept on walking until she was in front of Charlotte Avenue at the top of O'Connell Street; she turned in and made her way to number 9.

Angela was in the kitchen making a pot of tea.

'Hi, Gran.'

'Hello, love. Fancy a cup?'

'Sure.'

'Help yourself.'

'Thanks.'

Angela had picked up the newspaper when Marianne spoke again.

'Gran, do you think you could loan me a tiny amount of money? I've signed on and I'm looking for a job but it's going to take three weeks for anything to come through. Just to tide me over?'

If Angela hesitated before she spoke it wasn't evident to Marianne.

'Of course, how much do you need?'

'Oh, not much, just maybe ahm . . . maybe two hundred or something? I'll pay you back, I promise.'

'No problem, lovey, will I write you a cheque?'

'Oh . . . ahm . . . no. Do you mind giving me cash? It's just so much easier?'

'Maybe for you, dear, but not for me. I have to go to the bank and draw it out. I don't keep any cash in the house.'

'Do you have an ATM card?'

'I don't. I'm the wrong generation for ATM cards.'

'Oh. Well, a cheque's fine so. Thanks a million, Gran. I'll pay you back straight away, I promise.'

'I'm sure you will. Will I make it three hundred?'

'Oh, thanks, Gran, that'd be great.'

As she was making her way upstairs she noticed the open door of the dining room. She slipped in and closed it. She knew exactly where the blue velvet box was; it came immediately to hand when she opened the sideboard.

It was 'just in case'. Three hundred euro wouldn't go very far. And Granny would never miss these. The pastry forks were so damn ugly anyway.

13

The following Sunday the heat wave began. Up to now the weather had been perfectly good for the time of year but by noon that Sunday the temperature had reached 25 degrees and looked set to stay that way for a while. Normally Susan dreaded the arrival of a sunny spell – invariably, despite her best efforts, she would end up with heat stroke or sun stroke or an onset of freckles that her mother would insist were pre-cancerous moles – but this time, for no particular reason, she was looking forward to a week or so of hot weather. Perhaps it had something to do with the fact that now she actually had some clothes that were suitable for tropical living. Her typical summer wardrobe consisted of her winter wardrobe rolled up, or peeled off, or tied up, or sometimes even cut off. The result was never satisfactory. She was still too hot – denim just doesn't work above 20 degrees no matter how far up your white blotchy legs you roll them. Taking off her top layer (a jumper or a shirt) to reveal her next layer (usually a close-fitting vest top) made her feel just as hot and sticky and still didn't give her UV protection.

This year, however, Susan had all the gear. She had two, light as a feather, cotton dresses that covered her shoulders and went past her knees yet still gave the impression of being hardly there. She had several pairs of linen-mix trousers that positively wafted the air up her legs and a selection of colourful tops to alter her look as her mood or her day changed. She even had shorts, halter necks, tunic tops, swimsuits (a very flattering one-piece and a bikini), flip flops, and a selection of bangles and bracelets to set off each outfit. She had also invested in some top of the range sun protection; her confidence in it was such that she was willing to sit out and take some rays for nearly ten minutes at a time. Yes, for whatever reason, this year Susan was quite happy to watch the thermometer hit red.

It was noon and Susan was in her bedroom doing her exercises. The only hobby which she thought might be doable (flying lessons, snorkling and sky diving had all been dismissed for obvious reasons) was yoga. It was cheap, low impact and available on her way home from work.

After her first session she wasn't sure if she would be back. It was all very fine to get on the floor and have someone tell you to empty your mind, but what if you were afraid that if you emptied your mind you'd never manage to fill it up again?

But now she began to see why people went on about yoga so much. Everything irritated her a little less. It had been raining yesterday but she'd simply kept on walking and focused on the pattern the rain made as it crashed into the puddles. Paul had texted again but she deleted it without a moment's hesitation. Angela had taped over the episode of *Grey's Anatomy* she'd missed but she simply asked Felicity to tell her what had happened. And now that Marianne was home, she would concentrate on finding her centre and not allowing her sister to get at her. She was sure she'd be able to make it work . . .

Chakras engaged, Susan went to have a shower, then, still naked, she began to meticulously cover every inch of her skin in expensive sun block. It had become quite a ritual with her. It was almost as if, by coating her body in the sweet-smelling fluid, she was not only protecting herself against the harmful rays of the sun, but also preparing herself for whatever might befall her that day. It was something like the actor putting on his greasepaint; once in character, she was free to leave her old self behind.

She became aware of the sound of the mower and realized Gavin must be cutting the grass in the back garden. She hadn't had a lesson with him in nearly two weeks – he had been very busy at work and she had been lazy about getting into fourth gear – and even though he kept telling her she needed to keep up the momentum, she was slow to agree to a lesson. Now it was too hot for driving; whatever he said about his car having air-conditioning, she knew she wouldn't be able to concentrate.

Wrapping a towel round her, she went over to the window and watched as he systematically pushed the mower up the length of the garden and then down again, making neat lines of alternating green. He was moving rhythmically, almost as if in a trance, his limbs obeying automatically what his brain was telling him. Wearing loose-fitting Bermuda shorts, a white T-shirt and some sort of leather sandals, he looked cool, despite the hard work in the heat, and the sweat that was causing his hair to mat at the back. Suddenly he stopped and took a drink from the bottle of water that was in his back pocket. He poured some of it over his head, then pulled off the T-shirt, and used it to wipe his face.

She continued to look at him, as he stood there, half naked, leaning against the mower. She couldn't help it, really. And she couldn't help noticing that he had quite a good body, in an understated sort of way. He was definitely too thin to be considered hunky. His shoulders weren't particularly broad and while his midriff was flat it was certainly no washboard. His pecs didn't stand out or anything, and he probably had more hair on his chest than was currently fashionable. Yet there was something very appealing about him. She recalled the notion she'd had that first time in his flat, of him carrying something very heavy for a long time. You could just see him, unflinching and uncomplaining, even though the strain might become unbearable . . .

'I see the geek's got great gabongaes!'

Susan jumped.

Marianne was leaning over her shoulder peering out the window.

'Where the hell did you come from? Haven't you ever heard of knocking?'

'Keep your knickers on! I won't tell anyone you're eyeing up Gavin on the sly.'

'I am not! I'm just –'

'It's fine! I was eyeing him up myself, for God's sake! He's a very fine piece of manhood, our Gavin. Best thing I've seen in this dump for years.'

'Marianne! He's your cousin!'

'Lighten up, would you? I'm not looking to have his baby. I'm only saying he's a perfectly fuckable fella.'

'Honestly, you're gross!'

'Oh, get a life. So what if he's my cousin? All the royal families marry their cousins.'

'And all the trailer trash.'

'Yes, well, like I said, I'm not looking to have his baby. What I am looking for is a bikini top and a pair of shorts.'

'What? You mean you don't have one in those gigantic bags of yours? I thought you took everything with you.'

'Yeah, well, I packed in a bit of a hurry so I must have left them behind. Do you have a pair of shorts or not?'

'Let me have a look.'

While Susan rummaged in a drawer Marianne went back to the window.

'Aww, he's put his T-shirt back on. But it's all wet so now you can see the outline of his chest.'

'Here!' said Susan, thrusting at her a pair of shorts she had bought for two euro in Dunnes the summer she and Paul went to Marbella, and an old bikini top that had somehow become separated from its bottom.

'Thanks a million. I'll sterilize them before I give them back.'

'You can keep them.'

'You're too generous.'

'So why were you in such a hurry packing?' Susan ventured as Marianne was about to leave the room.

'I was late. I was late for the train. That good enough for you, Sherlock?'

Marianne went back to her room and continued to peer at Gavin who had resumed his mowing. In fact Marianne was the very reason Gavin was cutting the grass in the middle of one of the hottest days of the year. She had been messing about in the kitchen preparing a breakfast of organic fruit and non-dairy yoghurt when Angela had come in with him. He'd picked her up as she was making her way home from Mass. Angela was wittering on about what a life saver he was when Marianne got the idea that what they all needed was a party, a barbecue to be exact. Now, Marianne never ate meat, well nearly never, but wherever there was a barbecue, there was bound to be alcohol, and Marianne had decided that what this summer Sunday needed was alcohol.

Angela got into such a flap about the state of the garden and how a barbecue could be dangerous if the grass was too high that Gavin (who had been feeling guilty about not doing the garden) immediately offered to cut it. Then Angela got into a further flap about the heat and how he might kill himself until Gavin assured her he'd have it done in twenty minutes and that he didn't find it that hot anyway. Thus came about the spectacle of Gavin mowing his Granny's lawn.

'Yes,' Marianne mused as she observed him, 'he's a perfectly fuckable fella.'

Of course Marianne didn't have any desire to have sex with her cousin, per se, she was merely noting how the dynamic of a hot body and some cool alcohol might prove interesting in her granny's back garden when there was no possibility of getting to the beach. Both of her sisters could do with a good shag – they were far too uptight and Marianne had always been a great believer in sex as the cure for most of life's problems. It was a good relaxant, it was good exercise, it was cheap, it was companionable (even at times a group activity), it was psychologically cleansing (i.e. it stopped you hankering after sex) and it was very often a good laugh. However, she had never made the connection that most of the problems in her life were caused by sex. Not so much the sex itself (Marianne was usually very careful that way) but the people with whom she chose to have the sex, or the times she chose to have it. It wasn't the kind of thing she liked to analyse. It was the kind of thing she liked to just let happen.

There was a commotion downstairs as Susan finally answered a persistent ringing at the door. It was Bernie. And Carmel. And Brian. And another bloke who had the telltale look of someone who was being brought along as a present.

'Susan!' said Bernie with excessive delight. 'I'm so glad you're here! We thought for ages there was nobody home.'

'Hi!' said Susan, still adjusting to the light.

'We're on our way to Ballyconnell – thought you might come with us.'

'We're having a family barbecue.'

'Oh. This is Alan, by the way.'

The present stepped forward and offered his hand.

'Hi, Alan, nice to meet you.'

'Nice to meet you,' he said with a firm shake.

So this was the famous Alan. He seemed perfectly nice. Tall, tanned, inoffensive. But she was no nearer to letting anyone persuade her he was 'just what she needed' simply because he had turned up on her doorstep.

'Can we change your mind about Ballyconnell at all?' asked Bernie.

'I'm . . . ahh . . .' Susan had no idea how to get rid of them all. 'Come in for a minute, anyway,' she added aware that she was being rude. 'Everyone's out the back. Granny'd murder me if I didn't bring you out to say hello.'

She led them out to the garden where Angela was dozing in an armchair under the shade of the magnolia tree.

'Oh!' Angela said, shading her eyes as she looked up at the group in front of her, 'who have I here?'

'These are my friends, Granny,' Susan said, thrusting them in front of her. 'Bernie from work and her boyfriend Brian' – why did it feel weird saying that? – 'and Carmel, also from work, and this is Alan . . . their friend . . .'

'Hello, Mrs O'Regan,' said everyone.

'Lovely to meet you all. Sit down there under that gazebo thing and get a bit of shade. Are you all going to join us for this barbecue the girls have organized?'

'Oh . . . ah . . .' spluttered Susan.

'Actually,' said Alan, 'we were trying to persuade Susan to come down to Ballyconnell with us.'

'Alan has a mobile home there,' offered Carmel.

'It's my parents', but they're abroad at the moment.'

'You should go, Susan,' said Angela. 'The beach would be fabulous on a day like this.'

'I don't want to leave you and —'

'Oh, run off, would you!'

'Hello!' said Felicity joining the group, her slender figure draped demurely in a silk kaftan.

'Hi, Fliss. Wouldn't Ballyconnell beach be mad on a day like this?'

'Jointed I'd say. I wouldn't go near it.'

'There!'

'Is that where you're headed?' asked Felicity. 'You're more than welcome to join us if you want. There's tons of food and buckets to drink.'

'Oh, I'm sure they —'

'Are you sure? That would be so nice! What do you think, lads, will we stay?'

'That's really nice of you, Felicity,' said Alan. 'Are you sure we wouldn't be putting you out?'

'No! The more the merrier!'

'Thanks very much,' said Carmel. 'I'm not that gone on sand, anyway.'

'Now, where's Gavin, Susan? I'm afraid he'll have heat stroke from doing all that work in the sun.'

'I don't know. I haven't seen him.'

Gavin appeared just then, his wet T-shirt almost dry. Now that she was close to him, Susan could see a day or so's growth of beard and the thought occurred to her that it must make him even hotter.

'Hi!' he said immediately. 'I'm Gavin, Susan's cousin.'

They all shook hands. Within seconds they had established that Brian's brother worked with Gavin, and Carmel seemed convinced that she knew him from somewhere.

'Are you sure you didn't go to UCG?' she asked.

'No, UCD.'

'And you never lived in Corbally?'

'Never.'

'And you don't think you know me from anywhere?'

'I'm absolutely terrible with faces – but –'

They were interrupted by the arrival of Marianne, who bounded out to them, her breasts barely contained inside Susan's cast-off swimwear.

'Way to go, Suze! You managed to scare up a few men!' she announced, presenting said men with bottles of wine and a corkscrew. 'Now, let's get loaded!'

The afternoon began innocently enough – if you can call ten bottles of wine, a water hose and Marianne's bulging bikini top innocent. Susan was annoyed with everybody, at first. She'd thought she'd made it perfectly clear to Bernie that she had absolutely no interest in being set up with some sad sack friend of Brian's. Bernie had kept insisting how good-looking he was, and while Susan acknowledged that he was no elephant man, she just couldn't see the attraction. He was tall, certainly; a large man, perhaps in the style of a Clooney or a Ford although nowhere near that calibre. He was very well dressed. Susan thought she could recognize much of BT's basement hanging off him – the Paul Smith shirt, the Diesel jeans – yet somehow the clothes didn't seem to work on an actual live person. His hair was short, not thinning, just short – your average boring short hair. And his face was . . . well, his face was fine: blue eyes, straight nose, high forehead, nice smile, white, even teeth. You couldn't argue with the face. Susan simply wasn't interested in engaging with it at all.

Marianne, however, had no problem in engaging with

Alan's face, or with the rest of him either. That was the second thing annoying Susan. As soon as it became apparent that Brian belonged to Bernie, she homed in on Alan. She sat flush beside him, crossed her legs in his direction and allowed her calves to nestle against his Diesels. He didn't seem to mind. Nor did he seem to mind the vulgar way she was quizzing him.

'So what's it really like being a dentist? Is it completely gross, looking into people's mouths all day? Aren't people's teeth absolutely foul?'

When she didn't get a sufficiently demonstrative answer to those enquiries she changed tack.

'But you must make a packet. Surely that's the motivation? I'm not into money myself, but you'd have to get paid really well to do your job. So, how much would you make in an average week?'

Felicity told her to shut up at this point. She tried to take the wine bottle away from her but she had it between her legs. Marianne still drank like a student; she was never willing to share a bottle in case she didn't get her fair share.

Susan was also annoyed at Felicity. If it wasn't for her they wouldn't be witnessing this ridiculous spectacle. There would have been just the five of them, and Marianne might have kept her chest to herself.

As the food was served and the wine continued to pour, the group began to relax. Initially there had been a touch of an alpha male struggle between Gavin and Alan (somehow, Brian didn't feature). It was very subtle, barely perceptible to a casual observer, and it was probably only Felicity who was aware of it. Gavin seemed to be keeping Alan in his sights all the time, as if he didn't trust him, or wasn't entirely sure what he was doing there. Alan, meanwhile, wasn't as averse to Marianne's questions as he might have been.

'Oh,' he said casually to her money enquiries, 'you could hope to earn a very good salary once in your own practice. I'm working towards that at the moment.' And when Marianne asked him what he drove he very quickly told her it was 'An Audi A5 . . . but I'm thinking of upgrading.'

'That's got to be hard on petrol,' Gavin suggested, eye-balling Alan.

'It's a diesel,' he said. 'So I get very good mileage to the gallon.'

However, it wasn't long before the wine began to affect them too and they left each other alone.

Susan had known, from the moment she saw Carmel at the front door, that one way or another she was going to get another instalment of the Rob saga. The latest was that he'd gone back to his wife.

'I can't believe he's gone back to her,' Carmel had said to Susan, who had allowed herself to be pinned to a loo seat, earlier in the week, while Carmel held forth.

'I'm really sorry, Carmel,' said Susan, fishing in her pocket for a tissue and eventually proffering a piece of loo roll, 'but you know, I'm not all that surprised. He was bound to give it another go. He's only been married five minutes.'

'But I thought he loved me,' Carmel wailed.

'Maybe he did, but he loves his wife more. You see, that's the thing, she's his wife, he's obliged to make a go of it with her. Unfortunately he has no obligation to you.'

'That's so unfair.'

'Ahhmmm . . . I suppose it is.'

'He didn't even tell me to my face. He phoned me and said he was working it out with her. It's so cruel.'

'Look, Carmel, he's clearly a weak man – a silly boy who doesn't know what he wants. Even though he probably didn't intend it, he was using you to try and sort himself out. You are much better off without him. You deserve so much more.'

'But I wanted him . . .'

'You'll get over him, you'll see. He wasn't good for you. There will be others, believe me.'

'There'd better be, I'm getting fed up watching everybody else pair off.'

'There will be someone. Look . . . we'll go out some night. My cousin Gavin has a gig soon. We'll all go. There are always loads of good-looking guys at these gigs.'

'Yeah, but they'll all have long hair.'

'Just as long as they don't have wives.'

Carmel managed to crack a small smile at this.

'Come on, it'll be good craic; I'm sure Gavin has loads of hot single friends. Any guy would be lucky to go out with you, you know.'

'Thanks. All right then, I'll think about it.'

Now, as the sun reached its highest point in the sky, Carmel took advantage of a change in the seating arrangements – Marianne, who had been on one side of Susan, went to the loo, and Gavin, who had been on the other side, was giving Felicity a hand with the food – to position herself at Susan's right arm.

'So, I think I'm over him.'

'That's good.'

'I haven't called, I haven't even texted. I did compose a couple of really shitty texts, but I didn't send them.'

'That's really good, Carmel. You'll see, you're so much better off without him.'

'And you're right about there being loads of good-looking men.'

'Yeah, nice, uncomplicated men who won't wreck your head. It's not supposed to be so hard.'

'You're right. Great barbecue.'

'Glad you're enjoying it.'

Susan topped up their glasses. She hoped that was the end of it with Carmel. She had nothing left to give.

No one was absolutely clear how the hose appeared. It wasn't there at the beginning of the afternoon and then suddenly there it was, coiled up like a serpent, only inches away from the group. It was very clear who attached it to the tap – Marianne. 'We could all do with cooling down a bit,' she said, as she checked the pressure against the side of the house. Nobody objected – it seemed that the prospect of cooling down outweighed any thoughts they had on how juvenile or impractical the plan might be. But of course it didn't stop there. Soon the hose became a weapon and it became a game to chase each other round the garden and to wrestle it from whoever was holding it and then douse them in victory. It was amazing how naturally they all fell into the game. Felicity forgot completely that she didn't approve of this sort of thing; Alan forgot that his shirt was dry clean only; Gavin forgot that he had been feeling uncomfortable and Carmel forgot everything. Angela merely wrapped her newspaper round her legs and warned them to keep their distance. They were drunk and soaked and exhausted – and that's when the danger became apparent.

Marianne had the hose. Marianne had the hose for most of the game. Felicity was resting near Angela. Bernie and Brian were hiding out behind the gazebo. Alan, his clothes thoroughly ruined, was squeezing out his socks by the dying heat of the grill. Carmel was in the loo. That left Susan and Gavin as targets. She took aim and got the pair of them in her sights. They ran blindly away from the direction of the flow and both headed straight for the small, walled-in space by the side of the house.

For a moment they were completely obscured. Susan, panting uncomfortably (yoga wasn't sufficiently aerobic to improve her fitness), leaned against the wall and tried to get her breath back. Gavin was panting too, although more from excitement than from any lack of fitness. They raised their heads more or less simultaneously and as they did so something in the atmosphere changed. Susan couldn't tell whether it was the wine or a want of oxygen in her brain or if there really was something in the air between them. It was as if the garden, and all the others, and even the entire afternoon were a million miles away, and as if she and he were enlarged somehow, to inhabit the whole of everything. With his hair pasted to his face, all his features seemed hyper-real – his eyes bluer, his cheekbones sharper, his lips redder. Their faces were only inches apart; the tiniest movement would bring them into contact . . .

That's when Marianne's voice – now very loud, indicating she was close – broke the spell. The next moment Gavin was wrestling the hose from her and she was screaming blue murder. Susan took the opportunity to slip away, and compose herself under the shade of the magnolia tree.

14

Felicity didn't immediately make eye contact with Susan. For the moment she was still too preoccupied with her own thoughts to wonder what Susan had been up to by the side of the house. She was thinking about the last barbecue she'd been to.

Everyone had turned up. The year before's had been so good that it had entered office lore, and everyone who'd been square enough to miss it – for family commitments, minor operations, divorce proceedings – was determined to be part of the next one. Her budget was very generous. Tony knew how easy it was to make people feel they were being treated like kings merely by spending an extra couple of hundred. He'd get it back ten times over in unpaid over-time. So Felicity bought fillet steaks instead of sirloin; the champagne was a top of the range non-vintage and there was enough foreign beer to swim in.

Of course there was no beating the setting – the roof of the building occupied by thegoss. Tony had continued to fudge about the fire regulations, and Felicity knew, in her heart of hearts, that it couldn't possibly be legal, or safe, but it was too thrilling a location to quibble about such a small thing. Sometimes you just had to live on the edge. That was what she remembered – being on the edge. When everyone was nicely merry and becoming absorbed in their food, Tony had signalled to her to slip away from the group. There was a large structure in the centre on the roof area – a mainten-ance shed essentially – and once on the other side of it, they were out of sight and earshot of the rest of the group. He was carrying a bottle of champagne and they began to take swigs in turn. Then he poured a little of it down the front of Felicity's Ralph Lauren sundress and started to lick it from between her breasts. That's when he brought her to the ground, as close to the rail that divided them from the edge as he dared. Felicity only had to turn her head slightly to feel her cheek lift clear of the concrete and become exposed to the air, 100 feet from the ground. He had already removed her underwear and opened his fly, and now he slipped inside her. Felicity had never been more ready for him. It was a fast fuck, but it was glorious. She was convinced they came almost simultaneously, there on the edge of space and time. They could have fallen. The rail wasn't really a barrier. One sudden or uncalculated move and they would both be falling to their deaths. But they didn't fall. They got up and rejoined the party, sated and exhilarated.

Was that what her life had been reduced to? she wondered now, mindless thrill-seeking with a man who would have let her fall? This wasn't how she used to be. OK, maybe she'd been a little slow to get started, maybe she'd missed out on a few things when she was younger, but she'd always done what she thought was right. She'd always obeyed her instincts. But in the past year or so, she'd denied her instincts so much she'd lost her ability to know when something wasn't right. It was as if her sense of smell had been compromised by sniffing too many pungent aromas. She needed to get back to basics.

She looked round her. Marianne was still causing trouble. The game was over now, everybody had tired of it, but she still insisted on showering people with the hose and they were beginning to get annoyed. That was so typical of her – she never knew when to quit. When they were kids

Marianne had devised a game whereby she'd ring up people they knew – their friends' mothers, neighbours – and pretend they were ringing from the local radio station. Felicity had known about it and while she didn't approve, she didn't tell on her sister either. Susan was involved too, but only as a lackey. It was her job to look up the numbers in the phone book, while Marianne's knack for accents and quick thinking allowed her to take in all the neighbours.

'Hello, Mrs Murphy, you're through to Big L and our Dial-a-Dozen Quiz.'

'Now, Mrs Dowling, just answer the following question to qualify for our weekly draw. In what county . . .'

'Congratulations, Mrs Nolan, you've won our star prize – a holiday for two in the Bahamas!'

She had everybody going for weeks but instead of just letting it go while no one was the wiser, she'd started ringing teachers from school. And of course she was recognized, despite her talent for mimicry. There was war! But Marianne laughed it off. She took whatever punishment was given to her and probably used the time to plan her next caper. It must be lovely, Felicity thought, to have absolutely no care whatsoever for the consequences of your actions. It must be very liberating.

Marianne had dropped the hose and was now pestering Gavin to get his guitar. 'Oh, come on! Play something. This party needs some music, it's starting to die.'

'Leave him alone,' said Susan, emerging finally from the magnolia. 'You can't expect him to go all the way home for his guitar.'

'But there's one here. I found one in the wardrobe in my room.'

'Do you know what?' said Angela. 'I think that's yours, Gavin. It's been here since you were a teenager.'

'Is that the old nylon string?'

'I don't know what it is, love. Why don't you go and get it, Marianne? I'd love to hear Gavin play.'

So the guitar was found and after some minor adjustments Gavin began to strum.

'It's badly out of tune,' he said.

'Stop making excuses,' said Felicity, 'and play.'

'I could really do with a plec.'

'Play!'

He made a few more adjustments and then the strumming turned into something much more sophisticated and, after a while, when he seemed to be into his stride, Gavin began to sing.

Susan looked up immediately. At first she wasn't quite able to make out the words, but then it hit her. The song he was singing was Leonard Cohen's 'Suzanne'. When he'd said he played the guitar, Susan had no idea that he also had a voice. He mightn't ever be the lead singer in his band, but there was enough there to take everyone in the back garden of Charlotte Avenue down to his place near the river.

After 'Suzanne' he did another couple of Leonard Cohen songs – 'Sisters of Mercy' and a spine-tingling rendition of 'Hallelujah' – but the spell was broken when Marianne grabbed the guitar and crucified two Van Morrison tunes. Bernie grabbed it off her and presented it to Alan.

'Here, Alan,' she said with great pleading, 'do your Bruce Springsteen.'

And so the guitar continued to be passed from one to the other, until the mood became somewhat disjointed again and everyone began to move around.

'You were looking dreamy.' Felicity sat down beside Susan as the guitar was fought over by Carmel and Marianne.

'What?'

'You seemed very far away there for a while.'

'Oh . . . I've always liked Bruce Springsteen.'

'I didn't mean Bruce Springsteen, I meant Leonard Cohen.'

'What?'

'Did something . . . happen . . . there a while ago during the game?'

'What?'

'With Gavin?'

'What are you talking about?'

'I don't know. You just had a very odd look about you when you came out from behind the house. And Gavin has this – other-worldly – look in his eyes as well.'

'Does he?'

'He does.'

'Well . . . well, I don't know about him, but if I have an other-worldly look in my eyes, it's probably the yoga.'

'Yoga?'

'Yeah, it's made me very Zen. It's really made me think about things, you know, that I never really thought about before. Like . . . well, that maybe I have some control over what happens in my life.'

'Oh yeah?'

'I mean, I think it would be fair to say that ever since school I've been sort of drifting.'

'Not exactly. You went to college. You went travelling. You got a good job.'

'I know, but I only did those things because everybody else was doing them. I did arts in Galway because my best friend from school was doing it. Ditto the travelling. And I work for the tax office because it was the first job I got.'

'Still, it doesn't make any of those things bad choices.'

'No . . . but it doesn't make them *my* choices.' Susan sighed. 'That's why I'm so annoyed at Bernie foisting Alan on me. I don't want someone else deciding who I should go out with.'

'He seems nice.'

'He's fine. I'm just not interested at the moment.'

'Is that because of Paul?'

'God, no! I've no interest in Paul.'

'Are you sure?'

'Of course I'm sure! What kind of a question is that?'

'It wouldn't be unusual to realize after everything that maybe he is the one for you.'

'Listen to me. Since I broke up with Paul I've never had such a good time. I had got completely out of the habit of having fun when I was with him.'

'Poor old Paul.'

'Poor old Paul nothing! When I think of how dull, how boring, how meaningless life was with him . . .'

'Meaningless?' Felicity couldn't conceal a smile. 'What? Now he's gone your life is full of meaning?'

'Well, maybe not "meaning" in the big sense, but . . . you know . . . I don't feel that everything is already mapped out like I used to. I feel there are more . . . possibilities . . . for everything.'

'Like what?' Felicity was intrigued.

'Oh, I don't know . . . like I was saying, I think I need to decide for myself if this is what I want. I know that Paul isn't. At the moment that's the only thing I do know. I don't particularly want to buy a house. I don't want to be that person who never does anything just so they can own their own four walls. And as for my job, well, it's fine, but I might think about doing some courses, and I should probably apply for a promotion. I've just never been bothered before.

I've never had an overriding sense of purpose in my life, and I just want to take the time to think about whether I'm happy with what I have, or whether I want something else. You know? I feel I'm about ten years behind everybody else. It's time I caught up.'

'Listen, you're not behind anybody. I've just made a huge mess of everything.'

'What do you mean?'

Felicity took a deep breath.

'I'm here for so long because I had to take the holidays I'd clocked up. Sixty days. Can you believe it? How pathetic am I that I haven't had a proper holiday in three years?'

'You work hard.'

'I used to work hard. But then I started arsing around.' She paused. 'I've been having an affair with my boss.'

'Is he married?'

'God, no!'

'Well, then . . .'

'It's not just that . . . Look, I don't want to bore you with the details, but I managed to get myself royally screwed over. And it's all my fault. I kind of went off the deep end a little bit and right now I've no idea what to do next.'

'Oh, Fliss!' Susan gave her sister a hug.

'So at least you have some stuff you can decide whether or not you want to keep. Right now I have nothing.'

Just then, Carmel, who had been getting Gavin to teach her some chords, burst in on the girls.

'You'll never guess!' she said.

'Guess what?' said Susan, a distinct feeling of foreboding beginning to swell in her stomach.

'I did it!' she said. 'I did it! I asked a guy out and he said yes!'

'Who?' asked Susan, her voice beginning to wobble, her

eyes desperately trying to find the only two available men in the vicinity. 'Who did you ask out?'

'Well, actually . . . I hope you don't mind . . . but I asked out your cousin. And he said yes!'

15

Susan was speechless. What could she say? Her dumb friend had just gone and asked out her cousin. *Her* Gavin whom she'd been minding and looking out for and trying to protect from stray women. And yet, this was sort of what she'd told Carmel to do. So what could she say?

In the end she said something very silly.

'You take good care of him, now – he's very precious to our family.'

'Oh, I will,' gushed Carmel. 'He's so lovely. Do you know what he said when I asked him?'

'What?'

'He said he was flattered.'

'Oh.'

'Flattered, that I asked him out. I can't believe I did it! I've never asked a guy out in my life.'

'Well, that's great.'

'Oh, you were so right. I wouldn't have done it if it weren't for you. And you're sure you don't mind? Oh my God, we might end up being related!'

Susan swallowed hard and tried to keep from falling off the deckchair.

'Hold your horses there a minute, Carmel, nobody's proposed yet!'

Her voice was creaking under the strain of sounding jovial.

'I know, I know, I'm only joking! But seriously, I could really see myself with Gavin. He's totally different from all the other men I've known and he's *so* different from Rob. I realize now that he was only using me, but I just couldn't see it at the time. Isn't it amazing?'

'Yeah.'

'I can't believe he's not married, though. I mean, he must be in his thirties. He *is* in his thirties, isn't he? Don't tell me he's younger than me? Oh my God, he's only twenty-five, isn't he?'

'He's thirty-five.'

'Thank God! It's his hair. He has all his hair, so it makes him look really young. He has lovely hair, hasn't he? Have you ever noticed his hair?'

Susan was having extreme difficulty holding it together. She simply hadn't been prepared for this. In her wildest dreams she couldn't have imagined that Carmel would end up going out with Gavin. It was insane! She was insane! Who went around asking out other people's cousins they'd barely met? Carmel didn't have the sense she was born with.

'I am *so* glad I came today. I really wasn't in the mood. I was just going to sit out the heat with a tub of Pringles and a couple of DVDs – I was going to re-watch *Serendipity* and *Runaway Bride*. But Bernie insisted I come out. Ye were both so right – there's always someone just around the corner.'

'Yeah.'

'Oh, look. Marianne's let go of the guitar. I'm going to get Gavin to play again. He's really good, you know.'

Bernie joined Susan as soon as Carmel skipped her way across the garden and Felicity had gone into the house to make some coffee.

'Great news, isn't it!'

'What, Carmel? Yes . . . great.'

'I knew she just needed a new man to distract her.'

'Yes . . . great.'

Susan could feel her head beginning to swirl. Without realizing it she'd drunk an awful lot of wine. Bernie moved a little closer to her.

'Carmel was eyeing up Alan there for a while. I was sending her dagger looks but I didn't think she was taking any notice. Anyway, it's all worked out for the best. Alan's crazy about you, you know.'

'I've hardly spoken two words to him.'

'He's a good judge of character.'

'He must be bloody psychic.'

'So what do you think of him?'

'He seems very nice.'

'He's an absolute dote.'

'Yeah.'

'I knew you'd like him.'

'He's very nice.'

'He really deserves to be happy. His last girlfriend was an awful bitch.'

'Really?'

'She hurt him a lot. He's gone awful shy since.'

'Really?'

'Mmm . . . Brian was very worried about him.'

'Oh?'

'Well, they've always looked out for one another. They've known each other for years. Since school.'

'Right. So . . . what was wrong with his last girlfriend?'

'She was into this other guy the whole time, she was only going out with Alan to make him jealous and then she got back with him, the other guy, and neglected to tell Alan. An absolute cow.'

'Yeah . . . a real cow.'

'Because Alan is just so sweet, he'd never treat a girl badly.'

'No. No, I'm sure he wouldn't.'

'Hey, are you all right there, Susan? You seem to be swaying a bit.'

'Am I? No, I'm fine, but maybe I'll switch to water.'

'Great barbecue.'

'Bernie, you can't just will me into going out with Alan.'

'Oh, I know, I know. But it would be so nice if ye hit it off. I think you're made for each other.'

'Really?'

'Come on. I'm going to call him over and ye can have a proper chat. He's shy really.'

'Bernie, don't, please . . .'

'Alan, c'mere and keep Susan company a minute. I've been dying to pee for the last half hour.'

Susan couldn't tell if Alan saw the massive half-face wink that Bernie gave her as she skipped into the house, but she did notice that he moved the deckchair even closer to hers. So close that she was convinced she could smell mouthwash.

Her brain was really beginning to roll around in its socket now. What was going on? All she'd wanted was a quiet afternoon with her sisters – and her cousin – with no interference from matchmakers or do-gooders. What was she supposed to say to Alan, sitting beside her like a lap-dog? 'Sorry, Alan, you seem very nice but I have absolutely no interest in you whatsoever? Sorry your last girlfriend was a total bitch, but to be honest I really don't care? Hi, Alan, will you marry me? I can just see us together?' Why not? If other people could predict wedding bells on the basis of one meeting, why couldn't she? After all, she knew Alan exactly as well as Carmel knew Gavin. And why not, for crying out loud? There was nothing wrong with him. Wasn't he tall and good-looking? Very like George Clooney, actually. Wasn't he a dentist? Rolling in money, driving a big car and about to buy a big house? Wasn't he perfect marriage material? Why shouldn't she agree to snog the face off him? Why shouldn't she –

'Watch it there, Susan! I think that chair's about to disappear from under you. Here, that's steadied it.'

'I'm sorry, Alan,' she said, getting up quickly, 'but I really don't know you well enough.'

'Well enough for what?'

'What?'

'You said you didn't know me well enough. I was wondering what you didn't know me well enough for?'

'Oh! I don't know. I think I might have had too much sun. I might have a little lie-down.'

'Oh sure, sure. Is there anything I can do?'

'No. No, I'm fine, thanks.'

'Listen, would it be OK if I gave you a ring later? Maybe we could go out for a drink sometime?'

'Oh . . . sure . . . yeah, whatever.'

'Great. Are you sure you're OK?'

'Just the heat. Granny had the right idea, going inside. Ahm . . . nice to meet you, Alan.'

And so Susan wafted into the house, not even turning her head to see Gavin, his arms round Carmel's shoulders, his hands over hers as he demonstrated, once again, how to get a C major.

By the time the others had gone home in a series of taxis (leaving only Gavin who insisted on staying to help clear up), Susan had emerged from her lie-down.

'Hey, Suzy, you doing OK?' asked Gavin.

'I'm an idiot.'

'No, you're not. Alcohol and heat – it's not a great combination.'

'Yeah, but nobody else got themselves so wasted they had to get horizontal.'

'Hey,' he said gently, 'everyone needs a blowout every now and again. You've gone through a tough time recently.'

'Oh, Gavin, I . . .'

'Yeah?'

'All that stuff with Paul – what I said, I –'

'I know, you're not over it all yet. It just takes a bit of time.'

'Oh, Gavin, you are so *good*! And I'm so – you see, it's not exactly as I said.'

He leant over and kissed her on the forehead.

'You just need a night's sleep. I'll give you a ring later in the week and we'll go out for a drive. OK?'

'OK.'

'Sleep tight!'

'See ya. And Gavin . . . thanks.'

He blew her a kiss and walked slowly to the end of the garden, pausing briefly at the gate to wave one last time.

When Felicity joined her some time later Susan had barely moved in her wobbly deckchair.

'Interesting afternoon,' Felicity said, pulling up another deckchair and throwing down her dog-eared copy of *Gone with the Wind*.

'What?'

'I'd say this garden has never seen so much action.'

'God, yes. That was totally weird – Carmel asking Gavin out like that.'

'It'll be good for him. Gavin's lovely, but I think he's too shy for his own good.'

'Mmm.'

'Don't you think so?'

'I just – well, I'm just not sure if Carmel's the right one for him.'

'They're only having a drink.'

'I know. But . . . well . . . I don't think they have that much in common. She's not his type.'

'She doesn't have to be his type.'

'What do you mean?'

'Look, I'm not one for advocating the joys of casual sex, but sometimes –'

'Oh God, no!'

'Why not? Sometimes there's nothing like a little mutual ego boost.'

'Stop!'

'I think you're jealous, Suzy.'

'What!'

'Yes, I think you are. You're used to having Gavin all to yourself and now you don't want to share him.'

'That's not true – I just –'

'You're being a bit of a dog in the manger.'

'I am not!'

Felicity was laughing at her sister's discomfort. 'You're probably right, though,' she said.

'About what?'

'That she's not his type. But you must remember that *she* asked *him* out.'

'So?'

'Well . . . Gavin's been well brought up. So, if a girl goes to the trouble and risks the potential embarrassment of asking him out, he's not very well going to say no, now, is he?'

'No, I suppose not.'

'So they'll probably have a couple of dates, maybe even a little after-dark encounter, and that will probably be it.'

'Do you think so?'

'I do.'

'Yeah . . . he wouldn't say no, would he?' Susan sighed heavily. 'I'm just annoyed because I encouraged her to go looking for a man. I thought she'd find a stranger and not – Gavin.'

'He's a big boy. He might be well brought up but he's no eejit.'

'I know. I think I feel a bit protective of him.'

'I think you have a little crush on him.'

'A crush? I do not!'

'Just a little platonic one! It's no harm. He's the long-lost cool cousin you never knew you had.'

Susan looked worried. 'Do you think he thinks I have a crush on him?'

'I'm sure he has no idea. You're just the long-lost goofy cousin he never knew he had.'

'I'm not goofy.'

'Anyway, you should be saving all your crushes for Alan.'

'Please, my head hurts . . .'

'Anyway, honey,' said Felicity, uncoiling herself from the chair. 'I'm going to bed. Enough talk for one day. Don't worry about Gavin, he can take care of himself.'

Before going to bed that night Susan pulled out her list. She had only one thing to write and she wrote it repeatedly down the length of the page – <u>Stop Being Such a Fool</u> – under-lining in black biro as she went. It took her ages to get to sleep and throughout the night she kept waking from her dreams, her heart racing, her body streaming with sweat.

16

Later that night Felicity got a call from Sandra. 'You're a terrible bitch not to have phoned me,' she said warmly.

'I'm sorry, hon,' Felicity replied. 'I've no excuse except that I've been living in a bit of a bubble. It's as if the rest of the world doesn't exist.'

'I know the feeling!'

'I'm sorry. You were great.'

'Well, I'm still great. I'm trying to save your career here; I think you should come back.'

'What!'

'Things haven't been going all that well at thegoss since you left.'

'So?'

'It's a total mess. Apparently Tony has completely welched on the consultancy thing. They're paying him a massive salary and he's never there. Rumour has it he's involved with a new site. Some sort of high-end escort thing.'

'Look, that's nothing to do with me any more.'

'Of course it is. You're still an employee.'

'I couldn't go back! They wouldn't want to see me again.'

'I'd say they would. All's fair in love and war. I think they'd understand you were in a war zone. And nobody knows the business better than you.'

'Thanks for the vote of confidence, but I remember the look on their faces. They don't like hysterical types.'

'Yes, well, they don't like the types that shaft them either. You think about it.'

Felicity took a deep breath as she put down the phone. She wished she didn't remember the day she left, but it was still crystal clear.

She'd worn one of her best suits. Over the years she'd acquired a few very nice pieces – all part of the executive persona she was trying to cultivate. (Or was it just playing at dressing up?) It made her feel good to look in the mirror and see a woman who looked the part. Someone who, on *Dragons' Den*, would at least be told that she'd made an excellent pitch. She'd even had her hair done for the occasion – how ridiculous was that? Still . . . it was supposed to be the day she would become a millionaire . . .

She'd spent the morning dealing with a client. She couldn't recall whether this was a meeting she set up, or something Tony put in her way. The notes for the AGM were sitting on her desk. She'd glanced at them, but hadn't read the documents through in detail like she normally would have. She'd spent the previous evening at a party with Tony, something he'd persuaded her to go to, even though she would have been much happier at home going through her own notes. So, by the time she got to the boardroom that afternoon, she was ever so slightly less in control than usual. And she was tense. This was the biggest meeting of her life, yet there was also an unreserved excitement lurking inside her. It felt more like a sexual encounter than a business one, and perhaps that was why her eye wasn't quite where it should have been.

All the company shareholders were there as well as Sony Ericsson. But she'd known they'd be there; they and their cheque book were what this meeting was all about. It was the two men in the dark grey suits she hadn't expected. They moved through the first couple of items quickly; it could have been any run of the mill meeting of the shareholders. By the time they got to the fourth item on the agenda, organizational restructuring, she was feeling quite calm.

Olaf Spilling, Sony Ericsson's European vice-president, stood up. Felicity had decided that she was going to play it cool. She kept her head down and her hands folded neatly in front of her. She wasn't going to be caught with a smile on her face as Olaf Spilling announced the take-over at ten times the market value of the share price. This was all in a day's work for her.

But then, as Olaf's smooth Swedish accent continued to wash over her, she realized she hadn't quite heard the words she had been expecting. Had she missed it? Was it just a matter of mispronunciation? Or had he really said joint venture instead of buy-out? Her eyes shot up immediately.

' . . . so at the moment we are not seeking to increase our shareholding as we are not looking to buy out the company.' There was absolutely nothing wrong with Olaf's pronunciation. 'But we are delighted to announce that the brilliant Tony Whitby will be staying on as the titular head of the company for three years in a mainly executive and advisory role . . .'

Some low clapping was heard.

'We have come much to admire the dynamism and vision of Tony and his wonderful ability to create synergy in a company . . .'

Nods and grunts of approval.

'So it gives us pleasure to announce that Tony will also have the title of junior vice-president.'

Gasps and whispered murmuring.

'We hope,' Olaf paused to give a short laugh, 'that this will encourage Tony to stay with us and see the company through to the next phase.'

Felicity's eyes were flashing between Tony and Olaf but neither one would meet her gaze.

'In addition,' continued Olaf, 'we will appoint Doug Hewitt,' he gestured to his colleague sitting to his right, 'as chief financial controller. We look forward to our new time at thegoss.'

There was a loud clap which dissipated quickly as Doug Hewitt stood up and began to speak.

' . . . delighted to be part of the team. Of course I don't have Tony's innovation and vision but I will be attempting to bring some economies of scale to the company and incorporate an element of fiscal rectitude. But I would like you to be assured that business will continue as usual and I look forward to working with every one of you.'

She couldn't believe what she was hearing. Had she got it right? Tony and his venture capital team were selling their shares but only *their* shares to Sony Ericsson? Tony was being crowned king of everything with, no doubt, a king's ransom of a salary to go with his fancy title? She was now some nobody working for a big corporation where her role had become meaningless?

She wasn't the only one who looked round the room, dumbstruck, but she was the only one who stood up and asked what the hell was going on.

'I'm sorry, sweetheart,' Tony said. 'I'm sorry it had to be this way. It's better for the company. You'll be great. At least you still have a job.'

'How could you?' Her voice was getting increasingly more shrill.

'It had to be done. I'm sorry, this is just how business is.'

'Don't you tell me how business is! This is the most –'

But Felicity couldn't find the words. Her world was

collapsing round her and they were still only four items into the agenda.

'If we could continue . . .' There was a note of impatience in Olaf's voice.

'Shut the fuck up a minute, would you! I need to find out why this . . . cretin has shafted all of us.'

'It's a good deal. Nobody's been shafted. You're in a better position now than you were.'

'Don't you tell me what position I'm in! You're a monster!'

'I'm just looking out for myself. You'll learn to do the same thing. Best thing you'll ever learn in this game.'

That's when she fired the coffee pot at him. It was fortunate that it was nearly empty but she had a good aim, and the pot made contact with his head while the hot liquid splashed his face and his shirt front. She accompanied the gesture with a loud shriek; her voice was so far beyond shrill by now that everyone else round the table kept their heads and eyes very low.

'I just don't believe this!'

How could anyone stay calm in the face of such an underhanded ambush? That was the real insanity. The walls were beginning to close in, the air was becoming thinner, she was having difficulty breathing.

So she walked out.

'I'm taking my holidays,' was the last thing she said with any coherence as she left the room.

Two hours later she was wrestling with a security guard at Gatwick. What had happened in between, she had no idea.

17

The ring of the phone was insistent. Susan knew it was the call she had been dreading and she knew there was no point in pretending that the ringing would stop if she ignored it. She knew what she had to do.

'Hello?' she said expectantly as she pressed the green button.

'So . . . we had our first date.'

No preliminaries then, straight to business.

'Oh?'

She lay back on her bed feeling the need of support.

'I think I'm in love.'

She sat bolt upright.

'You what?!'

'I know, I know it's sudden. But, oh my God, he is just so gorgeous.'

'But you can hardly be in love, Carmel, you barely know him.'

'I know, but it's just one of those things. Remember I said to you the other night that I could just see it. All the other men I've ever known were shits.'

Susan sat on the edge of the bed. She didn't know if she was going to be able to listen to what she knew was coming.

'Just because he's not a shit, doesn't mean you're automatically in love with him.'

'He's got the most fabulous blue eyes. I never normally

notice guys' eyes but his are electric. Have you ever noticed?'

'Ahm, his eyes? Ahm, I don't know.'

Susan was feeling a pain across her chest as if her lungs were being squashed.

'Anyway, we met in Murphy's. You know – it's that old man's pub that's gone all clean and safe now? Well, he was waiting for me – my God, it is so nice to have a guy waiting for you – and as soon as I arrived he got me a drink – I'm drinking rum and Coke now. He was drinking Guinness – I love a man who drinks Guinness. And he started asking all about me – was I from Limerick, where had I gone to school, where had I gone to college – remember I thought I recognized him from somewhere? I still couldn't place him, but we had such an amazing talk. He is just so easy to talk to.'

Susan got up and began to pace the room. Why, oh why, had she ever got involved with this girl and her lunatic love life?

'Susan? Are you still there?'

'I'm still here.'

'So we stayed in the pub until near closing and then he walked me to a taxi.'

Susan couldn't bear to hear what was coming next.

'And he was such a gentleman. He just said good night and then kissed me on the cheek. Isn't that romantic?'

'On the cheek.'

'I never thought a kiss on the cheek could be sexy, but it was. It was *so* sexy. But then Gavin is so sexy. You probably don't realize it, being his cousin, but he has this air about him, he's just so masculine, or something, without being macho, you know?'

'I know.'

'So we're going to a play on Thursday. I can't remember the last time I was at a play. He suggested it and I thought how old-world to be going to a play with a man, on a date. You know what, Susan? I think I'm going to marry him.'

Susan gulped.

'I'm only joking, but I still can't believe that he's not married already. You'd think a guy like him would have been snapped up years ago.'

'Yeah, it's a wonder.'

'So has he had many girlfriends?'

'Ahm . . . not too many, I think. He's usually quite selective.'

'He is kind of shy as well, so maybe he doesn't find it easy to just ask girls out. I am so glad you encouraged me to ask him out!'

'I didn't exactly encourage you to ask *him* ou—'

'Oh my God, Susan, I have to go, talk to you tomorrow. Byeeee!'

'Bye.'

Susan threw the phone back on the bed and ran out of the room. She was vaguely aware of Angela and Marianne huddled over something in the living room as she grabbed her bag and fled the house. It was the first time in her life she wished she had a car. It seemed to take for ever to get to Gavin's flat and she was out of breath by the time she got there. She had to prop herself against the banister for a full five minutes before she had wind enough to ring the bell of number seven. Gavin answered in his bare feet with pliers in his hand.

'Hey, Sue,' he said, 'come on in.'

Susan stepped inside the door and immediately began looking round to see if anybody else was there.

'I hope you're not too busy,' she said, turning to face him, secure at last in the knowledge that the flat was empty.

'No, no, I'm just re-stringing my guitar.'

He held the pliers up.

'Oh. I was wondering what they were for.'

'I was about to make some coffee.'

'Lovely, yeah, coffee would be nice.'

She sat down on the edge of one of the armchairs and began picking at the guitar strings.

'Is this the one you were playing at the barbecue?'

'No, that's a bass, I was playing an acoustic on Sunday.'

'Oh yes, the bass. The cello.'

'What?'

'Nothing. You were really good.'

'Oh . . . not really.'

'No, you were.'

Gavin lowered his eyes.

'Thanks.'

Susan let her gaze travel across the room. It was remarkably neat. When do boys stop being slobs, she wondered, and become men who keep tidy apartments?

'So I hear you've had your first date with Carmel?'

'Oh God, it *is* true – girls really do tell each other everything.'

'No, no. It's . . . it's . . . she just – You know, Carmel and I are not that close.'

'Oh?'

'No, I've only got to know her since I came back to Limerick.'

'Right.'

Susan began to concentrate hard on the contents of the

coffee table: a newspaper, his glasses case, and an odd-looking thing like a miniature can opener.

'It's kind of funny,' she said after a while, 'you and her going out now.'

She was doing her best to keep her tone light and breezy.

'Kind of funny?'

'Well, you know, it's sort of . . . unusual. I work with her – you're my cousin.'

'But I thought you set it up?'

'Me? Oh God, no. I had no idea she was going to ask you out.'

'Oh? She kind of implied that it was all your idea.'

'No, no, it wasn't. I mean I sort of suggested she go out with *somebody* but I didn't for a minute think . . .'

'Right.'

'So it's sort of funny.'

'Right.' He paused. 'Is it OK?'

'Is what OK?'

'That I went out on a date with Carmel?'

'Of course, of course. Of course it's OK. Why wouldn't it be OK?'

'No reason.'

Gavin continued making the coffee while Susan went back to strumming the bass guitar.

'Actually,' she said abruptly, 'well – it's not for me to say. I mean – I was just wondering . . .'

'Yeah?'

'I wouldn't have thought she was your type, that's all.'

'Oh? So what is my type?'

'I don't know. Just not – I'm sorry – I shouldn't be saying anything. I don't even know what I'm saying.'

'I certainly haven't a clue what you're saying.'

The corners of his mouth were curling as he handed her the mug.

'I'm sorry.'

'There's no need to keep being sorry. You know, Susan, if it's a problem . . .'

'No, no, no problem – I was merely wondering where you might see it going?'

'It's going to a play on Thursday.'

'You're making fun of me.'

'I'm not.'

'It's fine. You do what you like. It's none of my business.'

'I really thought it was all your idea. You did say you were going to find me a woman.'

'Did I? When did I say that?'

'I don't know. It might have been that day we were sitting on Ballyconnell beach.'

Susan flushed at the memory.

'So you weren't trying to find me a woman?'

'I just want you to be happy.'

'I am happy, Susan.'

'Carmel makes you happy?'

Susan's brow suddenly became deeply furrowed.

'No. Not Carmel.'

'Oh?'

Gavin took the guitar from between her tightly knotted fingers.

'How about we go for a drive?'

'Oh God, Gavin, I don't think I'd be safe behind the wheel today. I have a bit of a headache.'

'No, I mean I'll drive. There's something I want to show you.'

'Oh?'

'Yes, a little trip down memory lane.'

'What is it?'

'You'll see.'

'Tell me.'

'You'll see it soon enough.'

They were standing by the edge of the lake trying to avoid the fuss being made by a swan who suddenly felt threatened by their closeness.

'None of that promenade thing was there then,' Gavin was saying, 'and this whole side of the lake was covered with picnic tables.'

'Yes, I remember,' said Susan, her eyes following the movement of his hand. 'And there was a sand pit here and a sort of a makeshift playground. Yes, I remember.'

'That's right, and up there where the hotel is now was where the camper vans and the tents used to pitch.'

'Oh yeah, and the ice-cream van and the chip van – Oh my God, those chips! They were so greasy but they were gorgeous.'

Gavin laughed.

'I think we got sick every time we had them. But we still had them. Every time!'

'Yeah. My mother used to get in such a state. She'd refuse to buy them and then she'd insist that your mother shouldn't buy them.'

'My mother was afraid of your mother.'

'But then your dad, who was definitely not afraid of my mother, would slip you the money and when no one was looking, you'd buy chips for everyone.'

'Mum would pretend to be furious with him but she was really delighted.'

'I can't believe I had totally forgotten about this place and we must have been here every second day in the summer.'

'It was probably only one or two summers. The pollution got so bad after a while they closed it completely to the public.'

'Really? I suppose that was before we started going to Ballyconnell. I still can't believe I had forgotten about it.'

'I know, I had forgotten about it too and I was much older when we used to come here.'

'How did you find it? How did you recognize it?'

'I didn't, at first. We came out here to do a survey and it was only when I looked up the old survey maps that it started to look familiar.'

The swan was starting to get very aggressive so they moved away from the lake and began walking up the hill towards the hotel.

'I had no idea the hotel backed onto this lake,' said Susan, beginning to struggle as the incline became steeper.

'You wouldn't have any idea from the road. The landscape round here has changed utterly since those days. Even the roads we used to travel aren't the same.'

'No wonder it took me so long to cop on to where we were.'

Susan was having great difficulty maintaining her balance over the rough terrain. The weather had changed in the last week and the rain had made the ground very slippery. Without her looking for it, and without him actually offering, Gavin took her by the hand and guided her upwards. When they got to the top he continued to hold her hand until they reached a bench, strategically placed for the full enjoyment of the panorama.

'Wow, it's beautiful!' exclaimed Susan.

'It's stunning all right, just a shame they wrecked the lake with slurry.'

'Is it completely ruined?'

'They've done a lot to reclaim it, and a lot of time has passed. It's OK for the swans, but there'll never be swimming here again.'

'We were together all the time in those days. Do you remember? Your dad had some sort of a hatchback and he'd carry all the picnic stuff and the deckchairs and the wind breaker – my God, we used to bring the kitchen sink with us.'

'It was a Volvo estate.'

'Was it? We had some tiny thing. There wasn't enough room in the back for the three of us.'

'It was a Datsun Cherry. And it wasn't that small. From what I remember no car would have been big enough with the three of you in the back.'

'We used to fight all the time.'

'That's how I remember it!'

'My mother was always saying "Why can't you be like your cousins? They never fight. Why can't you be more like your cousins?"'

'And we did fight. All the time. Or at least Luke fought with me. But if I fought back, I was picking on my baby brother. And Luke was vicious.'

'There was always a crisis, wasn't there?'

'I remember one time – we had spent the entire day here. Luke and I used to take a boat out and fish sometimes – not that we ever caught anything – while the rest of you swam and built sandcastles. It had just started to rain, and we were all packed up and halfway down the road, when your dad's car stopped in front of us – you had forgotten your sandals.

Your mother was in a panic and she made us all go back and pile out of the car – into the pouring rain – to look for your sandals.'

'No way! I don't remember that.'

'That's because you were in hysterics. You cried yourself unconscious.'

'Shut up!' she said, slapping him gently. 'You're making it up.'

'I am not, it's true. It all just came flooding back to me.'

'Someone must have hidden my sandals. Probably you and Luke.'

'Yeah, probably.'

'Did we ever find them?'

'Nope! You went barefoot for the rest of the summer.'

'I did not!'

'You did, I swear!'

'Gavin!'

'Well, that's how I remember it.'

She was still smiling to herself when she turned to him some time later.

'Thanks for taking me out here. Thanks for not bringing Marianne.'

'You're welcome. I thought you'd like it.'

'It's lovely. My headache's gone.'

'You want to do the drive home?'

'Maybe . . .'

'Even give fourth gear a whirl?'

'Maybe . . . but let's just sit here for another while.'

'Whatever you say.'

She turned to the scene in front of her and began looking back in time. She couldn't say that there was anything wrong with her childhood – it was bog standard stuff most of the time – but much of what she remembered was confrontation. Her skirt was too short. Her skirt was too long. Her hair was too messy. Her nails were too dirty. Her singing was too loud. Her dancing too noisy. Her breathing too breathy. Yet, looking back now to the lake days, she could remember the happy times. Sure, her mother was a control freak about most things but she was capable of spontaneous good humour on occasion. Like when their father would appear from the back of the car all decked out in his yellow spandex swimming trunks. Or the first time Felicity swam the width of the lake, or even the occasion when Susan had the best time for running the circuit through the small wood that backed onto the lake. It was a shame that she didn't remember these times more often. It was an even bigger shame that her mother seemed to have forgotten them completely.

'Is my mother an awful cow?' she asked Gavin, without taking her eyes from the lake, 'or am I an awful cow?'

'Ye're a right pair of heifers, the two of ye!'

'Gavin!'

'Oh, come on, Suze, ye're just a normal mother and daughter. Don't be so hard on yourself. You're just not that alike, I think.'

'Is that all it is?'

'Yeah, I mean, I think Marianne's more like her, and they get on better.'

'It's just that I never really feel like an adult when I'm around her. It's a terrible thing to say, but I think she brings out the worst in me.'

'You'll get there. You'll become one of those mothers and daughters who talk to each other five times a day. Just give it a while.'

'Oh God . . . that'd be much worse!'

She watched as a bird flew close to them, hovered for a moment and flew away again.

'Did you get on with your mother?'

'Most of the time. Mum was very easy going.'

'Yeah, I remember her as . . . happy.'

'She was. She was easy to be around because she just let us be ourselves. I don't think she was all that confident in herself, you know, so she never tried to force anything on us. You couldn't clash with her because she'd always back down.'

'I can't imagine you having a row with your mother.'

'I didn't, really. You just couldn't bring yourself to upset her. I remember once I came home drunk – I think I was in sixth year. At first she didn't realize I was drunk – she just thought I was being unusually talkative – but when I fell over my own feet and started to vomit into her geraniums, her eyes welled up and she went on about how she never thought she'd see her boy in a state like this. I swear to God I didn't drink for a year after that!'

'She was so gentle, your mother. So the opposite of mine.'

'Oh, Maureen's all right. She just has a different parenting style.'

'Parenting style – is that what it is!'

She turned her head towards the woods and the clouds that were building behind them. This was exactly what she needed. She loved the city, but sometimes you wanted a little dose of nature to clear the cobwebs. And the cobwebs *were* beginning to clear. Suddenly it became blindingly obvious what the problem had always been with Paul. He was just the wrong fit. Like he was Microsoft and she was an Apple Mac, both excellent systems but never meant to work together. She sighed.

'What's all the sighing for?'

'Was I sighing? Sorry.'

'I thought I was cheering you up a bit.'

'Oh, you are, you are. Don't take any notice of me.'

She smiled as she thought of what Felicity said about her having a little crush on Gavin. She supposed she did, a bit. Just a platonic one, of course. She wasn't perverted. But it was more that they were a good fit; they were two parts of the same system. It was a pity, in a way, that he was her cousin . . . but then, at least this way they would always be friends, no matter how many Carmels – or Alans – appeared on the scene.

'More sighing?'

'Oh, that was a sigh of contentment. Listen, I was just thinking . . . what about that dinner I promised you?'

'Yeah, I'm still on for it.'

'How about next Saturday night?'

'Next Saturday? Fine, I think.'

'No hot dates? Are you sure?'

'I'd cancel all my hot dates to see you cook.'

'You might be surprised. Felicity and I have been getting in training. We have five cookery books – Jamie Oliver, Nigella, Hairy Bikers, Rachel Allen and someone called Mrs Beeton.'

'Wow! I'm impressed. So we'll be reading not eating, then? I'd better bring my reading glasses.'

'Oh, shut up! You'll be sorry – you'll eat your words!'

'Hey, I'm sorry. Seriously, I'm really looking forward to . . . eating my words and some other stuff. Can I do anything to help?'

'No! Not a thing. This is our treat. And don't bring any wine. Felicity found a really good wine shop and she's mad to try it out.'

'Excellent! Can't wait.'

'Right then. That's settled. Come about seven o'clock.'

The rain had already started to fall and they could no longer ignore it. They ran back down the hill, Susan letting her arms splay out like wings, and reached the car just as hailstones began bouncing off the ground.

18

Angela had begun her day by strolling up O'Connell Avenue to get her hair done. She had been going to Petals for years. When the salon opened in the sixties it was a radical place where young women went to have bouffants put in their hair and pink lacquer on their nails. Angela loved it. She loved it then and she still loved it now. In those days it was a luxury she allowed herself, now it was part of a lifeline between her past and what was left of her future. Nothing had changed and yet everything had changed. Where once she was greeted as just another attractive client who was happy to chat about her kids and her holiday plans, now she was practically a celebrity, simply because she had managed not to die and remained quite attractive for a woman of her age.

'Well, hello, Mrs O'Regan,' she was greeted every Saturday morning. 'Aren't you looking marvellous!'

Angela welcomed their warm greetings and accepted them as sincere, but part of her knew that what the girls really meant in their cheery greeting was more like 'Isn't it marvellous you're not dead!' or 'We never thought we'd see you again!' or 'Don't you look great with them wrinkles and all that grey hair!' The truth was that the girls who had been cheery when Angela was a young mother were all gone – either dead or too decrepit to be thought of or spoken about any more. Angela was the salon's oldest client in both senses of the word and everybody was proud of her.

'Hiya, Mrs O'Regan,' Natalie said now. 'Has it been a week already?'

'Tempus is fugiting,' said Angela, settling into her seat at the sink.

'You're very funny, Mrs O'Regan, I don't know what you're saying half the time! Are we doing the usual?'

'We are. But make a special job of it. My granddaughters are having a party this evening and I want to look nice.'

'A party? For you? Aren't they very nice!'

'It's not just for me, it's for my grandson as well. Susan wants to thank him for teaching her to drive.'

'Isn't that nice of him, now. I wish one of my cousins had taught me to drive. Might've saved a fortune. The water all right for you?'

'It's fine. Oh yes, Gavin is very good. He's very good to me too.'

'Is he the one that cuts your grass?'

'That's the one. My other grandson is in the States.'

'Haven't you a daughter over there too?'

'I do. Kay is in Washington.'

'Have you been over to her recently?'

'I'm not one for travelling. But she emails me all the time.'

'Aren't you great to be on the email. I love my phone, I could text all day, but I'm just not into email. I don't know what it is. I just can't get into it. Will I put in conditioner?'

'You usually put in a small bit.'

'A small bit so. Who's coming to the party?'

'Just the children, and myself.'

'Are any of them married?'

'No. None of them married.'

'That's a shame. Wouldn't it be lovely to be having great-grandchildren?'

'You can't rush them. I thought Susan would be getting married soon but she broke up with her boyfriend.'

'Did she? What did he do?'

'My feeling is that he probably didn't do much. I think Susan just got tired of him.'

'Isn't she terrible?'

'She has to know her own mind. No point getting married if you're not in love.'

'You're a real romantic, you are. Sure, I don't love my husband at all and we get on great.'

'I'm sure you love him deep down.'

'I don't! Honest to God, I don't!'

'Ah, now, Natalie, I don't believe you.'

'It's the truth. I suppose you were mad about your husband, were you? God rest him.'

Angela couldn't answer a question like that immediately. Had she been mad about her husband? She'd been mad *at* him for years. Ever since he'd gone and died on her. She'd been furious. How could he do that to her? Going it alone hadn't been part of the plan.

'Yes,' she said to Natalie after a while, 'yes, I suppose I was mad about him. He made me very happy.'

'Ah, God help us – are those rollers all right? Not too tight?'

'They're fine, lovey.'

'And what about your grandson? Has he a girlfriend? Is he good-lookin'?'

It was one of the great troubles of Angela's life that Gavin didn't have a girlfriend. That indeed he wasn't married to a nice girl and having children of his own. For he certainly was good-looking, to her eyes at least. She'd always thought he had the brightest pair of blue eyes, even when nobody could get a decent look at them, and for some time now his smile had been the warmest thing in her life. She loved him; she loved him with more, possibly, than the usual love of an old woman for her grandson; she loved him with a tenderness that sometimes broke her heart. Yet despite all he meant to her, she would give anything to have him settled with a nice girl. She would surrender him quicker than his own mother would have, because she knew that having him was only a bonus.

There was that time a few years ago – well, several years ago now – that he'd been engaged, but the whole thing had fallen apart. It had upset him badly at the time but she wasn't sorry it hadn't worked out. She wasn't the right one. But Angela was constantly puzzled why the right one hadn't appeared yet. She had done her bit to put nice girls in his way – there was the niece of her bridge partner who moved back to Limerick just as Gavin was returning from Sweden – but nothing had come of all her promptings. He hadn't even asked her out. And then there was that nice estate agent girl who had been handling his flat – she'd been convinced something would happen there, but he never made a move. All Gavin would say was that they had nothing in common. 'How much do you need in common with a woman?' Angela had protested. 'Isn't it the differences that count?' 'Ah, Gran . . .' was all he would say in that soft voice of his, 'Ah, Gran . . .'

There was no doubt, however, that he was happier these days. That vague melancholy that so troubled her was absent. Certainly, the house being full of women and not just herself was helping. A doting grandma was no company for a young man, and she was concerned that she was the only woman in his life. And Susan, especially, seemed to bring a light to his eyes that she hadn't seen in a long time. Ahh, Susan, there was another one who didn't seem to know what she was at. Or did any of them? Felicity had been home far too long for a holiday and as for Marianne? She had written her another cheque, this time for a thousand euro, and she had the feeling she'd be writing another one soon. She didn't begrudge the child the money – wasn't she in the lucky position that she had some in the bank – but she worried that Marianne would never be able to manage on her own.

' . . . so is he good-lookin'? Would he be worth running away with?'

'Oh, he's very good-looking, but I wouldn't want him getting mixed up with a married woman.'

'You're very funny, Mrs O'Regan. Is that all right for you now?'

Angela glanced at herself. In the hand mirror Natalie was holding up behind her she could see the neat grey curls and delicate shoulders of some elderly woman. Surely nobody she knew. And in the mirror in front of her, by some trick of her eyes that didn't allow her to see things as they really were, she still found the face of the thirty-something who sported a beehive and a French manicure. There was no point in *really* looking in the mirror any more, it couldn't do any good, and who cared if an old woman was delusional if it managed to keep her sane?

'That's lovely. I'm presentable again.'

'Oh, you always look nice, Mrs O'Regan. You're not like an ould one at all.'

Susan wanted everything to be perfect. The Charlotte Avenue house was ideal for entertaining: not only did the high ceilings and large oval table in Angela's dining room make for the perfect setting, but Angela's cupboards were filled with all the props necessary for a faultless performance. She began by laying out the fine old Irish linen tablecloth. It had been a wedding present for Angela's grand-mother so heaven only knew how old it was. As she lifted the heavy folds of rich damask, Susan couldn't help herself indulging in a little 'olde worlde' fantasy. How delightful, she mused, if she were the lady of the house in the days when no lady could manage to dress in the morning and have a cup of tea, without at least three servants to help her. And she would be held in such high esteem by the gentlemen of the neighbourhood that all of them would be in love with her, but each would be afraid to ask for her hand for fear of being rejected. How delightful!

She giggled. She knew what nonsense it was. It was Marianne's favourite thing to point out to her (Susan's olde-worlde fantasies were well known to her family) that if she had lived in the nineteenth century, then it would have been *she* who was the servant, and *she* who would have had to help her mistress dress in the morning. But wasn't that the point of a fantasy – that it wasn't real and never could be?

Next came the silverware – Susan believed the canteen was one of Angela's wedding presents. It was Newbridge EPNS with delicate mottled bone handles. She wasn't sure if it was her imagination or not, but the pieces seemed smaller than modern cutlery, as if they were meant for more refined hands. She picked up a spoon and brought it to her mouth as if she too were a delicate, refined, fragile sort of thing.

And then came the glasses – positively ancient Waterford crystal. Susan had gasped the first time she saw these. It had been a ritual of her childhood, once a year, to empty the cupboards in Angela's dining room and clean the contents. All the girls were involved at one stage but by the time Felicity was too old or too busy for the task,

Marianne had decided it was just too lame to spend your afternoon dusting with your granny, so very often it was just Susan and Angela, dusting the china, polishing the silver, burnishing the crystal. The glasses she chose for tonight were small but very ornately cut – so different from the kind of crystal that was popular now. Not that Susan would exactly refuse a nice John Rocha tumbler or a Conran flute if they were presented to her, but the tiny proportions of these overwrought goblets seemed to exemplify drinking elegance. No matter what kind of wine Felicity brought home, it would taste like nectar in these.

She was looking for the water tumblers she knew matched the wine glasses but couldn't find them anywhere. Oh well, she thought, Granny probably put them back somewhere different the last time she used them.

She was very hopeful about their menu for the evening. They had done a thorough trawl of the recipe books and come up with a plan that was uncomplicated but should be very tasty. When Susan was buying the crab and prawns for the starter, the guy in Saddlier's fishmongers had shown her the simplest way to remove the shells and gave her a hint about adding lime juice even if the recipe said lemon. 'You still need some lemon juice,' he said, 'but the lime adds to the flavour and cuts down on the acidity.' Then, in O'Connell's butchers when she was buying the fillet steak, she was told how to vary the cooking times so that everyone got their steak just the way they liked it. Susan listened to all the advice and made a mental note not to bother with any more recipe books and just ask the people in the shops instead.

She visited the market next. She bought vegetables with actual mud on them, free-range eggs with feathers still attached and a selection of cheeses so stinky she had to double and triple check with the vendor that they had not gone off.

By the time she got home with all her produce she was very pleased with herself. The fact that Marianne still wasn't up and still hadn't cleaned the bathroom (her only task) didn't bother her in the least.

'She'll do it,' she said to herself philosophically. 'She won't let us down.'

Meanwhile Felicity had dropped into the baker, the florist and the cute guy at the wine shop. She hadn't realized that she found him cute, or that she had, possibly, been flirting with him on the two other occasions she had been in the shop, but she realized it with a bang when he greeted her with a cheeky smile and asked her if she thought her drinking was becoming a problem. She was scarcely done guffawing at his joke when he followed by asking her if she had any objection to drinking in places other than at home.

'Excuse me?' she said, not sure really if he was joking or filling out her application form for AA.

'I was just wondering,' he said slowly, 'if you would like to go out for a drink with me, sometime, to the pub maybe?'

'To the pub?'

'Yeah, the pub.'

'Ahm, OK,' she said, bewildered, flattered, amused. 'That would be nice.'

'Great! Maybe you could give me your phone number and I'll give you a ring.'

'I'll give you the house phone. I'm staying with my grandma – I don't have a mobile at the moment – I lost it – but you can leave a message here.'

'Great. Now, what can I do for you?'

'Do for me?'

'Wine? Did you come in for wine or just to ask me out on a date?'

Felicity couldn't keep up.

'Wine. Yes, lots of wine. I'm having a party – just a family thing or I would . . . Yes, I need some wine.'

And so it was that Felicity completed her first task of the day – the purchase of two bottles of a divine Sancerre, a sparkling white, four fabulous Italian reds from the south, two Pinot Grigio (for quaffing as they cooked) and a piquant Sauternes. It was surely more wine than they needed, even with Marianne, but better drunk than thirsty. Felicity had decided that she might as well enjoy herself while she was thinking over her next move.

When she got back to Charlotte Avenue she ran a bath (Marianne still hadn't cleaned it so she might as well use it) and poured herself a small glass of the chilled Sancerre. As she sank down under the bubbles, she began to realize that perhaps she had been making things needlessly complicated lately. She couldn't believe how easy it had been simply to agree to go out on a date. Why not? It was probably exactly what she needed. How long had it been since something so natural, so uncomplicated had happened in her love life? Perhaps a little diversion would be good for her. Surely she deserved a little fun before she faced her hard decisions?

Marianne did eventually clean the bathroom. Although she had to say that it hardly needed cleaning. Typical of her sisters to make her do a job that didn't need doing. She was a small bit put out by this entire dinner thing. They were making such a bloody fuss, the pair of them. And they were so pathetic with their books and their fine linen and their 'everything must be perfect' nonsense. Susan especially. If she really wanted to show Gavin how grateful she was for the driving lessons, why didn't she just pay him?

Besides, Marianne had her own problems. She had been offered a job and she wasn't sure whether or not she should take it. Her instinct was to refuse – she had never intended putting herself to work when she arrived back in Limerick – but she had ended up staying much longer than she meant to. And she couldn't keep taking money from Angela if she didn't show some sign of paying her way. At least it wasn't the worst job in the world – working the reception at the local community theatre – and even if the pay was awful it was more than her dole, and it would get her out of the house. She had realized that what she thought was the laid-back existence of a student, was in fact the daily routine of a geriatric. There was a fine line between watching *Countdown* with a knowing grin on your face and watching it in order to get better so you can beat your granny. And Angela had begun enquiring, ever so casually, what she needed all that money for, so perhaps it was time to create a little distance between them.

So it wasn't the job exactly that was the problem. It was the sense that she was settling in for the long haul. The feelings that had driven her here in the first place had faded and what she was left with was an overall sense of vagueness. Not that most of Marianne's life hadn't been conducted within a cloudy bubble, but now she was actually beginning to question her motives. Perhaps she shouldn't have come at all? Perhaps it would have been better to have stayed and dealt with what had happened? She had presumed that running away was the right thing to do – it was how she had always dealt with the crises of her life – and always before it had seemed like the best option. But this time, walking away from her problems hadn't made them go away.

However, today it was Marianne's turn to be the hero.

With all Susan's and Felicity's huffing and puffing they had gone and forgotten the dessert – tiramisu Susan had planned on making from scratch. But they'd totally forgotten to get the ingredients. Marianne came upon them in the kitchen while they were still staring helplessly at each other. Susan looked as if she was about to start blubbering.

'Oh, for crying out loud,' Marianne had said wearily, 'give me the keys to the Micra and I'll go down to Dunnes.'

'But you can't drive!' wailed Susan.

'No, darling, that's you. I can drive very well.'

So she was given the keys and when she came back she tumbled all the ingredients into a bowl and knocked together the yummiest tiramisu Angela's antique Royal Tara bowl had ever played host to.

'I didn't know you could cook,' said Susan incredulously.

'There's a lot about me you don't know.'

By the time Gavin arrived, bearing an oversized bunch of flowers, the pandemonium in the kitchen had subsided, thanks to Marianne's efforts and a bottle and a half of the Pinot Grigio.

Angela went into the dining room first and watched as each of her grandchildren sat at the table. They *were* a nice-looking bunch. Felicity was lovely in a silk patterned dress that reminded her of the sort of thing her own mother had worn. With her blonde hair rolled on top of her head and pinned in place with two diamanté combs, she had a real look of old-fashioned glamour about her.

Susan was wearing some sort of lace tunic over black leggings and little ballet pumps. Angela didn't understand what the get-up was all about, but she couldn't deny that she looked very fetching in it. And she'd noticed the look Gavin had given her when he thought no one was looking.

Obviously she wasn't the only one who appreciated the outfit.

Marianne, of course, didn't believe in dressing up. She had always prided herself on being a 'take me as you find me' sort of person, but she had washed her hair and put on a clean pair of jeans. Certainly none of the money Angela had given her had been frittered away on new clothes. Yet, as she stood at the top of the table opening the next bottle of wine, there was something a little forced in her efforts, as if maybe she felt she wasn't being found quite good enough.

'So, Gavin,' Felicity began with a cheeky glance at Susan, 'I hear you've been out and about lately. Going to the *theatre* no less!'

'Oh, go on, Gavin,' said Marianne, 'tell us *everything*. Is she a psychopath after all? Does she want to have your baby?'

'Shut up, Marianne!'

'You shut up! Go on, Gav, give us all the details.'

'We saw a play.'

'So what was it called?'

'*Dancing at Lughnasa.*'

'That old thing? I saw that years ago. Are they still showing it?'

'It was an amateur production, but it was very good.'

'That's a good play,' said Felicity, 'one of his best.'

'Yeah, I enjoyed it.'

'Did Carmel like it?' ventured Susan.

'I think she did. Though she was a bit confused by the idea of the boy being the narrator.'

'What's confusing about that?'

'I think it was something to do with them both being on stage at the same time.'

'I told you she was a psycho,' said Marianne.

'It's a very long play, isn't it?'

'Yeah . . . we weren't out of there until eleven o'clock.'

'Too late for a drink, then.'

'We got one in at the White House.'

'Just the one, was it?'

'Ahm . . . I think we might have had two.'

'What's with the third degree, Susan?' asked Marianne. 'Gavin's allowed to have a drink with his girlfriend.'

'I wouldn't exactly call . . . it's just that Carmel didn't come into work on Friday.'

'Aha!' said Marianne, 'maybe it's Gavin who's the psycho and he's done away with her. Where'd you hide the body, Gav?'

'Shut up, Marianne!'

'She was still alive when I dropped her off around half twelve. And I think she was probably alive when she texted me this morning to say she had a bit of flu. She was wondering if I was OK.'

'She doesn't have the bloody flu! She's such a hypochondriac, that one! She gets a little bit of a runny nose and calls it the flu. I'll bet she's never had a real flu in her life!'

'So . . . no hanky panky then?' asked Marianne.

'Marianne, lovey,' said Angela, 'you are a very nosey, very rude girl. You should leave Gavin alone and let him get on with his romance.'

'Oh, Granny, it's not a romance he's having, is it, Gav? It's just a bit of a fling, just a little bit of –'

'I think it's time you shut up,' said Felicity, gathering up the empty starter plates.

'Hear, hear,' said Susan.

'Oh, whatever! . . . Anyway, it seems it isn't only Gavin who's hitting the dating scene.'

'Why? Don't tell me you've picked up a man already?' said Susan.

'Nothing to do with me – just a message I picked up this afternoon when you were in the bath.'

'What message? Who from?'

'Somebody called Mark? He says it was lovely seeing you again and if Sunday suits you're to give him a ring on his mobile.'

'His mobile? Did he leave a number?'

'He did. But I forgot to write it down.'

'You what!!'

'Keep your hair on – I'm only joking. I wrote his precious number down. It's in the book beside the phone.'

'Marianne, why didn't you tell me there was a message for me?'

'Amn't I telling you now? This is the first chance I got.'

'Right, well, you might have told me sooner.'

'Who is he anyway?'

'Oh, just a guy I met at the wine shop. It's nothing. Just a bit of a date. He's years younger than me.'

'Sure, what does that matter?'

'I'm probably too old for him.'

'Oh, Felicity honey, would you get a grip? Though it pains me deeply to say it, you don't look bad for your age. You're *my* sister after all.'

'Anyway,' said Susan, 'he mightn't be as young as you think. If a guy doesn't lose his hair or get a belly, he can look twenty-five till he's forty.'

Felicity laughed.

'I don't want to feel like his mother.'

'Don't be ridiculous.'

'Thanks for the vote of confidence, but I do think age matters.'

'Age only matters to us, for God's sake!' said Marianne with a snort. 'Men don't care what age you are. Isn't that right, Gav? A man doesn't take one look at a woman, do a count of her fine lines, determine her age, and then decide if he finds her attractive or not. He either thinks she's sexy or he doesn't. It's just that most men are programmed to find young women sexy. But if you're hot enough . . . he won't care what age you are. Am I right?'

'Well, Gavin,' prompted Felicity, 'is she right?'

'Yeah . . . I suppose so. I mean, I'm no expert – obviously. But most men have no idea what age a woman is and it doesn't really matter – unless she's too young, of course.'

'So would you go out with an older woman?'

'Sure.'

'Even over forty?'

'Well . . . yeah. I don't think forty is what it used to be.'

'What do you mean?'

'Women sort of look the same no matter what age they are. I mean after a certain age. You know – the way they dress and the like. It's not like everything changes at forty.'

'Certain things are starting to change.'

'Like what?'

'Like having babies.'

'Yes . . . that just isn't as much of an issue for men.'

'But men want to have children too.'

'Sure, I suppose most men do – but it just isn't as big a deal, especially for single men.'

'So do you want to have children?' asked Marianne.

'I haven't given it a lot of thought . . . but yes, I think it would be nice.'

'But seriously, Gavin,' interrupted Felicity, 'surely you'd rather go out with someone who was thirty-three rather than forty-three?'

'Look, you're asking the wrong guy here.'

'Oh, come on, just answer the question.'

'I honestly think it would depend on the woman.'

'But the thirty-three-year-old would look a lot better than the forty-three-year-old.'

'I just don't think looks matter that much.'

'Of course looks matter! Look at the cosmetics industry. Look at the way every successful man ends up with a Barbie clone on his arm!'

'Oh, I know, it's all there. But Marianne's right about whether or not you find someone attractive. It really has less to do with how a person looks or what age they might be than how – than how they make you feel.'

'How they make you feel?' said Susan.

'Yeah. You know, a person – a girl – can be all hair and make-up and clothes and it doesn't mean anything. In fact sometimes it's a bit off-putting.'

'Off-putting?'

'Well, it's sort of hard to connect with someone who is so obviously caught up with how they look. I'm not saying it's not nice when women look well – because it is – it's very nice. But it can't be everything – you know?'

'I think you *are* the wrong man to be talking to. I don't think most men think the way you do.'

'Listen, Felicity, I don't have a clue what most men think, and I certainly don't have a clue what women think.'

'We should ask Granny,' said Susan. 'She has the most experience here.'

'Leave me out of it. I'm too old for anything.'

'But you're not, you're the perfect age.'

'Listen, I'm just a foolish old woman who still feels like going dancing and yet I can't even manage to go up the stairs without moaning and groaning.'

'That's just a bit of stiffness.'

'Listen to me, lovey, the most terrifying thing about getting older is that you feel exactly as you did when you were younger. Only nobody else sees you that way or treats you that way.'

'Oh my God!' said Marianne. 'What a horrendous thought!'

'Welcome to my world. Now where's that steak you promised me – I have my good teeth in!'

Susan was very pleased with the way her evening was going. Everybody looked so nice all dressed up – well, Marianne wasn't exactly dressed up, but she did look nice – and Gavin had made a real effort with that stripy mauve-coloured shirt and those dark jeans that swept cleanly across his behind. It was so damn easy for men. Felicity looked a million dollars with her hair that way, and Angela was dignified and womanly in an ancient silk wrap-around dress – the sort Diane von Furstenberg was now selling for several hundred euro.

The evening was in danger of continuing to go well, until Marianne (of course) decided to spoil it.

'So are you getting back with Paul, or what?' she asked, seemingly out of nowhere, as dessert was placed on the table.

'What on earth would make you think I was getting back with Paul? Are you getting back with any of *your* old boyfriends?'

'I just thought seeing as he's phoning you all the time.'

'What?'

'Oh, didn't I tell you? There was a message for you too: Paul says hi, and will you please ring him.'

'When did he ring?'

'Earlier today.'

'Marianne, Paul is none of your business.'

'Well then, you should have been here to take the call.'

'That's enough,' said Felicity. 'If you're going to answer the phone you might pass on people's messages properly. Otherwise, just let it ring.'

'So *are* you?' repeated Marianne. 'Cos if you're getting back with Paul you'd better tell Alan, cos he rang looking for you too.'

Susan was suddenly furious. 'Look!' she managed to say with forced calm, 'my private life is none of your business. So just butt out, would you. Now, can we please talk about something else?'

'Oh, that reminds me,' said Angela, putting her knife and fork down, 'I answered the phone today to someone looking for you, Marianne.'

'Oh?'

Marianne's glass remained poised midway between the table and her mouth.

'Yes, he just asked if you were there and I told him you weren't but you'd be in later.'

'Oh. Did he . . . leave a message?'

There was a distinct drainage of colour from her face.

'No, lovey, no message. And I never asked his name! Oh, I know I should have asked for his name. I'm sorry, Marianne, but he sounded a bit Cork, if that helps.'

'I'm sure it was nobody.'

'Tell us, Marianne, who's chasing you all the way from Cork?'

'Never mind! I thought we were changing the subject.'

But before the conversation could be steered into safer territory, yet another row emerged. This time about the girls' parents.

'I think they should just come back to Limerick where they belong,' Susan said emphatically.

'They're entitled to do as they please,' retorted Marianne.

'You only say that because that's all you ever do. You never think of anybody else.'

'I think a lot more of Mum and Dad than you do.'

'Oh, give me a break, Marianne, you're the most self-absorbed person I know. You never think of anyone but yourself.'

'How dare you say that! What would you know anyway? You who have no clue what's going on in anybody else's life. You always think you're the centre of everything, Susan, but the truth is, nobody cares about your petty little life. You're so pathetic you can't even break up with a boyfriend properly. I'm sure all Paul wants to know is if he can have your key back so he can give it to his new girlfriend.'

'Marianne, that's not fair,' broke in Felicity.

'It's plenty fair. I'm fed up with her making snide remarks about me. She should learn when to shut up.'

'I'm only saying what's true. You're making stuff up.'

'No, I'm not!'

'Yes, you are! Paul does not have a new girlfriend.'

'Well, maybe or maybe not. But you're totally wrong about Mum and Dad. You don't even have a clue why they go to Ballyconnell.'

'They go to Ballyconnell because they couldn't be bothered to be here with us.'

'Why would Mum want to be with you anyway? All you ever do is piss her off.'

'They should be here for Granny.'

'Oh, leave me ou—'

'They have to think of themselves too.'

'Clearly!'

'Oh, Susan, you're so dense! Mum and Dad bought the

house in Ballyconnell because it's something they've always wanted to do and – well – they might not have as much time as they thought.'

'What?'

'They might not – have as much time as they thought.'

'What do you mean?'

'They just –'

'What? Are they sick? Is Mum sick?'

'She was. Well . . . she thought she was. They didn't know for a while. So when she got the all-clear they decided to – to move to the seaside like they'd always wanted to do.'

'I don't believe it.'

'It's true.'

'Granny, did you know about this?'

'I did not, love.'

'So what was wrong with her?'

'She had a lump. But it turned out to be benign.'

'Why didn't she tell us?'

'Mum's very strong, you know, she didn't want to burden you all with it.'

'But she told you.'

'Despite what you think, Susan, Mum and I have always been close.'

'I had no idea she was sick.'

'I don't believe this,' said Felicity. 'She might have told us. We might have been able to help.'

'Well, she didn't.'

Nobody said anything for a while. Marianne's mouth kept twitching as if to remind herself that she had said too much and she tried to ease it by continually taking sips from her wine glass.

Felicity was still shaking her head, appalled that her sisters could row like that especially in front of Angela, but also a little hurt that their mother didn't confide her problem in all of them.

Angela didn't quite know where to look, not because she was embarrassed by the girls' display or upset by what had been revealed (she knew enough of her daughter-in-law to expect a constant mini-drama), but because, without realizing it, she had drunk far too much of that delicious Italian wine and now she was more than a little drunk. She was going to need to lie down soon, yet she felt she shouldn't leave the table.

Gavin *was* a little embarrassed by what had happened; he had become used to the background noise of bickering between the girls but this was something else. Some things were too private even for friendly cousins to hear.

As for Susan, she was still spinning: from mortification, rage, hurt, fear, self-doubt, a touch of self-loathing and something akin to total and utter befuddlement. She was exhausted. Without realizing it, she found herself reaching out to the, as yet, untouched tiramisu at the centre of the table, and begin to pick at the chocolate shavings with her fingers. She had scooped up all the loose ones and was beginning to swipe at the cream when Felicity gently nudged her elbow.

'Sorry.'

Susan was very sorry. For everything, but mainly that her lovely evening had turned out so badly. She had had such high hopes. She had seen herself as the perfect hostess: charming as she served the food, gracious as she received the compliments, gratified as she observed her guests enjoy their perfect evening. Trust Marianne to ruin it all. What on earth must Gavin think of them? What was the point in even trying to salvage anything of the party? It would be better if he just went home. And what was she going to do about her mother? Typical of her to be so secretive. You were supposed to tell your daughters about stuff like this so they could be supportive, but it seemed that she preferred to play the martyr and spin the story that nobody cared about her.

'You know,' said Gavin suddenly, without looking at anybody in particular, 'I make really good Irish coffees. It's the one thing I can do in the kitchen. Why don't you all go into the living room while I make the coffee, then we can make a start on this tiramisu here before Susan polishes it off.'

'That's an excellent idea,' said Felicity getting up. 'Come on, Gran, let's go and sit down, you could do with a comfy chair anyway. Coming, girls?'

'I'll give Gavin a hand in the kitchen,' said Susan, then added in a sudden attack of conscience, 'I'm sorry, Marianne. I shouldn't have accused you of being selfish.'

'That's OK, Sue. Sorry I goaded you about Paul. Of course he doesn't have a new girlfriend.'

'Thanks.'

When they were on their own in the kitchen Gavin burst out laughing.

'What are you laughing at?' asked Susan, incredulous that he could think there was anything funny in what had just happened.

'Oh, Susan, you two are hilarious. Ye're exactly what ye were like as kids. I mean, I'm sorry that your mother had a lump and all – I hope she's feeling well now, but . . .'

'Oh, Gavin, I feel terrible. I can't believe I behaved so badly.'

'You didn't behave badly. Sometimes it's hard not to revert back to being a child when you're with your family. Luke and I still do. We see each other maybe once a year, and we *always* have a row. I'm in my mid thirties and I still fight with my brother over the smallest thing.'

'Really?'

'Oh yeah. Last time he was home we nearly came to blows over the DVD player. I thought he'd broken it, he thought it was a piece of crap. You'd think we might sit down and remember Mum and Dad or something, but no, we had to have it out over a piece of cheap Japanese electronics.'

Susan laughed.

'I can't imagine you scrapping like that. You always seem so sensible to me.'

'That's the problem – Luke thinks I'm an old fart.'

'That's not fair, you're not an old fart.'

'No, I think he might be right.'

'No way!'

'Anyway, come on, let's bring these in. Let's throw a little more booze at the problem!'

Angela knew she shouldn't have accepted the Irish coffee – she'd already had more than twice as much alcohol as was good for her – but it smelled so nice. Sure, where was the harm really? At her age her liver was the least of her problems. Yet alcohol always had the effect of making her forget the things she should keep track of and remember the things that were best forgotten.

And so it was that Angela ended the evening by doing something very uncharacteristic indeed.

The girls were slumped on the couch and one of the armchairs, Susan and Marianne having made up enough to share a cushion, and Gavin was sitting on the floor with his head propped against her own armchair. Felicity had dimmed the lights and put on a CD of Doris Day's *Greatest Movie Hits*, all of which had the effect of disorienting Angela to a degree that she was not fully aware of where or when she was. It wasn't an uncomfortable feeling and she hadn't the will to fight it, but it did mean that she had no idea what she might do or say next.

The conversation in the room was moving between an appreciation of Victorian architecture and the latest person to get evicted from the *Big Brother* house. Angela didn't have a lot to say about either, so her own thoughts began to idle on the four grandchildren splayed across her furniture and how lucky she was to have them, even if they behaved like children half the time. Then she began thinking about them when they *were* children and then when they were babies, and that's when she remembered the thing she thought she had forgotten, or at least hadn't bothered to recall in many years, because, as a mere fact, it had become insignificant. So when Marianne asked her playfully which of her grandchildren was her favourite, this insignificant fact was foremost in her mind, and she duly blurted it out.

'Gavin's always been my favourite,' she said. 'But of course, he's not really my grandchild.'

19

Gavin was up early the next day. By eight o'clock he had showered and been out to the shop for the papers and a Danish. He turned on the TV and watched a pair of English presenters argue over George Bush's legacy to politics, but he didn't hear a word. There was still only one thing in his head: one sound and one image.

The sound of course was his grandmother's tipsy announcement regarding his birth. He had to smile. All these years she'd never said a word – in fact, she'd never even hinted that she knew. Gavin had pretty much convinced himself that she'd forgotten even though he didn't, for a moment, believe that his granny was doting. And he had kind of suspected that he was her favourite – grandson at least; Olaf's Susan was definitely the favourite granddaughter. He smiled again. What was that noise she made when she realized what she'd said? Sort of a gulp, or a squeak, almost as if she was actually trying to swallow her words. Of course they should never have let Angela drink so much, but it would have seemed mean to ration her wine when they were all knocking it back. He hoped she didn't feel too bad this morning; could you still get a hangover in your eighties?

Marianne, who had asked the question, let her jaw drop and just stared at Angela, speechless. It was the first time he'd ever known anything to shut her up. Susan said nothing either, it was Felicity who gave a forced laugh and told her granny not to be so ridiculous.

'Oh goodness me, yes, what did I say?'

'Nothing, Granny, you didn't say anything. I think you've definitely had enough of that whiskey,' and she took the glass, which was about to spill, from between her fingers.

'No, wait a minute,' said Susan suddenly coming to life, 'you did say something, Granny. You said that Gavin wasn't really your grandson. What did you mean? Gavin, what did she mean?'

Everybody turned to look at him then, even Angela, as if she too was expecting some sort of explanation.

'Yeah . . . technically Granny isn't my granny,' he said. 'Dad wasn't actually *my* dad. Mum had me before she married him. That's all.'

'So who is your father?' asked Marianne.

'Some guy. I don't know him.'

'Sorry, Gavin,' said Felicity. 'I'm really sorry about this.'

'It's fine. It's no big deal. It wasn't really a secret, you know. It just . . . never came up.'

'But still . . .'

'Honestly.'

'That's right,' said Angela, 'it wasn't a secret, was it? It never made any difference to me, you know.'

'I know.'

He tried to diffuse the situation by making a joke, by saying that he supposed that meant he'd have to do the washing-up now, but he only succeeded in confusing everybody.

'No way, no way!' said Felicity. 'You will not! You're our guest. We'll do it in the morning anyway. Everybody's way too tired now. It's well past Granny's bedtime . . . and we should probably all hit the sack.'

So Gavin left the house shortly after midnight not sure if he'd done something wrong, or if something wrong had been done to him, and really he wished they'd just forget about it and go back to arguing about their mother. Susan had rushed out of the house and called to him to wait. She was breathless by the time she caught up with him.

'Hang on,' she said again. 'No need to rush off.'

'It's late. It's been . . . a weird night.'

'Look, I can be slow on the uptake sometimes . . . does this mean that we're not related?'

'No. No, we're not.'

'Not at all? By blood, I mean?'

'Yeah. I mean, no. We're not related by blood. I suppose we're . . . step-cousins.'

'OK.'

And that was it. That was the image he couldn't get out of his head: his step-cousin, shivering in her flimsy lacy dress, her hands rubbing at her arms, her eyes wide with excitement and her lips drawn out into a ridiculous grin. He could be wrong, of course he could be wrong, he probably was wrong, but if he wasn't wrong, then Susan was ludicrously delighted that they weren't related. That was all she'd said. She'd said, 'OK,' hopped from foot to foot for a while, and then run back into the house.

Of course he'd never thought of her as anything other than his cousin, it would have been silly to do otherwise, but now . . . now that she, perhaps, didn't think of him as her cousin . . . So what exactly *did* he think of her, now that he could think of her any way he pleased? Well, clearly he liked her. He liked her more than any woman he had come across in a very long time. Did he fancy her? Well, who wouldn't? But you can fancy a girl and it doesn't have to mean anything. You can fancy a girl as she passes you in the street, but it doesn't mean you have any intention of running after her and telling her so. You can fancy someone for years and never do anything about it, but it doesn't have to mean that you're dying of love. Sure, he found her physically attractive. He'd always thought she was pretty and engaging and, yes, as he spent more time with her he thought her even more pretty and engaging, but that wasn't it. It was more what he had said earlier when he was treading very dangerous waters by being a lone man in a room full of women, daring to pontificate – it was how she made him feel. When he was with Susan he felt like the world was a beautiful place. It sounded like a cornball, but it was the truth.

He loved being with her. She made him happy.

He'd nearly said it to her the other day when she'd called over to his apartment in a flap about – oh God – Carmel. He'd forgotten about Carmel. He'd just have to deal with that later; right now all he wanted to think about was that look on Susan's face and what it might mean. And yes, without a doubt, the whole idea of something happening between them was weird and incestuous (even though it wasn't) and downright bonkers. Tom and Maureen would go nuts – no, no, of course it was out of the question. A mere matter of biology didn't change the fact that they were cousins. And he had probably, absolutely, been mistaken in whatever he thought he saw in Susan's expression. She was a daft girl at times, you wouldn't know what was going through her head. And didn't she have a new boyfriend anyway? And maybe an old one as well, if Marianne was to be believed. Yes, Alan was the man for her. Interesting and outgoing and not completely terrified of simply grabbing life with two hands and refusing to let go . . .

Gavin got up and walked over to the window. He loved this view of the square and the park. It made him feel as though he was in the middle of everything and yet entirely insulated from it. He began to wonder if it was time he moved away again. There was nowhere in the world he felt as comfortable, but sometimes comfort was the last thing you needed. Perhaps the States would be a good idea; after all, Luke never stopped going on about how great it was. He could easily get a work visa for a few years. Or maybe somewhere more exotic? Oh, what the fuck! What did it matter? He sighed and threw himself down on the couch from where he had a perfect view of the photograph of the man he'd adored all his life, as his father.

He hadn't thought about his father, his biological father, in a long time. As far as Gavin was concerned, Frank was his real father, no death-bed revelations could ever change that. In a funny kind of way he had always been grateful to his father; he had never taken him for granted the way a lot of children did their fathers. There was always something about him that made Gavin feel glad that Frank, and not anyone else, was his dad. They weren't particularly alike as men. Luke was like him physically and had inherited his ease with people and his sporting abilities. Luke and Frank went to rugby matches together, and there was that season Frank coached Luke's team to senior cup victory. Luke always cited his father as his most admired person . . . yet between Frank and Gavin there had always been a kind of unarticulated understanding that there was nothing they wouldn't do for each other. Frank mightn't have found much to admire in the music of Led Zeppelin or Rush, but it was he who bought Gavin his first guitar and his second (a moderately expensive Les Paul style electric). Whenever Gavin found life particularly complicated – like the time he was regularly doing the trigonometry homework of his best friend's sister but still hadn't managed to say a single word to her – he would look at his dad and think, one day, it would all be OK. One day, he would learn to take living in his stride. He laughed to himself; he wasn't there yet.

So, when his mother, who had only recently revealed to him how ill she was, suddenly turned round and told him that, actually, his father was some guy she had had an extended affair with in Dublin, it was more information than he could handle. It had often occurred to him since that he would have preferred it if his mother had said nothing. Of course, the truth matters. If the facts of life get muddled up you haven't a chance, but the only important truth for Gavin throughout his life had been that Frank loved him. The fact that there was a man out there who had the same genes as him was much less important. And yet he was supposed to care. He was supposed to be filled with a need to track down this man and look deep into his eyes and somehow find himself there. He sometimes wondered if that was the reason why his life still seemed incomplete: if he was more willing to know his real father he might have a better chance of discovering himself.

He sighed. This was why he didn't think about this stuff very often: it wrecked his head. He thought he was doing all right and then all the doubts and the questions and the insecurities came back. And the biggest of those, of course, was why hadn't his father come looking for him.

He was still sitting there when the doorbell rang sometime later. Susan! Perhaps she'd come to explain what she'd meant last night. As he opened the door he was grinning like a clown. It was the first thing Felicity commented on as she entered the flat.

'What are you so happy about?' she said.

'Nothing.'

'Look, I came here to apologize,' she said, seating herself

on the couch exactly where he had been slouched for the past half hour.

'For what?'

'For last night. For everything. For Susan and Marianne, and for . . . for Granny.'

'Honestly, Felicity, there's no need to apologize for anything. You especially.'

'Oh, look, someone has to take charge.'

'Really, there's no need.'

'But it must have made you uncomfortable – Granny just blurting it out like that.'

'It didn't. It's not a big deal. There's no reason why you shouldn't all have known years ago.'

'I knew.'

'Oh? Who told you?'

'Kay. It was when – years ago . . . when you were –'

'When I was dumped at the altar?'

'Well . . . yes.'

'Ah. One of my very finest hours.'

'You weren't exactly dumped at the altar.'

'As good as. Anyway that's when Kay told you the news?'

'We were just talking one day . . . she was mad at the way my parents were taking over and trying to tell you what to do. She felt they had no business interfering and then . . . I think it just slipped out. She told me to keep it quiet.'

'I didn't know myself until shortly before Mum died.'

'Really? It must have been a bit of a shock coming then.'

'It was. One of many shocks I got around that time.'

'I can't imagine . . . it must have changed everything.'

'You know, in a way, it didn't. I was still reeling from the fact that Mum was so sick – they'd kept that from me too.

But Dad and I had always got on so well . . . I mean, we'd clash, sure, but he always seemed to understand, or at least . . . try to understand what was going on inside my head. Luke was the one everyone liked – and he was Dad's natural son – but I always sort of felt . . . that he didn't need me to be like Luke, you know, he was fine with me just as I was.'

'Yeah?'

'So when it turned out that I wasn't his son, I suppose I thought . . . Well, he must just like me – for me. I know it sounds daft.'

'I don't think it does.'

'But I think it made it all the tougher when – when he – you know.'

'I'm so sorry, Gavin.'

'Please don't be sorry. That's the one thing I can't handle. Anyway, how's Granny this morning?'

'Oh, she's fine. I gave her an Alka-Seltzer and a plate of scrambled eggs. I don't know if she fully remembers what went on last night.'

'And Susan? And Marianne?' he added quickly.

'Haven't seen either of them.'

'Oh. And . . . what about your mother? I'd nearly forgotten about all that. Is she OK?'

'I think so. I didn't get much more out of Marianne. I'm just going to have to go down there and see her. I owe them a visit anyway. I've been a terrible daughter.'

He laughed.

'I think ye're all terrible daughters.'

'I think you're right. So listen . . . I just wish last night had gone differently.'

'It doesn't matter. I . . . I think I enjoyed it anyway. Great food.'

'Yeah, the food was good. Oh, you know . . . after nights like that I feel as if I've never left home. I feel like I'm still thirteen and haven't learned anything in twenty years.'

'Hey, don't beat yourself up about it. I feel like that all the time.'

'Thanks, Gavin. Maybe we'll do it again some time – and make a success of it.'

'It must be a bit weird for you being at home for so long. You're probably used to a much more exciting life.'

'Listen . . . it's the excitement I'm running away from.'

'Oh?'

'It all got a bit too much for me, you know. I handled things badly.' She began shaking her head. 'You don't want to hear about this.'

'No, I do. Go on.'

'Work stuff is always boring.'

'Not your work stuff. Weren't you about to be bought out, or something?'

'Yeah, it was what we were working towards. The website was doing really well – but the only way you make any real money out of that sort of thing is to get someone to buy you out when you're at the top of your game.'

'That was your thing, wasn't it – raising the profile of the site and the like?'

'I used to spend my evenings, God help me, designing questionnaires and little quizzes so I could get sneaky bits of information out of the users, so I could better sell the space. How sad was I? It's called customer relationship management and they were the only people I had relation-ships with. Apart from my sleazeball of a boss, of course.'

'Oh!'

'Clever move, wasn't it?'

'It doesn't really sound like you – if you don't mind me saying.'

'Oh, I don't mind! No, it wasn't a bit like me. But that was part of what I was enjoying. Do you ever get utterly pissed off with who you are? Like you just want to start again and be somebody else?'

'Yeah, I think I do. I think I've felt that way a lot of my life.'

'But, of course, it's ridiculous. You can't just not be the person you are. And you definitely can't do it by going out with someone you know is wrong for you.'

'I have direct experience of that.'

'Right, yeah – sorry.'

'It's fine – Go on, tell me more about Mr Wrong.'

'There's not much to tell – all very standard stuff, you know? Stupid girl's head is turned by sleazy successful older man.'

'You're not stupid, Felicity.'

'I was, believe me! I didn't know that Tony had sold off so much of his equity in the early years that he only held fifteen per cent, the same as me. I should have known that. That meant a buy-out was never going to happen.'

'Right.'

'I mean, we weren't in a terrible position – we still had jobs and our shares had increased and everything but . . .'

'That wasn't really the point.'

'No. It was much more about the man I was sleeping with screwing me over.'

'So you quit?'

'Well . . . I didn't exactly quit. It would be more accurate to say that I hit the roof. I had an utter and total melt-down.'

'Right.'

'Yes. I ranted – I screamed – I think I fired a pot of coffee at Tony – I fucked the European vice-president out of it – I behaved extremely well.'

'I'd love to have been there.'

'You wouldn't! You'd have been scared shitless!'

'Still . . . I'm sure you were something to see.'

'All my life I've been rational, cool, always the peacemaker, always able to see the other side. And then I flipped. It was as though . . . the last five years, being in boardrooms, talking millions . . . as though it was all pretend, and I was just some idiot who was really slow to cop on.'

'No wonder you've been taking a bit of time out.'

'Oh yeah, I've had a *lot* of time to think about it. But you know, once I got over the initial embarrassment, the worst of it really hit me. And it wasn't the three million – that only ever seemed theoretical anyway – it was that my job, my work . . . my life – was all gone. My job had meant everything to me. And it's not like it was a huge sacrifice or anything – it wasn't as if I had really wanted to get married and stay home with the kids – every hour I spent working I wanted to spend working. Because I was good at it. And it made me feel good to do a good job. I mean, I was dealing with the top executives at Coca-Cola. They were being convinced by *me*. I was making them part with huge amounts of *their* money. It was exhilarating, and everything else seemed . . . by the way. Unnecessary. Frivolous. And now all that's gone.'

'Can you . . . start again?'

'I don't know. Maybe I should go back to Sainsbury's where life was predictable. But I have to do something. I'm not cut out for watching *Countdown* and going on nice dates with boys I pick up at the off-licence. I don't know. I have to go back there anyway, I haven't actually quit yet. I'm still technically on holiday.'

'Have you spoken to . . . Tony since?'

'No. And he's made no effort to talk to me. What does that tell you?'

'I wish I knew how to help you.'

'Oh, you have! Just talking about it has been great. I . . . don't find it very easy sometimes to talk. I think I'm afraid of being seen as anything less than a runaway success. It's what comes of being praised too much as a child.'

'You are a success, Felicity, you've just had a bit of a glitch.'

'Thanks. I hope you're right – not that I need to be a success, just not an absolute failure.'

'I hear ya . . .'

As soon as Felicity left, Gavin decided he had to pull himself together. Everyone had problems, and at the moment his were all in his head. But before he got very far, a text came in from Carmel. She was big into the loving texts; so far, in the two weeks or so that he had known her, this was loving text number fifty-three. Up until recently he hadn't minded so much, he had thought it was just a girly affectation, but now it was beginning to grate on him. And what's more, she was starting to demand that he send loving texts in return. Usually he sent something like 'Got your text – thanks' or 'Shouldn't you be working?' These were in response to things like 'Tinkin ov U' and 'U have the sweetest eyes' and 'Cant wait to c u again'. It had been so long since he had been in any sort of relationship that he wasn't sure how he should proceed with these texts – the last time he had been with someone mobile phones weren't in common usage. Ahh, simpler times . . . when it wasn't possible to be so permanently contactable, so permanently in the grip of a microwave. And now here she was, sending things like

'Missing U where are U text me say something nice'. He couldn't help hearing Marianne's voice and thinking that perhaps she had a point. Of course the only reason he had agreed to go out with Carmel in the first place was that he thought it was Susan's idea. He really thought Carmel had said as much. He thought again. He couldn't quite remember what *had* been said that afternoon – all he knew was that there had been only one answer to Carmel's impassioned, 'So . . . would you like to go out for a drink sometime?' Oh, she was a perfectly nice girl and everything. And no, in spite of what Marianne might say, he didn't think she was a psycho, just a girl desperately in need of a boyfriend. And when you came down to it, wasn't he a boy desperately in need of a girlfriend? Hadn't he become pathologically afraid of doing or saying anything that might indicate he was anything other than quietly content with his lot? Wasn't he the guy who spent more time with his granny – even cancelled plans with his friends – than with anyone else, because it made him feel as though he had no choice? He had to look after her, she needed him, and if that meant his social life suffered, well, that was just the way it was. He was all she had.

He recalled the way he'd felt the other evening when he'd called over to the house to cut the grass and found Felicity had already done it. 'It's no bother,' she'd said. 'Sure I have the time. You're at work all day.' It was like she had taken something vital away from him rather than having saved him from a rather boring menial task. Yeah, if anyone needed to get a life, it was him. But he'd kind of lost the habit . . .

Clearly, the sensible, life-affirming thing to do was to try and make a go of it with Carmel. There was no reason why he couldn't summon the necessary courage to be whatever she needed him to be. After all, the hard part was done, or at least what was usually the hard part: they were already going out, it was already apparent that the girl liked the boy. In fact, the girl had been indicating very obviously just how much she liked the boy. That was one thing Gavin didn't believe he was mistaken about. What was it she had said to him? They had left the pub and were about to get into his car when she leaned across the bonnet and sort of whimpered (he assumed she thought she was being sexy): 'You know, you could save yourself the journey across town.' He had wilfully misunderstood. 'It's no bother,' he'd said. 'I wouldn't trust a taxi this late at night.' He hadn't given her a chance to say anything else, but had opened the door for her, got in himself and quickly turned the car in the direction of her house on the Mill Road. He could tell she was sulking by her silence (she wasn't a girl naturally set for silence) but by the time they got to her house she was ready for one more try.

'You can come in if you like. I think the girls are out.'

'Another time,' he said. 'It's late. But it's been a great evening.'

He really didn't know how much of a bollocks he was being. If a girl invited you into her house late at night, did you have to accept, or was there still a possibility that she might judge you to be merely acting like a gentleman in refusing her offer? Of course he wasn't being gentlemanly, he simply didn't want to join her in her boudoir. He had neither the ardour nor the curiosity for it.

And what, exactly, was his problem? She was attractive, personable, intelligent, she liked him, and, it would appear, she was up for it. Why the hell, then, didn't he just go for it? Wasn't that what the average red-blooded male was supposed to do? Did it really matter that he didn't find her particularly sexy? That, in fact, there was something about her that actively turned him off, something about the way she moved her mouth when she spoke as if she was silently over-articulating every word? It was only a small thing; most people wouldn't notice it, wouldn't even know what you were talking about if you pointed it out to them. What *did* matter was that he was an apparently red-blooded male who hadn't got his rocks off in an incredibly long time. The fact that he insisted on doing absolutely nothing about it also mattered. But what mattered most was that he had decided long ago that if he was ever going to be in that situation again, with anybody, it would have to be right. He simply wasn't strong enough (or horny enough, it seemed) to do otherwise. So what exactly, then, was the point of Carmel?

He absolutely hated being in this situation and he was mad at himself for letting it happen. He had let his guard down. He would never have said yes to Carmel, no matter how pathetic she appeared, if he hadn't been so . . . relaxed about everything. There was no doubt about it, ever since Susan had reappeared life had been different. He'd had no formal thoughts about her up to now, he simply knew that he was happier than he had been in a long time. He was more outgoing, more willing to just have a go. He had even told the guys in the band that he'd play with them full-time if they wanted and he'd been mad to go gigging. Now, though, he wasn't so sure. It was such a big commitment and he wasn't certain if he liked the idea of being a permanent part of something, of them having some sort of a claim on him.

But, whether he liked it or not, everything had changed. It didn't matter whether or not Susan thought of him any differently, because he couldn't help but think of her differently. All the ease he had once felt was gone. He couldn't pretend any longer that she was just his pretty cousin with whom he got along so well. Now she was this girl, this woman, with whom . . . with whom . . . yes, it was true – she was the woman with whom he had already fallen a little in love. And *what* was the point of that?

Being in love had never done him any good. Although, now that he thought about it, he wondered if he had ever really been in love before. What he had felt for Pamela had been much more like an inability to do anything other than reflect back what he seemed to be getting from her, and with Niamh, in Sweden, it was definitely nothing more than the desperation of the diaspora. And that was it. That was the sorry summation of his sex life.

Or was he over-dramatizing? Perhaps he wasn't in love with Susan at all; perhaps it was all a bit of a summer crush, perhaps there was nothing more to it than a simple lack of sex in his life. Perhaps there was a point to Carmel after all.

He had to get out. He grabbed his keys and left the flat. He was hurtling down the stairs, two at a time, a vague notion in his head of driving to Ballyconnell, even though he had neither surf board nor swimming gear, when he was accosted mid-flight.

By Carmel.

'Hey,' she said. 'Hi! It's me. Where are you going? I didn't know you were going out.'

It took him quite a few moments first to realize that a voice was talking to him and then to recognize it as Carmel's.

'Hi,' he managed eventually, 'did we have an arrangement?' He knew it sounded kind of crass but it was all that would come out of his mouth.

'Well . . . no. But I thought I'd surprise you.'

'Oh!'

'Surprise!'

'Sorry, Carmel, I just wasn't expecting to see you.'

'But I sent you a text. I thought when you didn't reply that it was OK.'

'A text? Oh yeah . . . I think I saw it . . . but I never got round to reading it.'

'You really don't pay much attention to your phone, do you?'

'Ahm . . . I suppose not.'

'So are you on your way out, then?'

'I don't really know. Ahm . . . let's get off the stairs anyway. We can decide later.'

'Decide what?'

'Nothing. Sorry. You've caught me at a kind of a bad time.'

'Oh. Do you want me to go away?'

'No . . . no . . . no. Come up for a minute.'

'OK.'

He opened the door of his flat not quite sure what had just taken place. He glanced at his phone and saw the message 'Mssng u OK if I call ovr'. *Why* hadn't he read it? *Why* hadn't he run faster down the stairs? *Why* hadn't he told her he was on his way out?

She stood in the middle of his living room holding her handbag as if it contained her life. He noticed that she was dressed less carefully than usual; every other time he had seen her she had been well groomed and clearly wearing her 'good' clothes. Today she looked as though she might have recently tumbled out of bed.

'Look,' she said before he had worked out what to say, 'I know I'm being a bit of a pain.'

'No, no. It's just that I was sort of in the middle of someth—'

'No, I mean generally. You're being very nice and every-thing – Susan was right, you're a totally sound guy – but I think I get it.'

'Get what?'

'That you're not really interested.'

'No, I –'

'It's OK. I don't mind. I'm not a nut job – I'm not great at choosing men . . . but I'm not a nut job.'

Gavin smiled.

'I didn't think you were.'

'You might have had your doubts.'

He smiled again. He was beginning to like this woman.

'Honestly, not one.'

'Anyway . . . I just went through this big thing with a guy and it was all messy and . . . not good. Basically he wasn't really interested, and well . . . frankly, I think I deserve better.'

'You do. Of course you do.'

'Yeah, well . . . I've kind of realized that you can't force someone to be into you and I get the impression you're not.'

Gavin sighed with something like relief.

'Actually, Carmel, I'm a bit of a mess myself. I think you're great. I've enjoyed our time together but, yeah, the truth is I'm sort of into somebody else. Only I don't think she's into me. Typical, isn't it?'

'Don't talk to me about typical. Actually there's another reason why I don't think it would work with us.'

'Oh?'

'You remember I thought I recognized you from some-where?'

'Yeah . . . I'm just so bad wi–'

'We did meet once.'

'Yeah?'

Carmel swallowed hard.

'You were engaged to my sister.'

'What!?'

'To Pamela.'

'Pamela is your sister?'

'Yeah. Now that's what I call bloody typical. The one nice guy I meet in ten years turns out to have been the one nice guy who got screwed over by my sister!'

'But . . .'

'I was in college in Galway. I hardly ever came home. Pamela and I aren't very close. And, well, you weren't together for very long.'

'So when did we meet?'

'That sort of engagement party thing my parents threw. My hair wasn't blonde then and I used to wear my glasses all the time – I've improved a bit since those days.'

'But I thought you were a fitness instructor, or something, and lived in London.'

'That's my other sister, Yvonne. She wasn't at the party.'

'I don't remember another sister.'

'Thanks.'

'I'm really sorry, that whole time is very vague.'

'Don't worry about it. Sure, I've only just worked out who you are. I kinda had the idea your name was Devin – I mean the guy my sister was engaged to – I always thought his name was Devin.'

'You really aren't a close family, are you?'

'I suppose not. But, you know, it wasn't something we ever talked about much. Everybody thought she treated you really badly.'

'So how is Pamela anyway?'

The minute he asked the question he wished he hadn't. It had simply been a polite reflex.

'She's fine. She's divorced. She lives in Canada now. She had a baby a year ago. Nobody's quite sure who the father is.'

'Right.'

'She would have been lucky to have married you.'

'I think we both had a lucky escape.'

'And you're just about to make your second escape from the Ryan girls.'

'Carmel, honestly, I —'

'It's fine. Really it is. It just wasn't meant to be.'

'Thanks. Thanks for being . . . so mature.'

'You didn't expect it of me, did you?'

'I . . .'

'It's OK. I didn't expect it of myself. Susan will be so proud. I could tell she was nervous of me with you. She probably thought I was going to break you, or something.'

'Come here,' he said, putting his arms round her. 'You're a fantastic woman. There's a lucky man out there for you somewhere.'

'I know,' she said, returning the hug. 'He just doesn't know it yet.'

'Come on, I'll walk you to your car.'

'So,' she said as he was grabbing his keys once again, 'who's this girl you're into?'

'Oh . . . I don't think it's anybody you know,' he said, banging the door shut. 'Nothing's going to happen anyway.'

20

Nothing was getting done at Charlotte Avenue. Susan had been out early for a walk, but ever since she'd come back she'd stayed in her room. Angela had taken a mid-morning nap and was feeling well enough to join the girls in the living room for a little brunch over the Sunday papers. Felicity, back from her visit to Gavin, had thrown herself onto the couch and was flicking through the style section of the *Sunday Times* as she sipped her orange juice and broke off bits of croissant. Angela was reading an article about Dickie Rock in the *Sunday Independent*'s 'Life' magazine, thus Marianne was forced to pick up a real bit of the paper, something she usually avoided. She couldn't really see the point of newspapers – couldn't you get all the news you wanted from TV, or the internet? What was the point of poring over it all a day and a half late? However, on this particular morning there seemed to be enough to hold her attention.

'Listen to this,' she said, leaning forward, 'it says here that Amy Winehouse has gone into rehab again and that, in order to counteract the effect of all the drugs on her skin, she's mixing her own urine into her face cream. Isn't that just bonkers!'

'What?'

'Her own urine!'

'That's rubbish!'

'It's not. It says so right here.' She turned a few more pages. 'There's a picture of Paul McCartney with a new woman – I think he looks much better since the divorce. All that worry must have been very ageing on him.'

'Is there anything other than garbage in that newspaper?' asked Felicity.

'Excuse me, missus! This is your bread and butter! But oh, I forgot that you don't actually approve of the stuff that's going to make you a millionaire. Of course, you're so much better educated than the rest of us. Here, I'll flick over to the financial pages for you.'

'Read whatever pages you like, Marianne, just read them to yourself.'

'No, no. Here is the news! Shares went up a bit yesterday and then – oh, my goodness! They went down a bit!'

'Very funny.'

'Look, here's a picture of a pervy-looking bloke. Oh-oh, says here he's been arrested. For insider dealing. Poor fuck – he does look a bit gormless. Runs some big internet company though, so I suppose he can't be that gormless. Here, look at him – doesn't he remind you of one of those priests who are always trying to be trendy?'

Marianne held the paper across the table, but the angle wasn't sufficient for the half glance Felicity gave it to reveal exactly who was in the photo. However, it was enough for her to grab the paper off Marianne.

'Oh my God!'

'Easy does it!'

Felicity stared at the photograph.

'Do you know him or something?'

'What?'

'Do you know him?'

'Ahm . . . ahm . . . yes.'

'Oh! So who is it?'

'It's my boss. My . . . former boss.'

'Just as well you're still on holiday then.'

'What?'

'Or they might suspect you of insider – whatsit as well.'

'Oh God,' said Felicity, leaving the table, 'I need to make a phone call.'

She rang Sandra immediately.

'Oh, thank God!' said Sandra somewhat melodramatically.

'What?'

'Oh, I'm just glad to hear from you. I thought you might be in prison. You're not, are you? You're not ringing me from prison?'

'Of course I'm not in prison. What's up with you?'

'I have some news about Tony.'

'I know. I read it in the paper. What's it all about?'

'I don't know much more myself. It seems he told somebody, one of his old cronies, that the share price was about to rise because of the buy-out. But it seems that the old crony told a few more of his old cronies and somebody got suspicious.'

'Wow!'

'I know! But listen – he's only been arrested on *suspicion* of insider trading. They don't *know* it was him. I think everyone's under suspicion.'

'Of course. I can see how it might look. In fact, it could look very bad for me.'

'Well . . .'

'I'm going to have to go back.'

'It might be a good idea before they come and get you.'

'Oh God, I'm not ready for this.'

'I'll keep you posted anyway.'

'Thanks, Sandra.'

Felicity went into the dining room and turned on the PC.

The broadband connection was good. She logged onto RyanAir.com and looked at flights to London. She clicked on a flight to Gatwick, departure time 06.55, arrival time 08.20, but when it came to filling in her credit-card details she stopped. She was nearly there. But not quite.

21

Susan was on the phone to her mother.

'. . . but it's all over now, love. I'm fine and there's nothing to worry about.'

'But . . . you might have been . . .'

'There's fear of me, love!'

'I know but – it would have been nice to know. I don't mean nice – I mean . . .'

'I didn't want to worry you.'

'We would have liked to have been worried.'

'Now that's just nonsense.'

'It isn't really. You're supposed to tell us. You told Marianne.'

'Oh, Marianne wheedled it out of me. You know the way she is, she can read me like a book.'

'I suppose . . .'

'I hope you're not cross with me, Susan, I've been through a lot.'

'Oh no, no, of course not.'

'Daddy thought we were better keeping it to ourselves. He thought it would be less stress on me.'

'Of course, yes. He's right. So . . . how are you feeling now?'

'I feel marvellous! I've never been fitter. It's the air down here, it's so much cleaner than the city. I've wanted to live by the sea all my life.'

'That's good then. I'm happy for you, Mum.'

'I know you are, love. So are you going to come down and get a bit of sea air yourselves?'

'Oh, we will, we will. We're just trying to organize it. We were thinking maybe next Friday?'

'Oh, your father has a golf classic all day, and then there's a do in the evening. We couldn't miss that.'

'No, of course not. Maybe we'll just come down on the Saturday then?'

'The Saturday? That should be fine. Oh no, wait a minute, we're hill walking on Saturday afternoon. Sure, why don't you just come down on the Sunday? I'll do you a roast. The local lamb here is lovely.'

'Sure . . . we can do that.'

'Do. Come down for lunch on Sunday. Will Angela come with you?'

'I don't think so, Mum. She seems tired these days.'

'I hope ye're not making work for her. Three girls in the house, she shouldn't have to lift a finger.'

'No, honestly, we have a rota.'

'Oh, wait a minute, love. Now that I think about it, Sunday won't do either.'

'Oh? What's on Sunday?'

'There's a farmer's market we've started going to in Ballyvaughan. I suppose we could miss it.'

'You shouldn't miss it on our account.'

'Would you be very upset?'

'No . . . we can come down another time.'

'That would be great, love. I'm sure we won't be as busy the following weekend.'

'Right. We'll say the following weekend so.'

'Wonderful. Have you any other news for me? How's Gavin? Is he looking after Angela's garden?'

'He is.'

'That's great, he's very reliable.'

'Yeah, he is. Mum?'

'Yes, love?'

'Why didn't you ever tell us that Uncle Frank wasn't Gavin's father?'

'What! Who told you that?'

'Granny let it slip the other night.'

'That woman!'

'She didn't mean to. And Gavin said it wasn't a secret. So why did you never say anything?'

'It just never came up. Well, actually, it's something we don't like to talk about. It caused a lot of hurt at the time. Your father's family was always very respectable.'

'Granny said she never minded.'

'Maybe she should have minded. Anyway, it's all in the past now.'

'You should have said something.'

'It wasn't my place to say anything. Maybe Angela should see a doctor.'

'Granny doesn't need a doctor, Mum.'

'Has Felicity gone back to London yet?'

'Not yet.'

'What's she at, that girl?'

'She's just having a holiday.'

'Isn't it well for some!'

'Well, at least she – anyway, I'd better go.'

'Marianne tells me you have a new boyfriend.'

'What!'

'Some dentist fellow. She said he offered to give her a check-up for free.'

'What?'

240

'Sounds like the sort of boyfriend that would be worth having.'

'Oh, Mum! Never mind what Marianne says.'

'They won't be queuing up all your life. Just as long as you realize that.'

'I really have to go.'

'Give my love to everyone.'

Susan put the phone down and sighed heavily.

She had eventually agreed to go on a date with Alan. Out of politeness more than anything else.

The problem with Alan was not Alan, it was entirely Susan. She couldn't help looking at him and thinking how eminently eligible he was, how adequately attractive, how pleasant he was to spend time with. And yet, not one fibre of her being could muster as much as a flicker of interest.

He'd asked her out to dinner in Brulées, one of Limerick's better restaurants. Sitting by the window at half past eight on a Friday night, a view of the bustling city before her, a 'to die for' menu in front of her, she'd had to admit (to herself) that one of the main reasons she'd agreed to the date was because he'd mentioned the restaurant first. It was one of the places she'd hoped Paul would bring her – she'd hinted heavily after his shambles of a proposal that they could do it all over again in Brulées – but he hadn't taken the bait. So now here she was, in a lovely new dress from Monsoon, her make-up expertly applied, her perfume wafting in subtle waves from each of her pulses, and the truth was that she was more interested in what the waiter thought of her dress than anything Alan might say or do.

'You look lovely,' he said, trying to draw her attention back from the window.

'What?'

'You look lovely.'

'Oh. Thank you.'

'I'm sorry it's all been so obvious.'

'What's been obvious?'

'This. Brian and Bernie trying to get us together.'

'Oh. Yes. I kept telling her –'

'It's OK. You can't force these things.'

'No. Did she tell you I just broke up with a boyfriend?'

'She did.'

'She's so love-struck herself she thinks everybody should be at it.'

'They seem very happy.'

'Yeah, they're looking at houses. Already.'

'I understand if you're not ready to . . .'

'Thanks. I sort of don't know what I want, you know?'

'Yeah.'

'Maybe in a few months?'

'What? Oh yeah. Yes. Definitely.'

'Anyway, we might as well order. The grub here's great.'

So they ate a very romantic meal of sautéed scallops, roasted pigeon and strawberry tartlets under very platonic conditions. Alan insisted on paying – he said Susan could treat him the next time – and he walked her back to Charlotte Avenue and saw her in without so much as a peck on the cheek. Susan could only wish him better luck on his next date.

She sighed once more and went in search of Angela so she could give a report about her mother. She found her in the living room with a tall, handsome, white-haired man.

'Come in, Susan,' she said, beckoning her into the room.

'This is Peter Gillespie, a very old friend of mine. Peter, this is my granddaughter, Susan.'

'Less of the old, now, Angela,' he said smiling, as he took Susan's hand, 'but, yes, we do go way back.'

'Peter's family owns Gillespie's Antiques, Susan. You know it there on Thomas Street?'

'Oh yes, yes, I know Gillespie's. It's been there for ever.'

'You might say for ever, love. I think I first met Peter when I was in the shop with my mother. Of course you were only a boy then,' she added with a giggle.

'Yes, your mother was a good customer of ours, Angela. I remember my father talking about her good taste.'

'Oh, she was fond of pretty things, my mother. Now, Peter, I was just about to put the kettle on, so I'll leave you Susan here to chat to. I'm sure you'd much rather chat to a pretty young one.'

The moment Angela was out of the room Peter Gillespie's manner seemed to change. He became less the genial elderly gentleman and much more the strict old schoolmaster. 'Your granny had a lot of her pieces appraised with us,' he said flatly.

'Oh,' said Susan, 'yes. Granny has some lovely stuff. I used to help her polish it all when I was younger.'

'Yes. Well, an appraisal means that you keep records,' he continued, without fully looking Susan in the eye.

'Right,' said Susan, nodding her head knowledgeably.

'So when some of your grandmother's pieces turned up in our shop a couple of weeks ago, we knew where they'd come from.'

'What? Was Granny selling some of her stuff?'

'It wasn't your grandmother who brought them in.'

'Who was it then?'

'I wasn't in the shop myself – my niece runs it for me now – but she says that it was a young woman. Of about your age, Miss O'Regan.'

'You think I was flogging Granny's stuff? But why would I do that?'

'Some of the pieces we bought were worth several hundred euro.'

'Oh my God! Look, Mr. Gillespie, it wasn't me who was in your shop but I think I might know who it was.'

'I'm just looking out for your grandmother. I want her to have her pieces back, but I'd also like to have my . . .' He took a piece of paper from his pocket. 'It all comes to nearly three thousand euro.'

'Oh my God! Look, Mr Gillespie, I'll see what I can do. Have you told Granny?'

'No. I thought maybe it could be settled without upsetting her. I don't have to tell you that she's an old woman.'

'Of course not. And what about the guards?'

'I haven't done anything there either. But I'm not afraid to. I want this settled.'

'Of course you do. Look, I'll see what I can do and I'll get back to you. Have you a card or something?'

He took a card from his wallet and wrote a number on the back of it.

'This is my home number,' he said. 'Hopefully I'll hear from you soon.'

'Definitely. I . . . appreciate you allowing us to sort this out ourselves.'

'Just as long as it's sorted.'

'What have you two been talking about?' said Angela, returning with a laden tray. 'I always knew Peter had an eye for the pretty girls!'

'Now, Angela,' he said, 'you know I've long given up on the pretty girls. Nothing but trouble, the pretty girls.'

The first thing Susan did was check the sideboard. The pastry forks were gone. And the sugar spoons with the cute little tongs. And the water glasses she hadn't been able to find the night of the dinner. She checked the cabinet. There was a series of miniature paintings missing and a few pieces of china. All nice pieces, but surely they couldn't add up to three thousand euro. Then she went back to the sideboard. There was a salt and pepper set she'd never liked much but which Angela always said was really valuable. She used to joke that it was her running-away money. It was nowhere to be found.

She went straight to Marianne's room and barged through the door.

'Excuse me! Ever heard of knocking?'

'You've been stealing from Granny!'

'I have not!'

'Yes, you have! Loads of her stuff is missing.'

'I didn't take it!'

'There was an antiques guy here earlier, a friend of Granny's. He said the stuff had been taken into his shop by a young woman.'

'It wasn't me!'

'Admit it. You did it. You sold a load of Granny's stuff.'

'So what if I did? It's never used. She doesn't need it.'

'That's not the point.'

'What does it matter? Granny has plenty of money. If I'd asked her, she'd have given it to me.'

'But you didn't ask her.'

'It's absolutely none of your business!'

'It *is* my business if you're ripping Granny off.'

'I'm not ripping her off. It's just a couple of things. I'll replace them.'

'No, you won't. You can't replace stuff like that. It's just lucky this guy knew it was hers. He wants his three thousand euro back.'

'I don't have it.'

'How can you not have it? You haven't spent one penny since you've been here.'

'I had some debts. All right!'

'What kind of debts?'

'Never mind what kind of debts.'

'Look, you either give this guy back his money so Granny gets her stuff back . . . or I'm telling Mum.'

'Don't you dare tell Mum!'

'If this guy doesn't get his money back, he'll be calling the guards. So it's either Mum or the guards.'

'Leave me alone. You're just worried about your precious inheritance.'

'Give me a break!'

'That's all you care about. In case Granny doesn't get to leave you quite as much loot as you'd hoped.'

'How dare you!'

'Get off your high horse, Susan!'

'You are not going to turn this round on me.'

'Whatever. I don't care. I'm so fed up with you and your . . . condescending attitude.'

'Condescending! I'm not condescending. Just because I don't think you should rip off your grandmother.'

'It's not just that. You take every opportunity you can to put me down. You think you're so much better than me.'

'I do not.'

'Yes, you do. You always have. You think everyone has

to behave the way you do. And look at you! What's so great about your life? What have you ever done that's so special? You with your safe little job and saving for a deposit on a crappy little house. You can't even hang on to your pathetic boyfriends!'

'Take that back, Marianne – you have no idea – how dare you lecture me!'

'Oh no, it's only you that's allowed to do the lecturing! Buzz off, Susan, and leave me alone. Go and ring Mum, if you like. I don't care! I'm just tired of looking at your face.'

'Fine! Fine! I will ring her!'

'You go and do that, you little tattletale!'

Susan's face was purple. She had charged up here full of righteous indignation but now all her fire was gone. She felt every word of what Marianne said. Her life *was* pathetic. Even more pathetic than Marianne's. At least Marianne had always done what she wanted. Susan had spent the major part of her twenties doing what nobody wanted, least of all herself. That had been the problem – she'd never known before what would make her happy. And now that she was beginning to realize what it was, she was also beginning to realize that she might never have it.

'Fine so. I'll tell her.' Her voice was quivering.

'You do that! Just don't bother me any more!'

Susan's hands were shaking as she picked up the phone. But she wasn't going to stop now. Marianne was not going to get away with this, no matter what spin she tried to put on it.

She dialled slowly. She was furious. But she was not backing down.

'Hi. Hi, Mum? Listen, there's something you should know . . .'

*

Afterwards she put the phone back in its cradle and walked slowly out of the house. She went down the path, through the front gate and on to Charlotte Avenue. The street noises were surprisingly soothing. She began walking, and pretty soon she knew where she was going. It probably wasn't a good idea but it was her only one.

22

Susan arrived at the building as someone else was coming out. She climbed the four flights and stood outside Gavin's door. Her stomach was twisted with apprehension but she wasn't going to walk away now. She rang the bell.

Several minutes passed. He answered the door looking slightly dishevelled in an old pair of jeans and a faded T-shirt, his hair falling over his eyes.

'Susan!'

'Hi.'

'Did we have a lesson?'

'No. No, I just . . . called round.'

'Oh. Come in.'

Susan walked ahead of him to the living room, as neat and bright and airy as it had always been. Suddenly she felt a tightness in her throat as if it were a fetid hovel.

'Do you mind if I open a window?'

'Sure. There's one open already, but I'll open the other one. It's a warm evening.'

'Thanks.'

Gavin lifted the sash as high as it would go and sat beside Susan on the couch.

'Is there something wrong?'

'I had a huge row with Marianne.'

'Well, that's never upset you before.'

'It's not funny.'

'Sorry. I didn't mean to laugh.'

'No, no. It's just that . . . it's so pathetic. I feel like all I do these days is scrap with her as if I was twelve again. But at least then I always thought I was right. Now I think maybe *she's* right. But, I mean, I *am* right – she was taking advantage of Granny.'

'Susan, what on earth are you talking about?'

'I don't know.' She sighed. 'Marianne was stealing from Granny. I mean, that's wrong, right?'

'She was stealing from Granny?'

'Yeah! I mean, that's terrible, isn't it?'

'What the blazes was she doing?'

'And yet she makes me feel as though *I've* done something wrong.'

'How do you mean?'

'I told Mum and Dad.'

'Well . . . I suppose you had to.'

'But she's flipping out now as if I'm not being fair to her.'

'Look, you did the right thing. Don't worry about Marianne. She's a big girl.'

'Yes, she is. But she still makes me feel like . . .'

'Like what?'

'I don't know. I think . . . I think I thought I would have my life a bit more sorted out by now. You know? Like I might . . . Well, I don't know exactly, but something more than living with my granny and my two sisters. I only meant to stay a week.'

'I thought you were having a ball.'

'I was. I've really enjoyed this summer. But the summer's over. I should be . . .'

'Marrying your boyfriend?'

'What?'

'Paul? You feel you should be getting back together again?'

'Oh no, God no.'

'What about Alan?'

'There's nothing happening with Alan. I've no interest in Alan.'

'Right.'

'So how are you and Carmel getting on?'

'Oh . . . that's over.'

'Really? Why?'

'I don't think she was that interested.'

'She kept saying she wanted to marry you!'

'I guess she changed her mind.'

'I can't make her out.'

'Actually, I really got to like her.'

'You did?'

'Yeah. I think she's a very nice girl.'

'Oh. So you're . . . sorry she broke it off.'

'No.' He shook his head. 'Did you know she is Pamela's sister?'

'Pamela who?'

'Pamela Ryan whom I was engaged to.'

'Oh my God! Her sister! She kept saying she knew you. I'm so sorry. I'd no idea. I don't even think I knew she had a sister. Well, I did but I never really paid any attention. That's just too weird.'

'Yeah . . . freaky.'

Susan got up and began fiddling with the curtains. She wasn't sure what she had intended when she came here. If she had thought that Gavin would magically make it all better, then she'd been wrong. She felt more confused and agitated than ever.

'What's up, Suze? What's really up?'

There was moisture in the corner of her eyes when she began to speak: 'I don't know what's wrong with me.'

'Susan?'

She was biting her lip and wringing her hands together.

'I mean, I kicked Paul out of my life – which was good because he was taking up all the available space – but I also kicked out my future with him. And while I didn't want that future . . . It's just that now there's all that empty space.'

Gavin got up and put his arms round her.

'Susan, you're an incredibly strong person. You can do anything you want. You don't have to be afraid of a little empty space. It can be a good thing.'

'Oh, Gavin,' she said sniffing, 'you always say the right thing.'

'No, I don't. I never have a clue.'

He bent his head until his chin was touching her cheek.

'I never know how to say the things I really want to say.'

He pulled away from her, still keeping his hands on her shoulders. He seemed to have stopped breathing. She was looking up at him, expectantly, as he cupped her face in his hands and kissed her lips.

'I've wanted to do that for a very long time,' he said.

'You have?'

'Yes. I probably shouldn't have but –'

'I'm glad you did.'

'Are you sure?'

'Oh yes.'

'I've wanted to kiss you for so long.'

'That day at the barbecue . . .'

'You felt it too? I thought it was just me.'

'No . . . not just you.'

'Or maybe I've wanted to kiss you since the very first day I met you. Hey,' he said, brushing his lips against hers, 'are you sure this isn't weird for you?'

'That's the weirdest thing . . . it doesn't feel weird at all.'

He kissed her mouth, he kissed her neck, he let his hand travel across her back while she allowed her body to go limp at every touch.

'I had no idea how you felt.'

'I felt guilty,' she said, pulling away from him suddenly. 'I felt guilty as hell that I was falling for my cousin. That's why when Granny said that stuff about your dad – well. But then I thought you wouldn't – that you didn't – that . . .'

He continued to kiss her as she tugged his T-shirt from his jeans. She was digging her fingers into his chest when he stopped her.

'Susan,' he said, as he placed his mouth over her ear and began to nibble gently at the lobe, 'you know I want to do more than kiss you?'

'I should hope so,' she said, smiling.

He pulled at the buttons on the short tunic thing she was wearing and it fell open revealing her pert little breasts in a barely-there black bra. He was monstrously turned on. He slid the rest of the garment from her shoulders while she lifted his T-shirt over his head. He was dazzled by the whiteness of her skin; every inch of her seemed to glow in the fading light. She broke away from him for a moment while she removed the rest of her clothing and then there she was, inches away from him, tiny and beautiful, and naked. He was about to burst.

That was when she unbuckled his belt and undid the buttons on his jeans one by one. When she touched him he believed he must have lost consciousness for a while – nothing on earth had ever felt so good. This was what he had been waiting for all his life. This was the ideal of sex he had formed somewhere in adolescence.

Every touch of Susan's was electric. She kissed him and held him and stroked him as if this was what she had been born to do. And he seemed to be able to please her. Always before, he'd been nervous about doing the right thing to the right bit, but now every move was natural to him, and every move seemed to be the right one. Susan made noises he could only interpret as indicating enormous pleasure, and when she screamed out loud 'Christ, that's amazing!' he had to take her at her word.

Once rested, they moved to the bedroom where diving into the clean white sheets set them off again. Gavin had never considered himself to be a 'five times a night' sort of guy, but he was beginning to see how it might come about. And there was nothing more intoxicating than hearing Susan moan with pleasure and seeing the look of artless ecstasy on her face. He had always thought she was beautiful, but now she embodied every beautiful thought he had ever had.

They fell asleep then, a deep empowering sleep. When Gavin woke Susan was searching for her clothes.

'You're not going?' he said.

'I have to. I can't just walk in the door in the morning. Granny'd freak.'

'No, she wouldn't. Anyway, haven't you done it before?'

'No, I haven't!'

'Sorry – this isn't a time for jokes.'

'No, it isn't. I don't want to go – believe me – but she's probably still half awake waiting for me to come in. And . . .'

'Yeah?'

'I'm half afraid my mother is going to turn up. I suppose

I should have thought things through a little bit. But I didn't know that . . .'

'That you were going to get seduced when you came over here to complain about your sister?'

'Well . . .'

'Here, give me a minute and I'll walk you home.'

'OK.'

Susan found most of her clothing and Gavin pulled on his T-shirt and the jeans that were still lying behind the couch.

'Here,' he said, handing her a jacket.

'Thanks,' she said. 'I love you.'

'Thanks,' he said. 'I love you too.'

And so, at approximately three thirty in the morning he dropped her off at Charlotte Avenue.

'Promise you'll call over in the morning?' she said, huddling close to him in the cold air. 'We can have breakfast. It'll be almost as if we had spent the whole night together.'

'OK,' he agreed. 'But as soon as breakfast is over I'm taking Granny aside and asking for her permission to keep you for the whole night.'

'I think you should run away with me.'

He buried his face in her neck.

'You know I really love you, Susan. I've never been this happy.'

'Me too. You make me forget what a mess I am.'

'You're not a mess. You're fabulous.'

'Oh, it feels good to hear you say that! Say it again!'

'You're fabulous, Susan! You're amazing! You're unbelievable!'

She laughed at him and wrapped her arms further under his T-shirt.

'Do you think my mother will go nuts?'

'Fuck your mother – if you'll excuse the expression. Your mother doesn't matter. Nobody matters.'

It was approaching four o'clock before she finally broke away from him and tiptoed into the house.

23

Felicity had a date that night, with Mark, the wine guy. They had agreed to meet in Tom Collins's, a pub Felicity hadn't been in since her early twenties when a gang from school used to make a pilgrimage there each Christmas. It made her feel old to walk through the door again and it didn't help that Mark, now in his 'weekend clothes', looked even younger.

He was waiting for her at a table near the door, his pint of Guinness almost empty.

'Hi,' he said getting up. 'I wasn't sure if you'd come.'

'Oh?'

'Yeah . . . I thought you sounded a bit doubtful on the phone.'

'Did I? Well . . . maybe . . . I'm just not sure if I'm going to be around for that much longer.'

'What? Tonight?'

'No, I mean I'm probably going back to London in a while.'

'But we have tonight, right?'

There was something so guileless and yet so hopeful in the way he said it that Felicity couldn't help indulging the feeling that maybe, for once, the present was all that mattered.

'Yes,' she said, 'we have tonight.'

'Great, I'll get you a drink. What'll you have?'

'The Guinness looks good.'

'Guinness it is.'

'You look great,' he said when he came back with a creamy pint and set it down in front of her.

'Oh – thanks!'

'You sound surprised.'

'Do I? I suppose I – I don't know. But thanks!'

'Don't mention it. If a girl looks good, I tell her.'

'That's very unIrish of you.'

'I'm only half Irish – my mother's French.'

'Oh, I bet you say that to all the girls.'

'Honestly, it's true. You should hear my French – it's flawless.'

'OK, then, let's hear your French.'

'Never on a first date. My mother taught me better than that.'

Felicity couldn't help but laugh out loud. She had no idea whether or not he was half French and she didn't care.

'So is that why you're working in the wine shop – because your mother taught you so much about fine wine?'

'Partly. And partly because my uncle owns the business and felt it was time I did some real work for a change.'

'What kind of artificial work have you been doing?'

'Strawberry picking, grape picking, apple picking – you can see the pattern. I was in a band for a while but I got kicked out because I couldn't sing or play.'

'So you're a bit of a waster, then?'

'Just a bit. So what do you do?'

'I used to help run a major website but, now, I mostly just hang around.'

'We've got loads in common then.'

'Loads.'

'So what's the website?'

'Thegoss. You probably haven't heard of it.'

'I have. I spend a lot of time online.'

'I wouldn't have thought you fitted the profile.'

'Oh, I'm into everything. And I love gossip. Of any kind. I'm a bit of a girl really.'

'Really?'

'Only in my taste for gossip, of course.'

'Of course.'

'It's a good site.'

'Thanks.'

'So what kind of stuff did you do?'

'Getting advertising mostly, finding out what our users were into – you know, designing little quizzes to extract information.'

'I'm sure I filled out one of those – I can't resist them. They always promise you'll win a prize. So far I've never won. Is there really a prize?'

'Of course there is – it's just that there's usually only one prize and thousands and thousands of little quizzes.'

'Sounds like a fun job. Why did you give it up?'

'You know what, Mark? That's a question I cannot answer.'

Felicity found the pints of Guinness Mark kept putting in front of her very easy to drink and his stories of bumming round Europe even easier to listen to. At the end of the night when he walked her to Charlotte Avenue and kissed her with a passion she felt certain was genuine, a large part of her wanted nothing more than to smuggle him up to her room and let him do whatever he liked with her, right through the night. But a much bigger part of her wanted to have done with all the things that were distracting her from the one thing she knew she had to do. The one thing, she realized, that she wanted to do.

So she pulled away from him.

'It's been lovely,' she said. 'It's been great. But I'm . . .'

'You're not really interested, I know.'

'No. No, it's not that. I need to get back. I've been away too long.'

He took hold of her again.

'Next time you're home, give me a ring. I'd love to see you again.'

'OK. Maybe I will. Goodnight.'

'Goodnight, Felicity. Don't forget about me.'

24

When Gavin woke it was already ten o'clock. He hadn't intended going back to sleep after walking Susan home. He'd lain on the bed so as to drink in her smell once more and try to convince himself that it had really happened. He still couldn't believe it. He wasn't supposed to be this happy. Only twenty-four hours ago he had been miserable.

He'd convinced himself that there was no point. Whatever he might have thought he'd seen in Susan's face on the night of the dinner party, he hadn't believed it would still be there in the cold light of day. She was clearly either still hung up on her old boyfriend or having a lot of fun with the new one. And fair enough, he'd said to himself. He couldn't miss what he'd never had. He could love her all he liked, but only as his cousin.

As his cousin. As his sweet, charming, delightful, gorgeous, captivating, utterly enchanting cousin. And he would remain ever dependable and reliable, ever the nerdy one who needed looking after, and had to be set up on dates to try and offset the loneliness of his life. But he was so tired of being that guy. It was one thing to be the all-purpose grandson who was always available to cut the grass or change a plug, quite another to be the all-purpose cousin who was always available to observe everybody else getting on with their lives. Yet that seemed to be the role he was destined to play. He couldn't go back to being something he wasn't. He couldn't pretend any more that he didn't have the feelings he did. So he had started staying away. Angela's grass got higher and higher and the mower stayed in the shed. When Susan's number came up on his phone he let it ring. He couldn't believe that the best few months of his life had now come to this. He had been thoroughly miserable.

So when she came to his door he couldn't work out immediately whether he was elated to see her face again, or if that wrenching feeling in his gut was actually a desire to make her go away.

She was hard to resist. She was genuinely flustered. Her pale cheeks had an unusual amount of colour in them and her lips kept forming a pout that he believed wasn't purely decorational. It was a no-brainer – he was glad she was here and he never wanted her to leave again. For the first time in his life he knew he was going to take control. For once he would say what he really meant. And if she laughed in his face, then so be it. He couldn't feel much worse than he did now.

But she didn't laugh at him . . .

And now it was ten o'clock. Susan would have been expecting him ages ago. He checked his phone but there was nothing there and he texted her to say he was on his way. He wanted to get there quickly, but he couldn't leave the house without having a shower. Although part of him wouldn't have minded going unwashed – he was convinced he could still smell her on his skin – hygiene prevailed. It seemed to take for ever and he was sure there would be a text from Susan or even a missed call but there was nothing. Of course it was more than possible that she was still asleep herself, despite her instructions to call over early. And ten o'clock was still early for a Sunday. He dressed quickly, ran his fingers through his hair and left the flat.

He hadn't been this excited visiting Charlotte Avenue

since Christmas morning when he was eight. He kept checking his phone but there still hadn't been a reply by the time he was walking up the path and ringing the bell at number 9.

He was greeted by a dressing-gown clad Marianne. 'Well, hello!' she said, folding her arms and leaning a hip against the door jamb. 'What brings you here so early?'

'I was looking for Susan. Is she up?'

'Oh, she's up all right but she's a little busy.'

'Oh?'

'Yeah,' she said, stepping onto the path and pulling the door to behind her. 'You'll never guess who called here this morning.'

Something went sour in Gavin's stomach.

'Who?' he asked flatly.

'Her old boyfriend, Paul. I knew it wasn't all finished there.'

'Oh . . . Paul.'

'Yes, she's in there with him now. They're "having it out".'

'I'm sure that's just their business.'

'Oh, I know, but I couldn't help overhearing a little. You won't believe this – it turns out the reason she and Paul broke up is because she slept with someone else! The best man at their friends' wedding. The best man! Can you believe it!'

Gavin didn't respond.

'That's just so typical of Susan, though. She's always the one lecturing people and giving out advice and being so high and fucking mighty.'

Gavin still couldn't find any words.

'But the best part is that he's in there forgiving her! He doesn't mind, he wants to start again. He wants to buy a house, for God's sake. She sleeps with a guy at a wedding and he wants to buy her a house!'

The colour had drained from Gavin's face and there was a muddy film over his eyes.

'I think I'd better go,' he said, his voice barely audible. 'Tell Susan I called.'

'Here they come,' said Marianne, opening the door wide. 'You can talk to her yourself.'

Marianne stood back against the door, her arms still folded, and revealed a startled Susan standing in the hall. Seconds later, a man appeared behind her.

'Oh God, Gavin!'

He looked at her just long enough for her to know that he knew. His look and Marianne's smug face told her everything.

'Gavin!'

It was too late. He was already halfway down the path. By the time she got to the gate it was rattling on its hinges.

'Gavin, stop, please. Let me explain.'

It was pointless; he was long out of earshot. All she could do was head for his flat and hope that he would be there. And hope that he would listen to her.

He didn't answer his buzzer and she had to wait for ages outside his building before she got in. She rang the bell to his flat; she knocked on the door; she called out his name.

'Gavin, please. Please let me explain. Don't believe whatever Marianne said to you. Listen to me, please.'

Eventually she heard the latch rising. He opened the door. His lips were blue and his eyes rimmed with red.

'Please, Gavin, let me come in and explain.'

He turned and she followed him in. He remained standing in the middle of the living room, his hands thrust into his pockets.

Susan swallowed. 'I don't know what Marianne said.'

'She said you fucked the best man at your friend's wedding. She said that was why you and Paul broke up. Not because he had cheated on you.'

'He wasn't the b— It was a mistake. I —'

'You lied to me!'

'I didn't lie to you. It was . . . I was going to tell you.'

'You lied to me!'

'I didn't mean to. I just . . . I didn't want you to think . . . last night wasn't the time.'

'You could have told me before last night.'

'I . . .'

'And so Paul wants to buy a house?'

'He's got some money from his parents. He wants me to move back to Dublin and have an — but none of that matters. Paul's not the problem, he just . . . I needed to finish things with him properly. I . . . I owed him that. It's just bad timing.'

'It's bad timing all right.'

'He was just there on the doorstep. I had to talk to him.'

'I don't care about Paul.'

'Oh.'

Gavin had been pacing the room. He paused now and buried his face in his hands.

'How could you not be straight with me?'

'I would have told you.'

'But you didn't.'

'I was going to.'

He started pacing the room again. He stopped several

times as if to say something, but the words wouldn't come out.

'I can't be with someone who can lie that easily,' he said eventually.

'Gavin! Don't say that!'

'Look . . . I thought last night . . . Last night was . . .'

'Last night was amazing. I love you! I love you so much.' She tried to make him look at her. 'Nothing has changed.'

'Everything has changed!'

'Don't say that. Please, Gavin, look at me!'

He shrugged her off. 'Leave me alone!'

Susan took a deep breath.

'Look, that whole thing at the wedding was stupid and foolish, and I shouldn't have done it and I definitely shouldn't have lied about it. But I was ashamed. I'd never done anything like that before. It was all part of . . . I was just realizing that I really didn't want to be with Paul any more. It was just mistake after mistake and I wanted to run away from it all and pretend it had never happened. Everybody makes mistakes.'

'I don't care any more, Susan. I can't trust you.'

'You *can* trust me. You can!' She was fighting back the tears. 'You *can* trust me. It's one mistake. I would never do that again. I would never do that to you. You must know that.'

He turned suddenly, meeting her eyes full on. 'It's not what you did. Of course everybody makes mistakes. I didn't think you were a nun.'

'What then?'

'I . . .'

'What?!'

'I've been lied to my whole life!' he flashed. 'Last night I thought for the first time . . .'

'But I would have told you.'

266

'It doesn't matter now.'

Susan steadied herself against the side of the couch.

'Gavin, did you mean anything you said last night? Are you going to throw me away for something I did when I didn't even know you?'

'I can't trust you.'

'Don't keep saying that. It's not true.'

'I . . . just can't.'

'So is this it?'

'Yes.'

'Please, Gavin. Don't.'

'I think you should go.'

'Gavin, no.'

The tears were rolling down her cheeks.

'It was a mistake,' he said. 'We were a mistake. You should go and buy your house with Paul. I have nothing to give you.'

'Gavin!'

He pried her fingers from his arm and placed her on the couch. Then he walked out, leaving her in convulsions in the middle of his own living room.

It was some time before Susan became aware that she was alone. She remained bundled on the couch, collapsing periodically into a crying mess. She couldn't believe this had happened. She had been here, in this very spot, only hours before, making love to the man she believed she would be with for ever. When she got into bed with that guy at the wedding she had thought she might be doing something to jeopardize her relationship with Paul – she had no idea she might be jeopardizing a future relationship too. Up to now, she hadn't truly regretted that night. She believed it had performed an important function in helping her figure out what she really wanted, but now she wished it had never happened.

She was truly taken aback when she opened the door to Paul that morning. Apart from that one chance meeting in the pub, she hadn't seen him since the night she left. She'd heard the doorbell when she was in her room and had practically galloped down the stairs, presuming, of course, that it was Gavin. For a split second it didn't register with her that it wasn't him and her high-intensity smile remained on her face.

He spouted some guff about text messages and the early bird catching the worm – she had to do a major mental readjustment before she was able to comprehend anything he was saying. She had been imagining diving onto Gavin and dragging him upstairs for an illicit pre-breakfast snog. Now she was facing the man whose very existence she had chosen to forget. He looked different. Perhaps he had lost weight, or perhaps it was simply that she hadn't seen him in a long time. When was the last time that she had really looked at him anyway?

She'd brought him into the dining room – she couldn't very well leave him on the doorstep – but she was immediately consumed with the same sense of panic she'd had on her very first morning in Charlotte Avenue. How could she be back here again? And how could he possibly think that she wanted to listen to anything he had to say?

'I wanted to talk to you,' he said, taking up a position at the far side of the room.

'Yes, I think you mentioned that in one of your texts.'

'I still think we can make a go of it.'

'Oh, Paul, I –'

'No, no, hear me out. Please, do me the courtesy of hearing me out.'

'But I –'

'Please!'

What could she do but stand there and listen?

'I went to my parents,' he began, 'and I put it to them that they might give us a loan. They have some money put by and a house would be a very good investment. But I think we should move back to Dublin. Limerick doesn't suit us. I'm up for another promotion soon, and you could easily get your old job back, or another one. What do you think? With my parents' money we could buy a house in Bray or closer even, if prices drop a bit more. We could be set up. We could have the life we used to have.'

'Oh, Paul . . . we're not getting back together.'

'Why? Why not? Give me one good reason why not.'

'You know why not.'

'We were always good together, Susan.'

'No, we weren't.'

'Come on, I've never stopped loving you.'

'I don't think you do love me.'

'That's a horrible thing to say. I've always loved you.'

'I don't know. Maybe we have different ideas of love.'

'I think you still love me.'

'How can you think that?!'

'I think you do.'

'Have you forgotten that I cheated on you? That I went off and slept with the bridesmaid's boyfriend at our best friends' wedding!'

Susan didn't realize she was shouting.

'I told you I forgave you for that.'

'I don't want your forgiveness, Paul. We were never meant to be together.'

'There were good times.'

'No, there weren't. There just weren't any bad times.'

'Oh, for God's sake, Susan, what do you expect?'

'I expect . . . I expect – Look, you should know that I've met somebody else. And I'm happy. I'm very happy. So, you see, I know the difference. What we had wasn't . . . well, it wasn't for me.'

Paul put his hands on his hips and surveyed the ceiling.

'Fair enough so. It was worth a try.'

'I'm sorry, Paul, I should have told you this months ago.'

'Yes, you should've.'

Susan sat on the edge of a chair. She was exhausted. She hadn't been prepared for this. She looked at Paul now, still standing with his hands on his hips, and she wondered how she had ever spent so much of her life with him. Only the thought of Gavin and what he meant to her kept her from despairing.

'Right so,' he said, 'I think I'll go.'

'Right. I'm sorry, Paul.'

He was about to walk straight past her but some impulse made him stop and hold the door open for her. She got up and walked through. That was when she saw Gavin.

There was nothing for it now but to walk out of his flat for ever. She contemplated waiting for him to come back – but what was the point? He didn't want to know. Nothing she could say would make any difference; she couldn't alter the past. And it was all her fault. She believed him when he said it wasn't what she had done that was the problem, but the fact that she hadn't told him. And she *had* lied. She hadn't wanted to see herself as the slightly slutty cheating kind. It was much easier to blame Paul than to take responsibility for what she had done. But it wasn't that terrible, surely?

She wasn't proud of it, obviously. She didn't want her mother, or anybody, to know, but surely other people had done worse? She had thought she could just wipe it from her memory and move on.

Oh, Gavin . . . If she'd known she would eventually meet him she would never have had sex with anyone. He was *so* worth waiting for.

He was every inch the fantasy she had first seen from her bedroom window when she arrived at Charlotte Avenue. Gavin – quiet, gentle, self-deprecating Gavin – who would have guessed that he was an Adonis? She had never seen anything more desirable than his naked body. She was consumed by love and desire for this man and with every passing second her feelings were amplified. He had touched her expertly, given her pleasure so intense she'd had to scream out loud; it had been the most stimulating and exciting sex she had ever had. It was, she'd realized, as she lay on the floor, his head resting on her belly, the first time she'd had sex with a man she loved.

She pulled herself from the couch and walked out of Gavin's flat.

She couldn't think beyond the necessity of putting one foot in front of the other but if there was anything she knew she didn't want, it was to see Marianne standing in the doorway of Charlotte Avenue. She wanted to kill her, to actually murder her with her bare hands, but she didn't have the fight for it. She was much too sad. Yet there she was, as if she'd never lifted her hip from the door jamb, her dressing gown still wrapped round her like a gossipy housewife's, barring the way to her bedroom, her only conceivable refuge at the moment.

'Just don't say a word.'

Susan tried to convey in her tone how much she didn't want to engage with her sister.

'Oh, why so glum? Did Gavin tell you off for being a slut?'

'Shut up.'

'Oh, for God's sake! Stop being so melodramatic. What does Gavin care anyway?'

'Just shut up!'

'What's the big deal? You're the one keeping secrets.'

'Marianne . . . would you just . . .'

And then it dawned on Marianne. Something in her sister's tear-stained face, in the shocking deadness of her eyes, gave the truth away.

'Oh! Oh. You mean . . . you and Gavin . . .?'

'Don't go there, Marianne. Just don't go there.'

'How was I supposed to know? Did he –'

'I don't care any more.'

'Look, Suze, I'm sorry, I didn't mean to –'

'Oh no! This is exactly the kind of thing you live for! For once in my pathetic life I find something . . .'

Susan wasn't able to finish the sentence.

'I had no idea there was something happening between you. Honestly if I'd known I'd never have –'

'Just save it, Marianne.'

'Let me explain to him –'

'Don't you dare say another word! Not to him! Not to me! Not ever!'

Susan climbed the stairs, blind with tears, and threw herself on the bed. That's it, she thought, my life is over. It would have suited her to black out and not wake up until the pain in her chest was gone, but she couldn't even close her eyes for a second without seeing his face, red and contorted, eyeing her with revulsion. She got up and went to the window where the only thing she could see was his figure, lost inside a waxed jacket, and his glance that, very briefly, on that first morning, had swung upwards, to her.

When the doorbell rang once again sometime later, neither Susan nor Marianne was anywhere to be seen. Felicity, who had stayed in the kitchen having a prolonged breakfast with Angela while trying to piece together a picture of what had taken place so far that morning, was on the verge of not answering when Angela suggested she see who was at the door.

'You never know who it might be,' she said. 'At my time of life, it's better not to ignore a call to the door.'

So Felicity sauntered through the hall, convinced that it was most likely a Mormon or a Jehovah's Witness.

He wasn't clean-cut enough for a Mormon and he looked a bit too normal for a Witness. Either he was lost, or she had completely lost her knack for sizing people up at a glance.

'Hello,' he said somewhat formally, 'I'm not sure if I have the right house. I'm looking for Marianne O'Regan. I was told she might be here.'

'Marianne O'Regan?'

'Yeah, ahm . . . I'm looking for her.'

'Oh yes? And who might you be, if you don't mind me asking?'

'Me? Oh no, no . . . ahm . . . I'm Eoin.'

'Eoin?'

'Eoin Connolly. I'm ah . . . I'm Marianne's husband.'

25

Felicity couldn't help staring. She wasn't entirely mistaken in her initial assessment – he certainly was a bit lost, but he did seem fairly normal. He definitely wasn't a Mormon – the baggy jeans and zippered cardigan, the scruffy jaw and unruly hair were not those of a missionary, yet there was something very polite about him. He had waited to be asked in, then waited to be told to go through to the kitchen. He waited again to be told to sit down, which he did only after shaking hands with Angela. She, meanwhile, was still looking at Felicity as if to enquire why she had asked the window cleaner in for a visit.

'Granny,' she said gravely, 'this is Eoin, Eoin Connolly. Eoin says he's Marianne's husband.'

'What, love?'

'I'm sorry,' she said, turning to Eoin, 'if we appear a bit odd. It's just that, as far as we knew, Marianne didn't have a husband.'

'Yeah, Marianne didn't want anyone to know. She said it wasn't anybody else's business.'

'That certainly sounds like our Marianne.'

'I'm a little lost,' said Angela. 'Are you trying to tell me that this is Marianne's husband?'

'That's right, Gran.'

'I'm sorry for the intrusion, Mrs O'Regan, and I'm sorry you weren't invited to the wedding – there wasn't much of a wedding to speak of – but I'm wrecked with worry over Marianne.' He paused. 'Is she here?'

'Look, Eoin,' said Felicity, 'you'll have to bear with us. We really have no idea who you are, and until we talk to Marianne herself – I'm not saying she's here now – you'll have to understand that we're not going to just . . . I mean, we have *no* idea . . .'

'Look, I know, I know. But maybe you'd just tell her I'm here, that I'm worried sick about her.'

'We can tell her that.'

'I never – it's not a case of – if that's what you're thinking . . .'

'I'm not thinking anything. We'll tell her. OK?'

'OK.'

He was just getting up to leave when Marianne herself walked through the kitchen door. She did a noticeable double take and then turned to walk back out again, but when Eoin called her name, she stopped. Felicity spoke.

'Marianne, we'll do whatever you want us to do. Eoin was just leaving.'

She turned round.

'It's OK,' she said, 'maybe you'd leave us alone for a while.'

'Whatever you want, hon, we'll just be in the living room.'

'Thanks.'

Felicity and Angela shuffled out the door. As soon as they were gone Marianne collapsed into her husband's arms and burst into tears.

It had all started a long time ago. Or at least it seemed a very long time ago now. She had met him during her very first week in Cork. He was a friend of Lorna's – the girl whose floor she was crashing on. An old boyfriend, in fact, but he'd remained a friend because 'he was like the boy next door I never had'. (Lorna was more into men who would make her cry than men who would see her home safely from the pub.) Marianne and Eoin were instantly attracted.

Marianne's modus operandi with men was simple. If she liked a guy, but felt that she was in some way inferior to him, she backed off immediately. It didn't matter if she thought he was a god sent from a Hollywood blockbuster; if she felt she couldn't hold her own with him, she simply moved on.

If, on the other hand, she felt that she was smarter, nicer-looking, further travelled – better in any minor way – then she went in for the kill. She was hard to resist when she was in attack mode. She was very predatory – she thought nothing of going straight up to a guy she'd barely met to tell him he had a fine arse – but she rarely came across as rude or vulgar. She had charm, and because she picked her targets, she had the confidence that she wouldn't be entirely rebuffed. So she went through men pretty easily. She liked variety and wasn't afraid of change. As soon as she detected that the honeymoon phase was coming to an end, she found a new target. Nobody ever got hurt; nobody ever took her seriously. She was great fun to be with in the short to medium term; nobody expected anything more.

Eoin saw right through her. He saw that she was masking her extreme vulnerability in the belief that she was invincible. He saw that she didn't have a clue what would make her happy. He saw that despite appearances, she was a woman desperate to grow up.

And she hadn't been able to fathom him. She couldn't tell if she was 'better' than him or not, she wasn't able to put him in a box, but for the first time she didn't feel the need for her usual games. She liked him – he made her feel comfortable, he made her laugh, he was nice to her – and very soon she found that he had become an organic part of her life. Ever before there had been Marianne – and there had been Marianne's latest boyfriend. Now there was simply Marianne and Eoin.

'I think you're like that onion,' she said to him one day.

'What onion?'

'You know, when people go on about people being like onions because they have loads of layers. Well, I think you're like that. I keep on peeling off another bit and there's another stinking layer underneath.'

'I'll give you stinking layers . . .'

By the time Eoin asked her to marry him Marianne had already been thinking that she could stay with this guy for a while.

Eoin wasn't foolish. He wasn't suffering from the illusion that Marianne was one of those girls who'd spent her childhood draping a net curtain over her head. Nor had he been one of those boys who'd felt that there was status to be had in a wife and all the trappings. He was simply head over heels in love with her and he wanted to keep her. He knew that proposing to a girl like Marianne might be the surest way to send her packing, but he also had a suspicion that it might be the very thing she'd agree to.

'Why don't we get married?' he said casually, as they were climbing Patrick's Hill one freezing day in December.

'Get married?' she said, without any surprise. 'What kind of a thing is that to say?'

'I thought it would be nice. You and me – Mr and Mrs.'

'You're having a laugh.'

'I'm not, you know.'

'Yeah, well, I don't believe in marriage. Marriage is only for people who are afraid of dying alone.'

'There's nothing great about dying alone.'

'Women live longer than men, so I'd end up dying alone anyway.'

'I thought you weren't afraid of that . . .'

'So you want to marry me for purely selfish reasons?'

'They're not all selfish. I want to look after you. Until I die first and leave you alone, of course.'

'Oh, great! But I don't need looking after, thanks very much. And besides you haven't even got a job.'

'Actually, I do have a job. I got one yesterday. I'm going to work in Carl's restaurant, as a chef.'

'As a chef?'

'Yeah. I did a cheffing course in college – well, six months of it.'

'You've never cooked me anything nice.'

'I cook for you all the time!'

'Yeah, but it's not nice! Not restaurant nice.'

'It fucking is! Anyway, the restaurant isn't nice. But that's beside the point. I think I might be able to keep you in the manner to which you've become accustomed.'

'Thanks a bunch!'

She didn't dismiss it though. For the next few days she couldn't think about anything else. She knew he was serious; the way he joked about it convinced her he was serious. Even though she had never imagined she would get married – it was so bourgeois, so conformist, so dull, so meaningless, *so* the death of good sex – all of a sudden the idea of being married to Eoin started to appeal to her. She began to see why people did this. It wasn't always for the big dress and the huge party and the expensive presents and the big mad 'look at me' walk up the aisle. Sometimes it really was because two people desperately wanted to be together and somehow getting a piece of paper made their chances of survival a little more likely.

So she agreed.

'OK,' she said three days later as they were walking home from the cinema.

'OK what?' he said.

'OK, let's get married.'

'OK.'

He stopped and kissed her. He backed her up against the wall of the Moderne and kissed her for a full two minutes and Marianne experienced a moment of absolute bliss.

Naturally, though, if they were going to do something as middle class as get married, they couldn't possibly tell anyone about it. Eoin wanted to tell the world, even if he didn't particularly want to buy them dinner, but he understood Marianne's issues with the whole thing.

'We can't go asking all your family if none of mine is going to be there,' she said, 'and I just couldn't face the look on my family's faces. They'd all think they *know* me, that I'm just like them, that I'm boring and stupid and –'

'It's OK. It can be quiet. I don't have much family anyway. Let's just pick two friends and leave it at that.'

'That'd be great. I mean, it's not about anybody else anyway, is it?'

'It's about nobody but us, girl.'

So they chose Lorna, and a friend of Eoin's he'd known for years. They went to city hall and in under twenty-five minutes they were married. Afterwards, the four of them went to Gruffalos and had pizza and three bottles of Prosecco. For dessert, they each had a chocolate brownie, and in the middle of the table a plastic bride and groom presided, until Marianne decided to throw it out the window for luck. Their guests were keen to continue the night in the Broken Inn, but the bride and groom insisted on going home. They had a marriage to consummate, after all, and besides, they had no interest in anything or anyone other than each other.

And that was pretty much how it remained for nearly a year. Eoin worked in Carl's restaurant and paid the rent. Marianne worked on and off whenever she felt like it and managed not to add to her debts, but did nothing to try and clear them. The debt issue had crept up on her. She wasn't a spendthrift, she didn't have expensive tastes, but when you refuse to work for any dedicated length of time, while spending as if you are steadily earning slightly above the average industrial wage, and when credit cards and other forms of finance are so easy to obtain, it's not hard to rack up a little debt. By the time she left Cork, she owed an accumulated sum of twenty-two thousand euro. Not a shocking amount of money, but the interest was rising sharply and she had no obvious means of repaying any of it. It didn't bother her hugely. It had never bothered her at all before, but now that she was with Eoin and everything between them was so good, she felt she should perhaps do something about paying off what she owed. She owed *him* that. She had only intended tapping Angela for a few small loans, but there was such a bloody palaver about cheques and ATM machines that it seemed easier to sell off a little of the junk. Granny was clearly happy to help her – what difference did it make if she cleared out her cupboards at the same time?

Besides, by the time Marianne came to Limerick, she had a lot more than a little debt on her mind.

*

'It's OK,' he said, stroking her hair, and kissing her cheek.

She continued to bury her face in his neck and sob pitifully.

'It's all right, girl, it's all right. No need to be so upset. I'm just glad I found you.'

'I'm sorry,' she said, eventually. 'I'm sorry I ran away.'

'Well, I've found you now. What made you run away? I was in bits with worry.'

'I should have told you.'

'Told me what?'

She was sobbing again and her breath began to convulse.

'Oh, Eoin, I should have told you. But I was so excited, you see, I was so excited at first.'

'What are you saying, love?'

'I thought I was pregnant. Well, I was pregnant – for a while. At first I wasn't excited – I mean, like before I knew for definite. At first I thought it was a really bad idea. I never in my life thought that being pregnant would be a good idea.'

'It's OK, love, it's OK. Tell me what happened.'

'But then it began to grow on me, you know? And I began thinking what you might say. Cos we'd never talked about it. But I thought you'd probably be pleased and then I did a test and it was sort of – faded. So I did another one and it was definitely stronger but I still wasn't absolutely sure. But then two days later . . .'

'It's all right, love. If you want to have a baby, we'll have a baby. I'd love to have a baby. I don't know why you had to run away, though. You wrecked my head.'

'I know. I don't know why. I just . . . ran.'

'You fuckin' eejit.'

'I know.'

They smiled at each other.

'So how'd you find me?'

'With great fuckin' difficulty!'

'Sorry. I didn't think I wanted to be found. I think I thought it was over.'

'Why would you think it was over? Aren't we married?'

'Sure, I don't know. I wasn't thinking straight.'

'Come 'ere,' he said. 'I presume you have a bed here. Let's go upstairs and have a lie-down. Your granny can't say a word to us seeing as we're married.'

'All right. That sounds like a good idea.'

As Marianne was guided upstairs by her husband she realized how glad she was that she'd been found. Why had she thought that it was all over, just because she got her period a week and a half late? Two weeks before that day she hadn't thought for one second about having a baby, so why was it such a disaster when it was clear that she wasn't going to have one? Had the intervening few days made such a difference? And why hadn't she just told Eoin what had happened, shared with him the thoughts that had been running through her head instead of packing a bag and heading for the hills?

She'd panicked, of course. She'd had a reaction to everything that had been happening over the last year. She had come so far in so short a time: she was settled, she was married, she was happy, she was all the things she never thought she'd be, and now she was also going to have a baby. It was only when one of those things was taken away that the whole picture collapsed. That couldn't possibly be her; that couldn't possibly be her life. Something was wrong and her only instinct was to run. She had no experience in talking over her problems. She had no background in facing issues full on and she certainly had no practice in sharing her deepest fears with someone who believed their only role was to make life better for her. It was easier to go back to what she knew and assume she was on her own.

It was only when she heard Eoin's voice in the kitchen and realized that he'd come for her that it began to click. She wasn't alone any more. Eoin was going to be there for all the bad times as well as the good times. She didn't have to pretend that she didn't need him. He really *did* know her and, despite everything he knew, he loved her. Oh, she had always known that her parents loved her and that Angela loved her and that her sisters, in their way, loved her too, but that was obligation. You had to love your daughter or else you were some kind of monster. With Eoin it was different; he had chosen her and it was clear that he wasn't going to wash his hands of her and tell her she was a contrary madam who insisted on making life hard for herself. As she nestled against him now, as chaste as a child, she began to truly understand what it meant to be married.

It was nearly a quarter to two when Angela began clearing away the breakfast things. She had checked on Marianne and Eoin (discreetly) a few minutes earlier and found them sound asleep. She really was a ticket. A husband no less! And her mother down there in Ballyconnell wondering if she'd ever marry any of them off. Well, she never lost it, anyway. Suddenly all the money stuff made sense too – not that Angela thought Marianne's debts were anything to do with a fancy wedding, but she could understand how she was finally beginning to take a little responsibility for her life. In Marianne's book, borrowing from Peter to pay Paul was a step in the right direction, especially if Peter was your granny and not likely to send in the bailiffs.

She sat down to gather the crumbs from the table with the side of an envelope. Well, the 'husband' seemed all right. In fact he seemed to be a lovely sort of fella. The way he'd held her and calmed her down was reassuring to see. Perhaps this whole marriage business would be good for her. Angela smiled to herself. The times move on but so much remains exactly the same.

She remembered when Frank came home with his wife, Gavin's mother. He'd been working in Dublin as an electrical engineer since leaving college, spending about one weekend in three in Limerick. While a lot of his time went catching up with old friends, he always devoted a good part of the weekend to hanging out with his old ma. He used to tell her bits from the office – like who was in line for the chop, or who had got a pretty new secretary, or what they all had to eat when they were taken out on the company dollar. She loved hearing him talk, it didn't really matter what he said, it was the blas he'd put on it for her.

And then he stopped talking about the office and when she complained that she wasn't getting her fix of her 'Dublin soap' he'd say there really wasn't that much going on, or wasn't it about time he actually did some work in that place instead of gossiping about it all the time.

Shortly afterwards he began talking about a move back to Limerick, which delighted her, of course. She was a little surprised, as he'd never mentioned the notion before, and he seemed to be having such a good time up there, but he was entitled to a whim, particularly one that brought him closer to home.

But when he finally did move back, she realized pretty quickly that there wasn't anything whimsical about it.

She'd known about the job for some time – a big post with the ESB in Ardnacrusha, that he was very lucky to get, apparently. He'd also mentioned buying a house, a nice spacious four-bedroom house with a big back garden not too far from her on the South Circular Road. It was clear, therefore, that he had some notion of settling down, but she'd no idea how soon. It was about a month before he was due to start the job that he first brought Grace home.

Angela would never forget the first time she met her. She knew they were coming – he'd simply said that he was bringing a girl for her to meet – so she watched them walk up the path together. Grace was wearing a cream-coloured wool coat that stopped just above her knees, with matching low-heeled court shoes. She held a bag over one arm and wore a scarf tied loosely at her neck. Angela's initial impression was that Frank had nabbed himself a film star. As they came closer, she could see that Grace's hair, which was blowing in the April wind, was probably not quite as blonde as it seemed, though there was nothing artificial in the way it swept along her cheek and down to her shoulders. And once she opened the door to them, Angela could see instantly in her calming blue eyes and her soft pink mouth that this was a woman she could like. She couldn't fully dismiss the film-star thing – there was something endlessly glamorous about Grace – but she came across as open and as guileless as a child.

'Hello, Mrs O'Regan,' she said immediately, 'it's lovely to meet you.'

'Hello, dear,' Angela said, holding out her hand. 'It's lovely to meet you too.'

Angela was relieved. She knew that she *ought* to like a girl that Frank brought home, she knew she would *try* to like a girl that Frank brought home, but she had no guarantee at all that she *would* like a girl that Frank brought home. For Grace was the first. There might have been other girls, other short-lived dalliances, but this was the first time that the girl had merited an introduction to his old ma. And it wasn't just Grace herself that she liked, it wasn't simply that she was warm and bright and chatty, it was the way her son, clearly, was completely in love with her. He adored her. Now, Angela wasn't one to classify adoration as a priority in a relationship, in fact she believed that most relationships would get on better without it, but Frank's attraction to Grace seemed to be a fairly solid thing. As for Grace's feelings for Frank, Angela didn't doubt them for a second. Naturally, as his adoring mother she considered him to be the best catch in Ireland and that any girl would be hugely fortunate to get him, but at least it looked as if Grace understood this as well.

By the end of that first visit Angela was happy that her son would soon be settling down with such a nice girl. She hadn't pried into their plans, she'd taken it for granted that when Frank moved down for his job, they'd get engaged and she'd move down as soon as they were married.

The next time Frank visited, he came alone. That's when he told her the rest.

'I've something to tell you, Ma,' he'd said after they'd spent a morning tending his father's grave. 'I don't think you'll have a problem with it because you're a sensible woman, but I just want you to know.'

'What is it, love?'

A few scenarios ran through Angela's brain; she didn't manage to come up with one that would present a real problem.

'It's about Grace.'

Of course it was about Grace.

'What about her?'

'I think you know how I feel about her.'

286

'I think I do.'

'I've already asked her to marry me.'

'Have you? Well, I'm delighted!'

'Thanks, Ma. And it's going to happen, no matter what.'

'No matter what?'

'She has a baby. He's over one now. She had him with – well, that doesn't matter. Obviously it didn't work out, and we've been together for some time now. I love her and I love her son and I'm going to marry her.' He looked his mother fully in the eye. 'I just want to have your blessing.'

'Well, son,' Angela said. 'You have it. A pretty girl like her can easily get into trouble, I suppose, and I'm happy for you to get her out of it . . . just as long as she really is the one you want.'

'Oh, she is, Ma, she is.'

'Well, then, bring her down to me so I can congratulate her properly.'

'Thanks, Ma. She's a wonderful girl, you know, she was taken adv– She's really very . . . You're sure you don't think any the less of her?'

'Of course I don't. And if anyone else wants to think otherwise they'll have me to deal with!'

Angela smiled. The only one who ever had an issue with Grace was Maureen. At the time she was barely Tom's girlfriend, but seemed to consider herself the future head of the O'Regan household. She'd let her feelings be known to Tom who was gormless enough to pass them on to his mother. Angela had made it very clear that Grace was like a daughter and if anyone thought otherwise they'd better keep it quiet if they had any notion of becoming a daughter themselves.

Of course the deal was sealed when Gavin appeared.

The very next weekend Grace came down for the official engagement visit and brought her fifteen-month-old son with her. Angela fell in love immediately. He was a small, round bundle of absolute perfection. She knew it was completely daft, but he reminded her of Frank at that age. He had the same blue eyes and the same roguish grin. It suited her to simply believe he was Frank's and leave it at that. And that's how it had always been.

She took a walk upstairs again and found Felicity ironing her clothes in her room – she was finally on her way back to London – and after knocking on Susan's door a couple of times had to walk away assuming she'd gone back to sleep.

'All quiet,' she said to herself, 'all peaceful, for the moment.'

26

Felicity breathed a sigh of relief. It was good to be home. The bright spaciousness of her apartment felt like clean mountain air after the heady atmosphere of Charlotte Avenue. She'd loved being at her grandmother's, but it was time to move on. Besides, the house was far too crowded now that Eoin had moved in (albeit temporarily), and living with Susan at the moment (although she loved her sister dearly) was a little too intense to be relaxing.

Poor Susan. Felicity had had no idea her feelings were so strong. Through a sustained bout of weeping and wailing she had managed to extract from her most of what had happened, but she was at a loss as to what to advise. Of course Gavin was behaving irrationally, but what could she do? In fairness, Susan was being as stoical as she could about the whole thing. 'He's the only man I've ever loved,' she said calmly the following day. 'The only man I will ever love, but he's gone. I just have to get used to that.' Then she'd gone upstairs and cried for an hour, but an hour later she was composed enough to help Felicity with her packing. Poor Susan.

Felicity had chanced calling to Gavin herself to see if she could persuade him to listen to Susan one more time, but he seemed to have gone to ground. She called twice to the flat without getting an answer and on her third attempt she noticed a For Sale sign on number 7.

Angela got a note from him to say he was sorry about the gardening but he had to go away for a while and that he'd be in touch. And that was it. That was all Susan had to keep her going.

Felicity took her suitcase into the bedroom and began to unpack. She opened the travel shopping bag first. She'd hardly worn any make-up the whole time she was away and what she had worn had been borrowed from Susan, so she needed a new supply. She opened the boxes and placed the day and night creams on her dressing table along with the light-reflecting foundation, the highlighting concealer, and the compact that contained three lipsticks, four eyeshadows, a mascara and a blusher. She would have fun tomorrow, painting her face, preparing herself, once again, for the battlefield. The cleanser and toner she placed by her bed along with a packet of cotton pads. It had always been a nightly ritual with her – she would pour enough of the cleanser onto the pad to just cover it and then massage the creamy emulsion into her skin until all the grime of the day was removed. Then she would repeat the process with the toner until her skin looked and felt like new again. She hadn't kept it up while she'd been away – somehow it had seemed unnecessary. What was there, after all, in Charlotte Avenue to make her feel dirty?

All her clothes she threw into the wash. She wouldn't be wearing any of these again for a while. Even for lounge wear, she fancied, she might go a bit formal. The laid-back, grungy look didn't suit her temperament, especially when she had something to prove.

She opened her wardrobe and surveyed the lines of suits and shirts, all as they had returned from the dry cleaner. All as she had left them. She reached out and touched the fabric of one, and knew immediately that it was her mid-brown Gérard Darel – the one with the tiny buttons along the pockets and the fluted edging on the cuff. She usually wore it with her white Missoni blouse – there it was, between the crazy multi-coloured Whistle's top that was perfect inside her grey Paul Costelloe, and the cream Ralph Lauren that went with everything. She touched another one – her black Marina Avram that doubled so well as evening wear – and another one – her moss green Quin & Donnelly that was really a bit dated now, but she couldn't get rid of it because it was what she wore the first time she made a killing for the company. Oh, it was good to be back! To know that she'd be setting her alarm for six the following morning. To know that she'd be climbing into one of these killer suits after her shower and that once she had her make-up on, she'd once again be the woman she thought she'd lost.

And now she was back. She'd contacted Sony the day after her date with Mark. She'd felt foolish as she dialled the number. Not because of the manner of her leaving, but because, if she'd only played it right, she might have got back in without too much damage done. That was impossible now. If only she'd been able to gather herself together when Sandra told her they weren't happy with Tony's management, she might have had a shot at getting her old job back. Now she'd be lucky if she didn't end up being charged with fraud. (Who would believe that Tony's right-hand man hadn't been involved in leaking the information?)

All she could do was present herself, her knowledge, her experience and her good name, and place them at their mercy.

She chose her gun-metal Vivienne Westwood. A conservative suit by Vivienne's standards certainly, and even more so when paired with a plain crisp white shirt, but there was enough of the brilliant libertine poking through the lining to give Felicity the verve she needed. She hoped.

27

Meanwhile, Charlotte Avenue had imploded – Maureen had arrived.

Curiously it was Maureen who had first contacted Eoin. When he set about looking for his wife he, naturally, came to Limerick and spent quite a few days walking the streets in the hope that he might simply bump into her. It was obvious after a while that wasn't going to work. He had absolutely no contacts for her, so eventually he went back to Cork. Lorna wasn't any help either; all she knew was that Marianne was from Limerick. Then Eoin had a stroke of genius – he looked up Marianne's last name in the phone book. And there it was: O'Regan, Thomas and Maureen, 53 Rosedale Drive, Clareview. So back he came to Limerick.

But there was nobody home. He tried for several days, but still nobody answered his knock. He could tell the neighbours were beginning to get suspicious, so on his fourth visit he told Martina Phelan next door (or Mar P as she was known to her neighbours) that he was an old college friend of Marianne's and he was trying to look her up. Mar could only pass on the information that Tom and Maureen were at their summer home in Ballyconnell and that she had no idea when they would be coming back. (Now, it had been rankling with Mar, for some time, that she not only had never received an invite to the Ballyconnell house, but that she didn't even know where the house was. 'Maureen has such notions,' she'd said to her husband every evening for a fortnight, 'as if I'd be down there knocking on her door. As if I have any interest, high up nor low down, in her precious holiday home.') So all she could do for poor Eoin (who came across as helpless but utterly harmless) was take his number and agree to pass it on to Maureen when she next saw her.

Which happened to be some considerable time later, when Mar popped out to Ennis for a bit of shopping, and bumped into Maureen herself in Chez Marie. So Mar passed on Eoin's number and that was how Maureen had her first conversation with her son-in-law. He seemed like a very nice boy, so Maureen saw no harm in letting him know that Marianne was staying with her granny in Charlotte Avenue.

When Susan's call came through about Marianne selling off Angela's antiques, Maureen didn't know what to think. She was inclined to believe it was all a bit of a misunderstanding, but Tom knew better what their daughter was capable of. When that was followed by another call from Angela telling her that Eoin wasn't just some random admirer (of whom, Maureen believed, her favourite daughter must have several) but an actual husband, an actual relation of her own, and when she heard further about the miscarriage and then the business with Susan and Gavin, she simply had to get on that dual carriageway and see what her family was coming to.

She arrived in a flurry of concern and condemnation. As a mother she was concerned that her family was falling to pieces; as the notional head of the household she was highly critical of the way everything had been handled.

'Mum!' wailed Marianne as soon as her mother appeared at the door.

'Marianne,' she said, without returning her daughter's fervour.

'Mum!' she wailed again. 'It's been terrible.'

'Marianne, I'm not at all happy with what I've been hearing.'

'Oh, Mum! Everything just got a little bit out of hand.'

'Let's have a chat about it and we'll see what we can do.'

'How are you, Ma?' asked Tom genially as he squeezed through the door behind his wife and made his way to the kitchen where Angela was standing, calmly observing the scene.

'Good, son. How are you?'

'Oh, divil-a-bit, you know.'

'I know.'

'And Susan and Felicity? Are they around?'

'Oh, Felicity's gone back to London. And Susan's at her yoga class. She'll be in later.'

'Good, good.'

'Come on in, let ye,' she called to the two women who were by now locked in a teary embrace, 'and we'll have a cup of tea.'

'So where's Eoin?' asked Maureen, her voice considerably louder than it needed to be.

'I'm . . . ah . . . here?' he suggested, rising from his position at the kitchen table. 'It's great to meet you at last.'

Maureen surveyed her son-in-law. From his voice and manner on the phone she had expected someone slightly better dressed. His accent, while decidedly Cork, was soft and almost cultured, and he had been impeccably polite. Yet his frayed jeans and faded sweatshirt suggested someone who might not be professional.

'Hello, Eoin,' she said formally, holding out her hand. 'It's good to meet you too. Though I have to say it should have been sooner.'

'I know, and I take full responsibility for that. We shou–'

'Yes, well, no point in going over it now.' Maureen knew that it was very unlikely to be Eoin's fault that their marriage had been kept a secret, but she appreciated his willingness to take the blame. She took it to be a good sign.

'I'm totally mad about Marianne,' he said quickly. 'I'd do anything for her.'

'I'm sure you would, Eoin.'

'Anyway,' said Angela breezily, 'the tea's made and I have an apple tart in the oven. All I need is someone to whip the cream.'

And so, over Barry's tea and Angela's home-made pie, Eoin was initiated into the O'Regan family. Maureen had to admit that he seemed all right. The bottom line was that he made Marianne happy. It still bothered her, though, that she couldn't quite 'place' him. Clearly, he was from good stock – his father worked for the department of justice (Maureen managed to glean that he was quite high up) and his mother's people had originally come from a big farm on the Limerick/Cork border. He had a brother a doctor and a sister a solicitor but as far as she could gather, while Eoin had spent some time in college, he had never got a degree. Just like Marianne, then, but you expected more from a man. What were his prospects, after all, if he didn't have anything on paper?

The same thing was on Tom's mind when he took his son-in-law for a walk round the area later in the afternoon.

'I'll get straight to the point,' said Tom, before they had even crossed the road. 'I want to know what your plans are.'

'My plans?'

'Your plans for yourself and Marianne.'

'Well, we'd planned to go back to Cork yesterday, but when we heard —'

'I mean your long-term plans.'

'Oh . . . right . . . well . . . ahm . . .'

'What line of work are you in?' asked Tom casually.

'I work as a chef . . . in a bistro . . . on McCurtain Street.'

'And do you enjoy the work?'

'I do.'

'That's good for a start.'

'Actually, to be honest, I don't.'

'We want you to be honest, Eoin.'

Tom was quite pleased with the way he was proceeding. He had persuaded Maureen to let him do the talking as far as Eoin was concerned. He felt that a man to man thing was called for. He also felt – though he didn't say this to his wife – that it was an opportunity for him to be seen as 'the boss'. He'd never been seen as the boss in his own home, and now there was another man in the family, he felt that a small stand was timely. Maureen had agreed. Seeing as her husband had never asked for anything in his life, she thought she should allow him this. Besides, she wasn't entirely confident of her skill with a man of the new generation.

'I had a bit of training, you know, as a chef, but I was never keen on it. I only took the job because . . . well . . . it's a steady . . .'

'I know what you mean, son. So what kind of work would you be interested in?'

It was a difficult question. To his recollection, he hadn't ever been asked it before. At school, when it became clear that he wasn't going to follow his brother into medicine or his sister into law, he'd kind of got forgotten about. He'd filled in his college application with a series of courses he'd picked at random: arts (perhaps, subliminally, because arts seemed to be the opposite of medicine), computers (because everybody was doing it), sound engineering (because he liked music) and catering (because he liked food). That's how his cheffing career had begun.

'I'm not sure . . . it's hard to say.'

'I used to work at Murphy's Builders Suppliers – I used to run the place at one time. How about I see if I can get you a job there?'

'All right, Mr O'Regan, I'll give it a go. I'll give anything a go.'

'Call me Tom, son.'

'Thanks . . . Tom.'

In the meantime, Maureen and Marianne were having a chat in the living room, though from Marianne's point of view it wasn't going quite as well.

'Twenty-two thousand euro! I can't believe it, Marianne.'

'It's not that much.'

'It's not much if it's the amount of money you've saved over a lifetime. If it's the amount you owe, however . . .'

'It just crept up.'

'It crept up, Marianne, because you let it. Do you think it's been easy for your father and me over the years? Do you think we let ourselves get into that kind of debt?'

'Well, no, but –'

'And do you know why?'

'Well . . .'

'Because, if we couldn't afford it, we didn't buy it! It's as simple as that, Marianne. Oh, we were far too indulgent with you. Letting you find the sort of job you were interested in instead of insisting that you stuck at one thing. We have a lot to answer for, I know, but so do you. You've been doing your own thing for too long now.'

'But, Mum, everybody has a little debt.'

'Maybe they do – God knows in this country of ours it's hard to stay straight – but do you know what people do, Marianne, when they get into debt?'

'What?'

'They get out of it! One step at time. Ten euro at a time, if they have to. What they don't do is go stealing from their granny!'

'It wasn't stealing!'

'What else could you call it?'

'I wasn't thinking straight. I was upset – after the baby . . .'

'I appreciate that you went through a difficult time, but I will not let you shirk your responsibility on this one.'

'I'm sorry.'

'And what about all of Granny's lovely antiques? Is she ever going to see them again?'

'I don't have the money. I put it straight into the bank. I was trying to clear the debt.'

'You're just lucky that Mr Gillespie is a friend of your grandmother's. Otherwise he'd have gone straight to the guards. He might still; there's nothing stopping him.'

'He won't go to the guards.'

'That's where you're wrong, Marianne. He is in receipt of stolen property, and he knows who stole it! Not I nor your father nor your grandmother is going to get you out of this one!'

'Don't tell Granny, please.'

'She ought to know.'

'Mum, please . . .'

'You've gone too far, Marianne. You're too old to act like this.'

'I just got confused. I was trying to do the . . .'

The tears she had been fighting were in full flow now. Maureen watched for a while as her daughter's shoulders moved slowly up and down, then she sat beside her and put her arms round her.

'You know it happened to me once,' she said.

'What did?'

'A miscarriage.'

'Really? When?'

'Between Susan and yourself. I was barely the six weeks, like you.'

'Oh, Mum . . .'

'So I know what you're going through.'

'You never told us.'

'A mother doesn't tell everything.'

'Thanks for telling me now.'

'Your old mother has her uses.'

'I know it was wrong . . . about Granny's stuff.'

'Well, that's good, Marianne, because for a while there I didn't think you did know it was wrong. That's a start at least.'

It was a little later in the afternoon, when Tom and Eoin had returned, that the four of them sat down for a chat.

'I just want to say,' Tom began, 'that despite everything, we're very happy that you're married. You seem to be a good sort, Eoin, and hopefully we'll get to know you better.'

It was the closest he'd come to a 'father of the bride' speech and he felt very proud.

'That's all very well,' said Maureen, 'but none of us can rest easy until this mess is sorted out.'

'I know, Mum. I'll do my best.'

'It occurred to me,' she said with a sigh, 'that we might

loan you the money, Daddy and I, to clear the debt, and then you could pay us back. Every single penny. But we wouldn't charge you interest like the bank.'

'Oh, Mum, that would be –'

'No.'

Everyone turned to look at Tom.

'What?'

'I don't think that's the way it should be done. You said it yourself, Maureen, that we've been at fault for indulging her, and I think that should stop now.'

'Have a heart, Tom. I think she's learnt her lesson.'

'No. I don't think she will learn her lesson unless she does it the hard way. I'm not saying we won't help at all, I just think she should prove – to herself – that she can do this.'

'What are you suggesting?'

'That Marianne goes into the bank herself and gets one of those consolidation loans – from the bank, mind, not from one of those dodgy companies. And she has to get a job.'

'I agree with you there.'

'And every week she pays off a bit of what she owes.'

'It'll take years!'

'Yes, Marianne, it will take a long time. But that's real life.'

'I don't want to do that! I don't want to work in some god-awful job just to give all my money away.'

'Sorry, Marianne, I don't think you have any choice. Otherwise your mother and I won't buy back Granny's antiques, and Mr Gillespie will go to the guards.'

'Tom!'

'I'm only saying what you've already said, Maureen.'

'I know, but can't you see she's sorry?'

'She needs to be very sorry.'

'Can we at least . . . do the other thing we were talking about?'

'The house?'

'Daddy and I thought that you could live in our house, in Clareview. It would save you paying rent, so you could put more money into the loan.'

'What? You mean move in with you and Dad?'

'Sure, we live in Ballyconnell now.'

'But won't ye be coming back?'

'We're very happy in Ballyconnell, love. It's what we've wanted all our lives. And if giving ye the house for a while helps ye out, then we're happy to do it.'

'But, Mum, we live in Cork.'

'Can't ye move to Limerick? What have ye in Cork to keep ye?'

'Well . . .'

'Well, nothing. Here you have family, a comfortable home, and a way out of your debts.'

'But –'

'Just think about it, Marianne.'

Marianne did think about it. And Eoin thought about it. And by the end of the afternoon, Marianne had reluctantly agreed.

'But I don't have to take the first job I see. Let me just find one that I like. Then I'll be much more likely to stay at it.'

'You'll take the first job that comes your way and if you don't like it, you'll just have to stick at it until you find one that you think you'll like better.'

'Dad!'

Maureen smiled at her husband.

'There's just one more thing,' she said, 'and your father

and I are adamant about it. We want you to have a proper church wedding.'

'Mum!'

'The church might not mean much to you, but to me and your father, it's still a big part of our lives. We just want to see things done properly. For your own sakes.'

'Honestly, Mum. We're already married. What's the point of doing it again?'

'In the eyes of the church you're not married. Now, I'm no prude. I know the world we're living in – heaven help us – I'm only thinking of your souls.'

'Oh, give me a break. Our souls are fine.'

'It's not a terrible idea, Marianne,' Eoin suggested, from the far corner of the room, 'it might be nice.'

'It's a church! A wedding in a church!'

'Where's the harm?'

Marianne hoisted herself up on her soapbox.

'A wedding is a ridiculous charade of middle-class pretentiousness, a travesty of clerical hypocrisy, a monument to all things vulgar *and* it's a diabolical waste of money.'

'Daddy and I would pay for it. Right, Tom?'

'Right.'

'But, Mum . . .'

'Marianne, love, we're not talking about anything vulgar, give me that much credit. All I'm talking about is a private service in Ballyconnell Church, followed by a little walk to the beach and then maybe a little picnic or something.'

'The beach?'

'I don't see why not. It's the most beautiful spot in the country – why shouldn't we have your wedding there?'

'I suppose if it was on the beach . . .'

'The picnic would be on the beach. The service would still be in the church.'

'Well, you know, there's all that new legislation now that says you can get married anywhere. What if I agree to a priest and you agree to a beach?'

Nobody had quite agreed to anything by the time Susan came home.

She had contemplated not coming home at all – nothing good could come of a meeting with her mother now – but curiosity got the better of her. And, perhaps, a small touch of loneliness. After all it was months since she'd seen her mother; there was a chance she'd have changed. All through her yoga session she'd tried to focus on the good things she could remember – it had been one of her toughest sessions yet.

'Susan? Is that you?' Maureen called out as soon as she heard the hall door open.

'Yes.'

'We're all in here.'

'I'm coming in. Just putting my bag down.'

Susan came into the living room and surveyed the party. Maureen was perched on the edge of the couch by the arm, a position that allowed her to dominate the room. Marianne, beside her, was under her protection, although Eoin, on her other side, was under the impression that she was under his protection. Tom sat on one armchair, his feet crossed in front of him, just enough distance from the couch so Maureen could catch his eye whenever she needed to. Angela had joined them when she'd felt it was safe and was now sitting on the other armchair, at enough of a tilt from Maureen so that she had no idea Angela had been asleep for the past twenty minutes.

'Hi, Mum, Dad,' Susan said, crossing the room to kiss them both. There was no obvious place for her to sit so she remained standing, uncomfortably, somewhere between the two armchairs.

'Have you got thin, Susan?' Maureen asked as she observed her daughter.

'Ahm . . . I don't think so. How are you, Mum? You're looking very well.'

'Oh, thank you, love, I daresay I have a bit of a colour. We've had marvellous weather in Ballyconnell, much better than here.'

'It hasn't been too bad here either.'

Susan couldn't quite believe it. Was she really having a conversation with her mother, whom she hadn't seen in several months, about the weather?

'Of course, you never take the sun, do you, Susan? Always running away from it.'

'Well, actually –'

'And what's all this I hear about you running around with your cousin?'

'He's not my cousin, Mum. He's absolutely not. And you've always known it.'

'Well, maybe not by blood . . . but in every other way.'

'I think that it's really only the blood way that matters. Anyway, none of it matters, because he's disappeared.'

'Gone to ground has he? You must have really frightened him.'

'Gavin was always a good lad,' said Tom, uncrossing his legs. 'He'll turn up. He's always been the sort to like a bit of time on his own. I wouldn't worry, Susan. He'll be back.'

'Thanks, Dad, but I really don't know if he will.'

'Susan, why do you always have to complicate things? What was wrong with that lovely dentist?'

'Mum!'

Susan had had enough. It was bad enough that she was in pain, it was too much that her mother saw fit to ridicule her pain. She excused herself from the room (just as Angela began talking in her sleep) and marched quietly up the stairs. She went to her bedroom, pulled out the Dunnes suitcase she had arrived with, and began to pack. In less than twenty minutes she had left Charlotte Avenue for good.

28

Felicity's interview with Olaf Spilling and Doug Hewitt wasn't what she had been expecting. She went in there, that Monday morning, in her fancy Vivienne Westwood suit fully expecting that in half an hour she'd be flogging the same suit to try and pay her rent for the month. She was aware, as she surveyed Olaf, and made the mental observation that he looked rather like a young Christopher Reeve, that the last words she'd said directly to him were 'Shut the fuck up a minute.' As for Doug Hewitt, all she could say of him was that he looked remarkably like Joe Pesci – at his shortest and fattest.

Olaf, however, was all smiles and polite enquiries about her holiday, while Doug seemed content to let his colleague do the talking.

'You heard about Tony Whitby's arrest, I presume?' said Olaf, after she finished telling them about her three-hour delay in Shannon.

'Yes,' she said. 'I have to say I was very surprised.'

'We were not,' said Olaf.

'Oh.'

'Yes. It turned out Tony Whitby was not everything we thought. He didn't keep his part of the deal. He seemed to think, Ms O'Regan, that it was a good management style to be always on the golf course.'

'Right.'

'And we have concluded our investigation regarding the leaks surrounding the share price.'

Doug Hewitt was nodding throughout the exchange, but otherwise he didn't seem to have anything to contribute.

'Oh yes?'

'So that leaves us without a manager.'

'Indeed.'

'We like thegoss, Ms O'Regan, we think it has the potential to become global. And we think you might be able to do this.'

'Right. I mean yes. Yes. I could do this – that – for you. Do you mean you want me to come and work for you?'

'You already work for us, Ms O'Regan. I mean that now you would work for us in the capacity of executive manager. Do you think that is something you could do?'

Before Felicity could answer, Doug Hewitt leaned forward and began to speak.

'I've been right through the books,' he said, eyeballing her at last, 'that's what I do. I get right down to the nitty gritty of a company and I don't come up for air until I know every bitty thing that's gone on, right from the beginning.'

'Right.' Felicity was finding it difficult to vary her vocabulary.

'So you see, Ms O'Regan, we know that it was you who was responsible for the intrinsic success of this company. No doubt your former boss had much to contribute, but without your understanding of the business, this website would never have become what it is.'

'Right . . . ahm . . . thank you. Thank you for saying that.'

'So I can only echo Olaf's wish that you come to manage thegoss. What do you think?'

'Ahm . . . I think . . . yes. Yes. I would love to manage thegoss.'

'Excellent, excellent. This is very good.' Olaf Spilling's grin was particularly Superman-like as he shook her hand.

'I'm really looking forward to working for you,' said Doug Hewitt.

'Working *for* me?' asked Felicity.

'Of course! I'm a mere accountant. The success of the company lies in your hands.'

Her shock was only marginally less than it had been the day Olaf and Doug first appeared on the scene, but at least this time she did play it cool. She let the two men shake her hand repeatedly and when they took her into Tony's office and asked her to make a list of what she'd like to change, she merely smiled and said she'd like a plant or two.

She settled in immediately. After all, she'd practically been running the place before. She found it a little bizarre, at first, to be sitting at Tony's desk, looking out at his view, replacing his business cards with hers. She half expected to see him walk through the door telling her what a gullible fool she was to fall for the joke. But the feeling didn't last long. Soon, any sense of dislocation was replaced by a very real feeling that she was where she belonged, doing what she was good at.

Part of her wouldn't have minded if Tony had walked through the door, if only so he could see what she was making of his company. She had spent much of the summer having heated imaginary exchanges with him, but she realized now that it was pointless. Tony wasn't the kind of man who was capable of giving you an explanation for his actions. He was a primitive, she'd decided, he acted on his instincts. He was a survivor and he did whatever he had to do to get by. She didn't blame him. And she had finally stopped blaming herself.

29

Susan walked barefoot along the deserted beach, and with every step she began to see why her mother had so readily forsaken the city. There was something very soothing about the green, rock-laden landscape on one side, and the endless blue on the other. It was good for the soul.

Her soul had taken a bit of a bashing recently, but she was beginning to rally. Her parents suddenly being so understanding helped, and even Marianne had done her bit by apologizing for her behaviour, or at least by coming as close to an apology as it was possible for her.

'I wasn't being malicious,' she'd said, after Susan finally agreed to listen to her. 'I was only repeating what I heard. You were the one telling lies.'

'Thanks, Marianne, now I know where telling lies can get you.'

'I mean, I'd no idea. I really wouldn't have said anything if I'd known. You do believe me, don't you?'

Susan sighed. 'Yes, I probably do.'

'So . . . how did it happen?'

'I don't know. It just did. I just . . . fell in love with him. He's like nobody I've ever known.'

'Yeah . . . he's one of the good ones.'

'He's amazing. He's . . . everything. Anyway . . .'

'If I can do anything?'

'It's fine.'

'I hope you get back together.'

'Thanks, Marianne.'

Susan had left Charlotte Avenue with as little idea of what would happen next as when she had arrived. Finding her case much heavier than she remembered, she'd hailed a cab halfway down the avenue and when the driver asked for an address, she gave the first one that came to her mind. And that's how she ended up moving in with Carmel.

'Oh well,' she'd said aloud as she dragged her case over Carmel's threshold, 'we were both dumped by Gavin. At least we have that in common.'

'Well, actually,' Carmel pointed out, 'I was never dumped by Gavin. I dumped him. And you know what? It was a very empowering experience. I think I've changed the way I view men. I think this might be the start of a whole new era for me.'

In fact, Carmel was full of useful advice.

'Clearly Gavin's main problem,' she said one evening as they shared a bottle of wine and a take-away pizza, 'is that he has abandonment issues.'

'Abandonment issues?' asked Susan.

'Oh yeah, I mean it's classic. His mother dies, then his father dies, then he finds out his father isn't actually his father and that his real father abandoned him years ago. Then his fiancée abandons him – very publicly and for another man. Then for years he doesn't allow himself to get close to anyone and as soon as he does – you go and abandon him. Classic abandonment issues.'

'Oh. I never really thought of it like that. But I didn't abandon him, he abandoned me.'

'You proved yourself unreliable. He wasn't able to trust you. It amounts to the same thing. One way or another you were going to let him down.'

'Oh.'

'Sorry, sweetie.'

'That's OK. It's just that I always thought of Gavin as . . . so strong. So . . . sane. I didn't think he was the type to have issues.'

'We all have issues, Susan. Some of us hide them better than others, but we all have issues.'

'Right.'

Carmel's own love life had taken such an about-turn that she had even managed to get herself a new boyfriend. She had met him through an on-line dating service though it turned out he lived only three streets away from her on the Mill Road. 'He's thirty-eight,' she told Susan another evening they were sharing a home-made curry and a six-pack of Bud Lite, 'non-drinker, non-smoker, regular saver, and a small bit receding. He's perfect.'

'I'm happy for you,' said Susan. 'I really am. I hope it works out.'

'Do you know what? I think it will. I think he wants it to work just as much as I do. It's like – yeah, sure, there's better-looking, richer, more dazzling people out there – but who cares? When you've found someone a bit like yourself, someone you're comfortable with, it really doesn't get better than that. I think we're very lucky.'

'Yes,' said Susan wistfully, 'I think ye are too.'

Susan had barely unpacked at Carmel's when she had a visit from Maureen to talk about 'the Gavin situation' as she put it.

'I don't approve,' was the first thing she said after stepping inside the door and surveying the house with a glance.

'I know.'

'I still don't think it's right.'

'It's irrelevant now.'

'But I want you to know that I'm sorry.'

'For what?'

'I'm sorry it didn't work out. If you really think he's the one for you, then . . . I'm sorry it didn't work out.'

'Thanks, Mum.'

'It's not easy finding the right person. I had thought you were all settled with Paul.'

'Please don't talk about Paul again.'

'I'm not going to. If you say he wasn't right, then I believe you. I . . .' She started to fidget with her handbag and ran a hand across her throat. 'I think it's time . . .'

Susan had never seen her mother have such difficulty getting a sentence out.

'I think it's time I started to trust you a little more,' she said eventually. 'You're old enough to know your own mind and make your own decisions. And if I don't approve of everything you do then . . . well . . . I understand that it can't be helped. You have to live your life.'

'Thanks, Mum. That means a lot.'

'I know I've been hard on you. I see myself in you, that's all.'

'What do you mean?'

'I was a bit like you – couldn't settle down – couldn't decide what I wanted.'

'But didn't you and Daddy get married really young?'

'We weren't that young. But I mean before that. Before we got married. What I mean is, I'm so glad that we did and yet . . . at the time I nearly convinced myself that I didn't want to settle down.'

'Oh.'

'All I'm saying, love, is that it was really good for me – getting married to your father and having the three of you – and I just thought that it would be good for you as well.

That's why I was so keen for you to settle down with Paul.'

'Oh.'

'I just want you to be happy, Susan.'

'I hope I will be eventually. It seems to take me longer than everybody else.'

'You'll get there.'

The two women hugged each other; a warm, all-encompassing hug that did both of them a lot of good.

'I've decided to do a yoga-teaching course,' said Susan, emerging from her mother's embrace.

'Oh?'

'Yeah. I mean, I'll have to do advanced yoga first and a lot more practice, and it'll probably take me ages, but it's something I'd really like to do.'

'That's great, love!'

'Yeah, I'm quite excited about it. I never thought I'd get into it so much, but it's really cool. You'd probably enjoy it!'

'I'm too old for that sort of thing. A good walk on Ballyconnell beach is all I ask for. Now, is there any chance of a cup of tea?'

As Susan boiled the kettle and rummaged through the few groceries she'd bought, she reflected that the previous twenty minutes or so was probably the longest she'd ever spent in her mother's company without wanting to slit one of their throats. 'Perhaps we're both growing up a little,' she said to herself as she added tea leaves to the pot. 'Maybe there's hope for us yet.'

'This is lovely,' Maureen said, as she sipped from her china mug (the best Susan could find in Carmel's presses).

'I think you're right about leaves being nicer than a bag.'

'I've been saying it for years.'

'Anyway . . .'

'Do you know what I was thinking?' said Maureen, placing her mug on the table.

'What, Mum?'

'I was thinking you should come down to Ballyconnell with us for a spell. It would do you good to get out of the city for a while and I could do with your help if we're really going to have a wedding on the beach – God help us!'

'I don't think I can take any time off work at the moment.'

'But you've had no holiday this year.'

'True, but a few of the girls are still on holiday so I wouldn't be able to get away.'

'Perhaps in a couple of weeks? I think a change of scene would do you good.'

'Maybe. Sure, I'll think about it. Come the end of the month they'll all be back from their holidays anyway.'

'That would be a lovely time to come. I'll pencil you in so.'

'OK, Mum, I'll see what I can manage.'

In the end Susan got away easily enough towards the end of September. As she was bundling herself on to the bus, it struck her that maybe she would have been better off taking a cheap flight to a sun-drenched resort on a distant coast, but she was committed now, and besides, a holiday like that would only remind her of what she didn't have. She'd had a glimpse of what it might have been like to be truly happy, but now that was gone and she was adjusting to a life less stunning.

The first few days of her holiday went perfectly well. Her mother was making a real effort not to mention Gavin's – or

Paul's – name, and she did everything she could to distract Susan with trips to the local harbour and fair-trade coffee mornings in the village with her cronies, and even a visit to the local beauty salon for a facial and a manicure, two things Susan had never done before. Her father was acutely aware of what mustn't be said and at every opportunity he let his daughter know what a treasure she was, assuring her there were plenty more fish in the sea.

Susan was grateful for it all, but by the evening of the fourth day all she wanted was a quiet walk on the beach. On her own.

She continued walking even though the light was beginning to fade. She had long passed the exposed part of the bay which was used by surfers (she could nearly swear she passed the very rock where she and Gavin had stopped that day) and she was now walking in a straight line without any thought that she might lose her way.

That's when she saw him. At least she thought it was him. A figure emerged from the sea and walked to a small bundle on the sand where he began pulling on some clothes as he dried off with a towel. No, it probably wasn't him. What would he be doing here in the middle of the week? But as she drew closer she became more and more convinced that she recognized those shoulders and that long arching back. By the time she was level with his position on the beach, he had turned round and was heading for the rocks.

She turned away. Even if it was him, she had nothing to say.

'Susan!'

She started walking.

'Susan, wait!'

She kept walking.

'Susan! Susan, wait!'

She wouldn't wait. He had to run to catch up with her.

'Please, Susan, stop. I – I want to apologize.'

Susan's pace slowed. He stood in front of her, barring her way.

'What are you doing here?' He was out of breath.

'I'm staying with Mum and Dad.'

'Oh.'

'What are *you* doing here?'

'I . . . I've been . . .'

Susan suddenly realized that she couldn't meet his eye and all she could think about was how devastatingly miserable she had felt the last time he had stood in front of her.

She turned and started to walk away from him again.

'Susan, please wait! Let me talk to you.'

She stopped and stood to face him.

'For what? So you can chew me up and spit me out all over again?'

'No, I –'

'Nobody knew where you were! You just – disappeared!'

'I sent Granny a note . . .'

'So you were just going to leave and run away from everything – again.'

'I – Susan, it was all my fault – all my shit. All my . . . I just went a bit nuts and I took it out on you . . . I –'

'Well, it's done now.'

'Susan, please.'

'Look! It's over and done with! I can't be the person you need me to be so there's no point.'

'Susan, you are everything . . . You make . . . Susan, I love you. Just listen to me. Let me tell you how sorry I am.'

'You can't be all that sorry if you're out here swimming and surfing.'

'I didn't know what else to do. I've been trying to work up the courage to talk to you. I've been writing you a letter but – Look, I know you don't owe me anything, I know I don't deserve anything, but . . .'

Susan stared at him, her bottom lip trembling.

'You have transformed my life. From the minute I met you again, the only thing I've wanted is to be with you. You've made me happier than I ever thought was possible. I know I don't have anything to offer you, but if you could just – maybe think about giving me another chance.'

She shook her head furiously.

'Don't decide now. Just think about it.'

'I can't go through that again. How do I know there isn't something else I did – ten years ago – that you're going to object to?'

'Susan, I flipped out! Look, I don't have any excuses. That night when we were together was the most incredible night of my life. And when Marianne said that thing I thought – just for that moment – that you were laughing at me. That it hadn't meant as much to you. I know it's all my shit – I know it all. It's just so pathetic that when the best thing – the absolute best person in the world comes along – I find a way to fuck it up. It was easier to feel sorry for myself than . . .'

Susan wiped the tears from her eyes.

'I never laughed at you.'

'I know! And I never – I – it's none of my business why you broke up with Paul.'

He reached out and took her hands in his. She still wasn't able to look at him.

'I really thought you hated me,' she said.

317

'How could I? It's myself I hate.'

He folded her head into his chest while his tears fell into her hair.

'I've never stopped loving you.'

She looked up at him.

'I've never stopped loving you.'

'Can you forgive me?'

'I want to.'

'I know I'm a bit of a nut job, but you're good for me.'

'I think you're good for me too.'

Suddenly she pulled away from him.

'But I can't take the responsibility.'

'What do you mean?'

'Well, what if it doesn't work out? What if we're terrible together? I can't handle it if you're going to fall apart again.'

He held her at arm's length in front of him. 'I'm not looking for any guarantees from you. I'm not tying you into anything here. If you get tired of me in six months or six weeks or six days, then that's fine. I'll count myself lucky to have had you for that long. But if you thought that you might want me to stick around for a while, then that would be brilliant.'

'I don't know . . .'

'I don't blame you. But I promise I won't be any trouble.'

She smiled at him.

'I suppose we could see how it goes.'

He put his arms around her again and bent his head so it just touched hers.

Susan looked up and peered into the deep, underwater blue of his eyes.

'I want to be with you for ever,' she said.

'Oh God, Susan . . .'

They kissed fiercely, their bodies locked together.

'Come on,' he said, 'I'm taking you home with me.'

They set off across the rocks, her small body cradled in his, leaving the beach deserted once again as the sun finally slid below the horizon.

Epilogue

It couldn't have been more perfect. The sun had been threatening to come out since early morning on this late-October day, and just as their lips parted from their first (officially official) conjugal kiss, the sun appeared, duly radiant, from behind a bank of cloud. Eoin and Marianne looked at each other. Marianne was so happy her mother had persuaded her into this wedding and even happier she had persuaded her mother into having it on the beach. As the remainder of the cloud dispersed over Ballyconnell Bay, it seemed to be written in the very sky that this was something special. Everybody shed a tear, Maureen was positively blubbering, and all the time the happy couple never took their eyes off each other.

Angela was charmed. It was a while since she'd seen so many of her family gathered together, and all of them so happy. She couldn't get over the change in Marianne. She'd gone from behaving like a wayward, directionless adolescent to a sensitive, maturing woman almost overnight. She'd come to her in tears about the things she'd taken. Honestly, a few oul' bits of rubbish she never used from one end of the year to the next – she could have had the lot of them if she'd only asked. She wasn't surprised that Marianne had debts, but at least she was trying to do something about them. Angela had offered to clear the debt for her, but Tom wouldn't hear of it. He'd actually been furious with her for offering. 'She has to learn her lesson, Mam,' he said. 'You wouldn't have had it any other way for us.' That was true, but your grandchildren were different – you were entitled, even obliged, to indulge them.

So Marianne had knuckled down to a job in Dunnes. She worked overtime when she could get it, and not one penny of what she earned was spent on herself. But that was never Marianne's problem – she was utterly unmaterialistic, to give the girl her due. But now she seemed to understand the laws of cause and effect a little better. And of course she had Eoin to guide her. He adored her, but he had exactly the same idea as Tom with regard to sorting out her money problems. And it wasn't a one-way street there, either. She could see that Eoin was a bit of a lost soul and Marianne provided him with a way back in. They were a sweet couple; thanks be to God they'd found each other.

Angela glanced at Maureen who had finally stopped weeping. She looked every inch the mother of the bride. She'd bought her outfit in Ballyconnell's only boutique – Maureen believed in shopping locally – a fabulous ensemble in peaches and cream. The only problem was that it didn't really need to be worn; it was the sort of thing that looked much better in the shop window. But Maureen was beatific. It was the happiest day of her life and if she had her time over again, Angela was convinced, this is how she'd have got married.

It was a good day for her son as well. The pair of them had every right to feel proud as they surveyed their three daughters, each one radiating the happiness they felt. God knows it isn't easy being a parent in this day and age and they'd done as good a job as anyone.

Felicity had flown in for the weekend but she was going to have to leave the wedding early in order to catch a flight to the States. There was a taxi picking her up at the beach to bring her straight to Shannon. Apparently there was some very important meeting she had to be at – something about her company going global – whatever that meant. She was a changed woman since the summer. You could see the light in her eyes and feel the energy pulsing out of her. This job meant everything.

Of course Angela had tried to wheedle out of her if there was anything (or anyone) else causing her to have such a spring in her step, but Felicity had nothing to reveal.

'Maybe one day, Gran,' she'd said when they were sharing a pot of tea the night she'd arrived, 'but for now there just isn't time. I know you think I should be settling down, but I *am* settled. I'm settled in this way of life and I like it.'

'But what about the future, love?'

'Granny, I don't have any regrets now, and I don't think I will in the future. Look, if the love of my life appears, I'm not going to send him away, but right now, I'm not going to go looking for him either.'

'And what about children?'

'I'm not over the hill yet, Gran. If it happens, it happens. *With* the right person. And if it doesn't, it doesn't.'

Angela didn't much like hearing this flippant philosophy from her granddaughter, but she knew that Felicity believed what she was saying. What would she know about high-flying careers anyway – the only work she'd ever done was type letters for an accountant.

And then there was Susan. And Gavin. Well, it certainly was odd, the way life worked out sometimes. From the very beginning there'd been something between them. It was as though each of them was more themselves when the other one was around. Gavin often crumpled up with shyness, but when Susan was in the room he wasn't afraid to relax and just enjoy himself. And Susan? Well, it wasn't clear if Susan had had any idea who she was over the past few years, but with Gavin, it became easier for her to discover what she wanted. It was just a pity, really, they hadn't got together long before now. But that was life, again, getting in the way.

Angela smiled to herself as she looked at Gavin. She knew exactly what was on his mind. He'd admitted to her only the other day when he was at the house fixing her central heating, that he was desperate to ask Susan to marry him. He'd even bought a ring, but he was afraid a proposal would seem too needy and scare her off. 'I think we just need to be together for a while,' he'd said, 'you know, with no crises, or anything.'

'So how are ye getting on, living together?' Angela had asked.

'Great. Wonderful. It's like every day is the best day of my life.'

'Susan said something similar to me only last week.'

'Really?'

'She said being with you makes her feel as though there's nothing in the world she couldn't do.'

'She said that?'

'Sounds to me as though she might like a proposal.'

He'd continued tinkering with the boiler and said no more about it, but Angela wouldn't have been a bit surprised if there was news there soon. If they both knew it was right, why not just go ahead and get married? After all, you never know what's in the future; you have to make the most of every minute.

The day was turning cold, despite the sun, and Angela pulled her scarf closer round her. They were setting up the gas heaters (Marianne claimed she wouldn't drive, fly or eat foreign food for a year, in order to even out her carbon footprint. Angela gave her a week). It was in the winter she missed her husband the most, and her son, but it wasn't a bad position to be in at eighty-six years old, stuck in the middle of a family that still thought you were worth having around.

She caught Susan's eye as the happy couple sailed past them, and gave the girl a wink. Susan took Gavin's hand, which had been tightly entwined in her own, and kissed it. Oh yes, she thought, it won't be long now.

Acknowledgements

Everybody at Penguin: Michael McLoughlin, Patricia McVeigh, Cliona Lewis, Brian Walker – a very talented team who have done so much to support my writing – but in particular Patricia Deevy for having faith in me. My editor, Alison Walshe, for her endless patience and expert guidance. Liz Davis for her expert copy-editing.

My agent, Ita O'Driscoll, who is ever full of good advice and encouragement.

Claire Culligan, who has become my official unofficial reader, for her warm reassurance at the times I needed it most, and also for a crucial breakfast scene!

Everybody at school and at County Limerick VEC, who have been hugely supportive of my writing. And they bought loads of books!

Joan McKernan, who is a tireless champion of the arts in Limerick.

My extended family, who are full of encouragement, but a particular thank you to Elaine Singleton for our yoga conversation.

My writing group, who have been very understanding all the times I haven't turned up – they haven't kicked me out yet!

So many friends, who are always there cheering me on, and in particular Geraldine Rooney – whose name slipped off the page last time!

My parents, Jim and Anne Cosgrave, and James' parents, Geoff and Mary Griffin, without whom we probably wouldn't be able to leave the house!

My gorgeous daughters, Dharma and Maya, who give me so much joy.

And James, who for this book provided me with not only love and reassurance and the time to do endless rewrites, but also gave me the benefit of his knowledge of the internet. Thank you, James, for everything.

Also a very big thank you to everybody who bought *Desperately Seeking . . .* Hope you enjoyed it!

He just wanted a decent book to read ...

Not too much to ask, is it? It was in 1935 when Allen Lane, Managing Director of Bodley Head Publishers, stood on a platform at Exeter railway station looking for something good to read on his journey back to London. His choice was limited to popular magazines and poor-quality paperbacks – the same choice faced every day by the vast majority of readers, few of whom could afford hardbacks. Lane's disappointment and subsequent anger at the range of books generally available led him to found a company – and change the world.

'We believed in the existence in this country of a vast reading public for intelligent books at a low price, and staked everything on it'
Sir Allen Lane, 1902–1970, founder of Penguin Books

The quality paperback had arrived – and not just in bookshops. Lane was adamant that his Penguins should appear in chain stores and tobacconists, and should cost no more than a packet of cigarettes.

Reading habits (and cigarette prices) have changed since 1935, but Penguin still believes in publishing the best books for everybody to enjoy. We still believe that good design costs no more than bad design, and we still believe that quality books published passionately and responsibly make the world a better place.

So wherever you see the little bird – whether it's on a piece of prize-winning literary fiction or a celebrity autobiography, political tour de force or historical masterpiece, a serial-killer thriller, reference book, world classic or a piece of pure escapism – you can bet that it represents the very best that the genre has to offer.

Whatever you like to read – trust Penguin.